Dear Mystery Reader:

The Gourmet Detective, an ex-chef who makes his living as a menu consultant for the most chic restaurants in London, has an appetite for mystery.

This time around, a shady deal between two Provencal vineyards has him jetting off to France to do some sleuthing. No sooner does he arrive then the corpse of a vineyard worker turns up. Was he gored by a wild boar? That's what the locals are saying but the Gourmet Detective knows better. En route to the truth, the Gourmet Detective finds himself embroiled in a delicious mess. With his own life at risk, he still manages to find time to sample world-renowned cuisine.

If you're hungry for a good mystery, look no further. DYING ON THE VINE is a main course to savor.

Yours in crime,

Joe Veltre

Joe Veltre
Associate Editor
St. Martin's Press DEAD LETTER Paperback Mysteries

Other titles from St. Martin's **Dead Letter** Mysteries

Dead Letter is also proud to present these mystery classics by Ngaio Marsh

I passed two rows of vats. The lids were open to permit air to be ingested, and the contents bubbled gently. Clouds of sweet, fruity vapor swirled slowly and an insistent hiss indicated that fermentation was at a high level. A piece of cloth caught my eye. It was tied to the top of the rail and I went to inspect it. It was a scarf, once white and now stained with dark red. Wine stains, I told myself firmly. . . . I was looking at it to determine why it was there when to my horror, it moved. . . .

It was too late by the time I realized that it was not only the scarf moving but the rail. Then I was moving with it as the result of a strong push in the middle of my back. My fall was like slow motion and there seemed to be ample time for the realization that the metallic sounds I had heard had been the removal of the locking pins from a detachable section of the rail.

The rail fell away and I fell after it.

The surface of dark liquid soared toward me and a thick warmth was all enveloping . . .

"The Gourmet Detective is . . . a delight. [This series] provides terrific writing, characters that come to life on the page, and wonderful information on gourmet cooking and the food industry."
—Stuart Kaminsky, author of *A Fatal Glass of Beer* and *Bullet for A Star* on *Spiced to Death*

"Leads readers on a cook's tour of haute cuisine, replete with tantalizing descriptions of food and its preparation, robust wit and an appropriately culinary murder."
—*Publishers Weekly* on *The Gourmet Detective*

DYING ON THE VINE

PETER KING

St. Martin's Paperbacks

DYING ON THE VINE

Copyright © 1998 by Peter King.
Excerpt from *Death Al Dente* copyright © 1999 by Peter King.

Library of Congress Catalog Card Number: 97-34992

ISBN: 0-312-96683-0

Printed in the United States of America

St. Martin's Press hardcover edition/April 1998
St. Martin's Paperbacks edition/April 1999

10 9 8 7 6 5 4 3 2

Chapter 1

The view from the top of Partington Tower was breathtaking, especially as it was one of those rare days in London when you could actually see the view.

The weather was clear and crisp and the windows had just been washed. The Thames was having one of its turgid days, looking like thin brown soup as it swirled languidly past. I amused myself by picking out the individual buildings in the complex that had begun as the Festival of Britain in 1951. The National Theatre and Festival Hall loomed as massive blockhouses of dirty concrete, but in contrast were the garish colored glows of the neon signs over the Hayward Gallery and the National Film Theatre.

In the other direction and past Blackfriars Bridge, the massive curved roof of Waterloo Station glinted green while close beside it was the soaring expanse of glass covering the International Terminal where the Eurostar trains crouched, ready for their three-hour dash to Paris through the Channel Tunnel. Between the two bridges, restaurant boats sat at anchor, dreaming of their younger days on the open sea and now condemned to serving beer and sausage rolls to tourists lolling under gaily striped umbrellas on the upper decks. Up here at the top of the tower, a pretty young secretary came to escort me into a nearby office.

The room had large windows, almost floor to ceiling, so the view was even more impressive from here than from the lobby. That was fair enough considering that this office belonged to the chief executive—the man who had phoned me yesterday and asked me to come here to discuss a sensitive matter.

They always were, I thought as I studied the man at the big mahogany desk with the antique leather inset top. He had a head of silvery gray hair and a strong nose. His slightly red face was from a mixture of good living and exposure to rays, natural and artificial, but his skin was smooth and unlined. He probably worked out in a gym more than once a week which helped to keep his Savile Row suit such a good fit. An aura of aristocratic breeding sat lightly on his shoulders and his voice was deep and authoritative.

"Frankly, I'm not sure whether you can do anything for us or not . . ."—he smiled disarmingly, showing even white teeth that probably got as much attention as his clothes, skin, and health— ". . . but we have to do something," he concluded.

In other words, I was the bottom of the barrel. They had already tried everything and hiring me was just window dressing. I smiled politely and waited for him to go on.

"It concerns the Willesford Wine Group. As you may know, we have distilleries, a soft drinks group, and a fruit juice division. But wine was our business for years before the others were added. My grandfather bought this vineyard in Provence and it brings in sixty percent of our wine revenue, the balance coming from Chile, Australia, and Italy as imports."

I nodded to show I was listening. I had run a quick check on his company after yesterday's phone call and it confirmed what he was telling me now.

"The problem is basically a simple one; the solution to the problem is, however, proving unexpectedly elusive. There is a vineyard adjacent to ours. It belongs to a group called Peregrine. Peregrine made an offer—quite unsolicited—to buy out our vineyard. It was marginally below what would be a market price. I say 'would be' because we had no interest in selling and turned the offer down flat."

I was not only listening now, I was hanging on Sir Charles's every word. This was different from what I had expected. Maybe this was going to be an intriguing case after all even if my chances of succeeding were small.

"We received another offer—this one substantially higher—and we turned it down too. Then we had another and yet another. The amount of money was now more than twice the market value. The fifth offer was much higher again." Sir Charles paused.

"What communication did you have with this Peregrine group while these offers were being rejected?" I asked.

"None. We tried to find out who the group consists of and who is behind them. All we learned is that Peregrine Holdings is Monte Carlo based. You know what that means."

"A closed door," I said. "Like trying to get hold of a copy of the Vatican's tax return."

"Indeed. We even couched one of our refusals in terms that suggested we might be interested if we could parley. Just to draw them out. No response."

"It's a fascinating story," I admitted, "but before you go any further, I should tell you that I'm not sure it's in my line. I'd be willing to look into it but I'm not a financial analyst. I seek out rare food ingredients, things like exotic spices. I advise on markets and opportunities for unusual foods and wines. . . ."

Sir Charles was already waving a hand to stop me.

"I know what you do. I investigated your background very thoroughly before I asked you to come here. 'The Gourmet Detective,' that's what they call you, isn't it? I think you're the right man for this; you see, the financial part of this business is not critical—what I want to know is *why* these Peregrine people want our vineyard."

"Maybe they just want to expand and think this is the best way of doing it, even if it does cost money."

Sir Charles pushed his chair back and rose to his feet. "Come with me. I want to show you something."

He led the way to a richly carved mahogany door and we went into a large conference room with wood paneling, a long table with chairs around it, and a blackboard on one wall. It was actually light green but I can't think of them as anything but blackboards.

A rolled map was clipped to the top and Sir Charles pulled it down. It was big, about four feet by three feet, and appeared to be a French Ordnance Survey map. It had been hand-colored in red and green. The red area was roughly circular in shape and about the size of a tennis ball. It sat in the very center. The rest of the big map was shaded in green, dwarfing the tiny enclosed shape in the middle.

"This shows our vineyard and Peregrine's vineyard," Sir Charles said.

I studied it. A "D" classified road ran across the top from east to west. Smaller, unclassified roads ran from it into each area. To the northeast, the land rose rapidly, reaching nearly four hundred metres or well over a thousand feet.

"It reminds me of the classic old Western movies," I commented.

Sir Charles looked a little blank. Perhaps he wasn't a movie fan.

"The tiny family ranch, completely surrounded by the vast acres owned by the wicked land baron who's determined to acquire it by any means at all," I explained.

"Ah, I see . . . no, no, you have it all wrong," he said, shaking his head.

"Have what wrong?"

"That is the Peregrine vineyard there." He tapped a beautifully manicured finger on the miniature red circle in the center. "And this"—the sweep of his arm encompassed the endless rolling acres around it, colored in green—". . . this is Willesford property."

Chapter 2

When we had returned to his office and his secretary had brought coffee, I said, "I must say you surprised me. That little pip-squeak actually wants to buy *you* out?"

He smiled slightly. "I think that map helps you understand our predicament."

"It is a puzzler," I admitted, "if the idea of Peregrine wanting to expand is ruled out."

Sir Charles pursed his lips. "Their latest offer is nearly a million pounds over true market value. They can't be *that* desperate to expand."

"And all attempts at contacting them have failed?"

"Completely without success," said Sir Charles. "There's one other thing I should tell you . . . we hired a private detective, a Frenchman, formerly with the Nice police—a man with a very good reputation."

"And what did he find out?"

"Nothing." A brown folder lay on the desk. Sir Charles put a hand on it. "Here are copies of his reports. You can take this with you. But I can tell you that it contains nothing of any real help." He hesitated. "There's another factor influencing us in hiring you. This French detective has had no contact with us for some time." I felt a pang of alarm but he added quickly, "That has no sinister connotation. We have checked and he has been seen recently in Nice. His last report was thoroughly negative and he inferred he wanted to drop the case due to his lack of success."

"Sir Charles," I said. "I'm not a detective. Oh, I know I use that sobriquet, the Gourmet Detective. It's good for business but I'm not really a detective at all and—"

"I know," said Sir Charles firmly. "As I've just told you, we hired a detective, a good one, and he got nowhere. Maybe a different approach is needed. Maybe some detail would be obvious to a man like you with a knowledge of the wine business where a detective might go right past it."

We both seemed to be assuming that I was going to take the assignment. I had already decided to do so—it was an intriguing problem even though the answer might turn out to be, as Sir Charles said, obvious.

"Tell me about your vineyard," I invited.

"The names and positions of all the staff are in that folder too," he said. "We have 147 acres under cultivation. We produce five wines. Top of the line is our Sainte Marguerite—an excellent white. It's an 'appellation controlee,' a very good 'vin de paille' made from Savagnin grapes. We bottle only one red but it's a near-classic and many critics have compared it to a Crozes-Hermitage. Then we have two white table wines, both made from Chardonnay grapes and with a good reputation in the neighborhood, in the Paris region and here in the U.K. We call one Pont Vieux and the other Bellecoste. Then we have a rose which we call Val Rosé. It's not bad as rosé wines go though we probably should discontinue it and switch that effort to another white, but it sells well. And—as I'm sure you know—rosé wines are very profitable."

I knew what he meant by that last remark. Grapes that might not be good enough for any of the white wines could be used in a rosé and a clever wine maker could use up one hundred percent of his produce that way, getting rid of even the poorest-quality grapes. Furthermore, as rosé wine has no vintage, the cash flow is excellent, there being no delay between bottling the wine and putting it on the market for immediate sale.

"You're quite sure that there are no exterior factors which might make the vineyard desirable?" I asked. "Nobody wants to build a mammoth shopping center there, for instance?"

Sir Charles laughed, a deep, throaty chuckle. "Not a chance of that."

"Sean Connery doesn't want to build a golf course there then?" I persisted.

"The former 007 has bought several parcels of land in Provence for that purpose but none are in this area."

"What about an industrial park? Land can be very valuable to a group contemplating one of those."

"What is probably the largest industrial and scientific park in Europe is already not far away—at Sophia Antipolis, near Antibes. A second would be out of the question."

"The route for the alternative A8 autoroute must run somewhere through there—"

"Much farther north," said Sir Charles. "Believe me, we've considered a great many such possibilities and we could find nothing. We've talked to all the local authorities and we also had Morel—that's the French private detective we hired—we had him check independently."

"No possibility of gold or oil deposits?" I smiled to show that I wasn't really serious even though I was.

"We had a geological survey conducted recently, just in case modern techniques might show up something that had not previously been apparent. There was nothing—and even if there were minerals of any kind, under French law the right to exploit them doesn't have to be sold with the land."

"Hmm," I said, "I think I'm running out of ready answers."

Sir Charles waved a deprecatory hand. "My dear fellow, perfectly reasonable suggestions, all of them. No," he went on, "we've spent a lot of time, money, and effort trying to guess what's behind these offers. We've come up with absolutely nothing." He glanced at me sharply. "Which is why we hope that you can do better."

"When you say 'we,' who does that—"

"Our board of directors. It consists of my son, Nigel; Richard Willoughby; Tommy Traynor, who recommended you; and myself."

I had known Tommy Traynor for many years. He was a good businessman and a shrewd judge of wine—not to mention horses and women. Willoughby, I had heard of and knew to have fingers in many pies.

Sir Charles was still regarding me keenly.

"If I take this assignment, I would want to know how many people are aware of it," I explained.

"Of course. When we hired Morel, we didn't impress upon him any particular need for secrecy. I know he didn't go around Provence trumpeting who was paying him—he is, after all, an experienced private detective. But when he asked questions; people knew who he was. With you, we want to use a different approach."

"What exactly do you mean?" I wanted to know.

"One of Richard Willoughby's interests is a publishing chain, magazines and newspapers mainly. We propose to arrange a cover for you as one of their reporters—doing a series of stories on vineyards in Provence owned by Englishmen."

"Oh, that's all right," I said, relieved.

"So only the four of us on the board and Willoughby's senior editor will know about this."

"Good."

"So what are your terms?" he asked.

"A hundred pounds a day plus expenses."

He nodded, but before he could speak, I added quickly: "Plus a bonus of five hundred for a satisfactory answer to the question 'Why does Peregrine want to buy you out?' "

He hesitated, then nodded again.

"When can you start? The sooner the better as far as we're concerned."

"Today's Tuesday. I have a few loose ends to clear up . . . I can do that tomorrow . . . I could leave Thursday morning."

He pushed the brown folder over to me.

"There's a voucher for first-class return travel on British Midland, Heathrow-Nice in there. They'll exchange it for a ticket when you tell them which flight you want to take. Mildred will give you a week's advance in cash and she will make a reservation for you at Le Relais du Moulin. It's one of the better places in the area and convenient for both vineyards. She'll also reserve you a car at Nice airport."

I don't have a car in London. I hate driving and in a metropolis like London, a car is more trouble than it's worth, but in a widely spread region like Provence, I knew I had no choice.

"I suggest you phone me in two weeks," said Sir Charles. His tone implied that if I didn't have any results in that time, I wasn't going to get any. "We can decide then if we want to continue."

It wasn't very long but it wasn't altogether unreasonable. I might not have solved the whole case by then but I should have some clues as to where the answer might lie.

I picked up the folder and we shook hands.

Chapter 3

By choosing the first flight departure of the morning for Nice, I hoped to avoid any "delays due to late arrival of incoming aircraft," but it still didn't work out that way. We left twenty minutes late, but the breezy voice of the captain assured us that we would make up the time, and so we did.

The snowy masses of the Alps were slipping away to our left and the blue sparkle of the Mediterranean was straight ahead as we began the descent. We swung out over the water then turned in for the run to Nice airport which, despite its popularity, seldom seems crowded.

Passport control was a mere glance and a wave through to the glass doors into the baggage claim area. Next to it, the car rental desk was empty of customers and within ten minutes, I was on the Promenade des Anglais and edging into the autoroute lane marked Autoroute du Soleil, A8—direction Aix-en-Provence.

I had temporarily forgotten how traffic moves in the South of France. It's fast and furious, with little regard for the other driver and the devil take the hindmost. I was taking it carefully until I became readjusted and that meant I was attracting glares and squawking horns, a few shaken fists and—from the numerous convertibles—some choice epithets blended from bawdy provincial French and contemporary porno TV.

After an hour's driving, though, I was getting the hang of it all over again. My speed had crept up and though I wasn't zigzagging from lane to lane, I was no longer a target of abuse. I exited through a busy tollbooth and went north on a country road into Provence, leaving most of the vehicles to head south for the beaches.

The sun shone without hindrance from a cloudless azure sky. The road curled through fields of thyme, mustard, and sage while swifts hurtled over the car in ones and twos, suddenly uniting into orderly formations. I passed an ancient church with a grizzled old man in blue denim overalls repairing the gate. The inevitable half-finished houses dotted the landscape here and there, some old, some not so old, but each one hiding a story of heartbreak or unfulfilled dreams. The countryside dozed in the soft warm air and the road climbed steadily higher.

The village of Saint Symphorien straddled the junction of three minor roads, and it was evidently market day. Cars and people filled the streets; stalls lined both sides, occupying every inch. Each kind of merchandise had its own location. Cheap clothes and toys were set up in the square by the church. One street was ablaze with flowers and the next with fruit. A covered market was in a cast-iron frame building that must have survived World War I and it evidently sold food, for women were coming out with string bags and straw baskets, bulging and heavy. Music blared out from speakers attached to the lamp standards and half a dozen young men were setting up a platform, presumably for a show.

I edged the car cautiously through the melee and came upon D235, which the map in the car showed led to Ducasse, another village. The Relais was on that road and I found it without difficulty—a typical Provençal auberge converted from a weathered old stone farmhouse with a red tiled roof. It looked cozy and inviting and the cobbled courtyard in front had several rows of cars.

The entrance hall was cool and quiet, huge flagstones covering the floor and massive oak beams supporting the low ceiling. A fireplace of walk-in proportions was in one corner and the walls were festooned with farm implements. In contrast to these reminders of past centuries, behind the reception desk a fax machine, a small but efficient switchboard, and a computer with a color screen added touches of modern technology.

Madame Ribereau was lean and athletic with a strong-boned face and gray hair. She had worked in the local vineyards as a girl, she told me, and I supposed that must have been when Sir Charles's father owned one of them, later buying up the others. She and her husband had rebuilt the Relais from a shell and I congratulated her upon such a magnificent job. The smells coming from the adjacent dining room reminded me that it must be lunchtime and Madame said that today's specials included *soupe de poissons,* fillets of red mullet with raspberry butter, and leg of lamb with rosemary.

That decided it. I quickly checked into the room: small but adequate, immaculately clean, and with a view from the tiny mullioned window out over the hills. I headed for the dining room, was shown to a table, and ordered a Kir. They don't make them the same anywhere else, I reflected. The bishop of Dijon had done mankind an inestimable service when he had originated the drink, often copied but never improved. This one had just the right number of drops of Cassis and a good Montrachet had been used, rather than any old white wine the way so many bartenders make it.

I had the fish soup—I find it irresistible when heavy with garlic and liberally laced with *rouille,* the spicy red pepper sauce. The lamb was pink and succulent, the meat even redolent of the wild thyme and rosemary that the cattle of Sisteron love. Sisteron provides all the South of France with lamb, and in the past it must have been a spectacular sight when the huge herds were driven down to the coast to escape the Alpine winter.

A half bottle of wine from the Willesford vineyard went well with it, though I noticed that the label said St. Estephe, no doubt asserting to local consumers how French it was. A tiny cup of very strong black coffee helped me to feel very conscientious as I signed the bill to my room because I headed for the car and drove toward the Willesford vineyards. On the job already and only four hours in the country!

The roads were almost empty—every self-respecting Frenchman was eating lunch. The BMW that scorched past me leaving a trail of dust had German license plates, but otherwise traffic was sparse. The scent of lavender was in the air and the road still climbed. Then I saw the vineyard signs, proclaiming Tasting and Sales in French, English, and German.

I drove in slowly through the wooden gates. The road was unpaved but packed hard. It wound through groves of oak trees, on and on, finally opening into a big courtyard with winery buildings on two sides. A tractor stood next to an open-bed Renault truck. A heap of rusty iron parts was piled high, the metal bones of dead vehicles and equipment. Next to it was an ancient wooden cart with large wheels.

I could see no sign of people, but lunchtime explained that. Flying insects droned and whined, the only sounds etching themselves across the silence. It was warmer now and I could feel a prickle of sweat as I got out of the car.

It was then I saw that I was mistaken—the courtyard was not deserted. A man stood by the old cart, leaning against the wheel, staring at me.

"Bon après-midi," I greeted him. He didn't reply, just kept staring. I walked toward him. He was wearing ragged old gray pants and shirt with a floppy loose jacket, but what caught my eye was just how ragged they all were. Torn and ripped, soil-stained and dirty—they looked as if their owner had been in a fight.

"Where are the offices?" I asked him in French.

He said nothing. He had a slack mouth and a long jaw. His dark hair was untidy. His eyes were expressionless and his stare was almost insolent, as was his attitude. He leaned against the big wooden wheel of the cart, one arm draped over it.

It struck me that most French vineyards use a lot of foreign labor. Perhaps the man didn't understand French. *"¿Habla Español?"* brought no response and *"Fala Portugues?"* was equally unsuccessful. I was about to try German, the lingua franca of eastern Europe, when the bark of a dog split the silence.

It was loud and shattering, an aggressive, brittle sound. It was coming closer, then it burst into view—a large black animal of indeterminate breed. It bounded toward us and I told myself that it couldn't be dangerous, too many visitors came here to taste and buy.

The dog stopped, a few paces away, still barking furiously—but not at me, the stranger. It was barking at the man by the cart, who ignored it completely. I realized that he had not moved or changed his expression since I had first seen him. The dog sidled to him and nuzzled his leg.

The arm draped over the wheel fell slowly to his side. His knees buckled and he slid very slowly to the dusty ground. His eyes were still on me and his face didn't change.

It was then that I saw the smears of blood around the tears in his clothes. I put my fingers on his neck, against the artery. I could feel nothing and I tried again. The dog's barking was now hysterical. It had already known what I knew now. . . .

The man was dead.

Chapter 4

"Annabel!" It was a woman's voice and went on in French: "Stop it! Stop that noise and come in here!"

The dog stopped barking and looked back toward the voice. It looked at me, then at the body slumped on the ground, and resumed barking.

"Annabel!"

She came out of the nearest building, calling the dog's name, and saw me.

"Do you want something?" she called out, and further words drifted away when she saw the body.

"Who are you? What's the matter with Emil?"

"I don't know. I was coming to talk to you when I found him here—dead."

She regarded me suspiciously when my accent identified me as English. In an earlier era, she would have been a fervent supporter of Joan of Arc. Kneeling by the body, she drew in a deep breath when she saw the bloodstains. She took his wrist and her fingers moved as she tried in vain to find a pulse.

She stood up. "He's dead," she said. I just nodded.

A voice called out from the nearest building. "Over here, Marcel!" the girl called out sharply. "Quickly! It's urgent!"

Marcel was elderly and overweight. An accelerated ambling gait was the best he could manage and even that made him wheeze. He had a chubby face and thinning hair. He wore a pair of old black pants and a sort of smock with wine stains on it.

He looked with horror at the body. "What's the matter with Emil?"

"He's dead," said the girl, matter-of-factly.

Marcel's eyes were roaming over the rips and tears, the smears and splashes of blood. "But how? What happened to him?"

The girl didn't respond to either question. "Call the police," she said firmly.

Marcel looked appalled at the idea. "The police?"

"Yes, the police. At once."

He threw a baffled glance in my direction and hurried off. The girl turned to me.

"Who are you and what are you doing here?"

She was medium height and had a strong sturdy body. Her hair was cropped short and a dark blond color. She was attractive, her features strong and bold.

"I'm a journalist. I'm doing a series of stories on south of France vineyards owned by English. I walked in here looking for—well, you, I suppose . . . are you Simone Ballard?"

"Yes." Her eyes searched my face. "You must be the man I received a fax about yesterday." Her suspicion eased fractionally but I wasn't off the hook yet. Maybe I should get my questions in first. "Is this man one of your workers?"

"Yes. Emil Laplace. He's been with us a long time." Still shaken, her gaze went back to the body. "What do you suppose happened to him?"

"I don't know. He's got a lot of injuries, probably

internal too. He must have lost a lot of blood as well."

She shook her head. "He wasn't due to come on duty for another two hours. He liked to spend his spare time gathering mushrooms."

These didn't look like injuries that might be considered an occupational hazard of picking mushrooms. Behind the vineyard buildings rose high hills.

"Could he have fallen?" I wondered aloud.

She shrugged. "But how did he get here?"

A young man came running across the yard and went straight to Simone.

He stopped in front of the body. Gasping, he asked, "Is Emil dead?"

"Yes."

"I found him, up near the caves." Getting his breath back, he went on. "He was alive though very badly hurt. I couldn't carry him. I remembered this old cart in the storage shack up there. I put him on it and brought him here."

"He was on the cart?" Simone asked.

"Yes."

He must have recovered just enough to climb out, I guessed. He had flung out an arm over the wheel to steady himself and died in that position.

"I phoned for an ambulance," the young man said.

Another man came walking out. "What's all the excitement?" he wanted to know. He spoke French but with an English accent. From the list of staff names that Sir Charles had given me I knew he must be Lewis Arundel, the business manager.

He was lean and lanky, with slick dark hair and a thin saturnine face. He was probably about forty.

His eyes flickered from me to Emil's body and back.

"What's happened?"

"Emil's dead," Simone said. "Jean-Jacques found him up near the caves and brought him down here. He was still alive then but he must have died while Jean-Jacques was phoning for an ambulance. This man found him here dead."

"Who's he and what's he doing here?" His eyes searched me.

"He's that journalist we got the fax about."

He looked at me, full of suspicion. He studied Emil's body, cataloging every rip and every bloodstain, and looked at me again. More workers came strolling into the yard, probably to start their shift. They came over to stare, wide-eyed, at Emil's body and whisper to each other.

Marcel came back and proposed carrying the body inside, but Lewis Arundel quashed that idea before Simone could speak. It must be left here for the police, he said. They would want to see it exactly as it was found. He looked at me as he said it, and if it had been a trial and he were on the jury, I'd have been hanged right there on the spot.

There were desultory conversations in muttered tones and long, nervous silences. At length, the ambulance arrived in a swirl of dust and two young men in white uniforms joined our rapidly growing group. There was a spirited discussion about priorities and responsibilities. The two wanted to put the body into the ambulance but Lewis Arundel said, "Not until the police have seen it." Marcel called for respect for a colleague who had been well liked. One of Emil's two co-workers referred sadly to a soccer bet that Emil had lost and not yet paid.

The French temperament includes a masterly ability to compromise, and the ambulance men decided that they would wait for the police but they wouldn't leave without the body. Yes, they said in answer to a question, they were authorized to transport dead bodies as well as live ones. This congenial arrangement had finally been reached when a dark blue Renault sedan with a flashing light on the roof roared to a dusty stop alongside the ambulance. Seconds behind it came a tiny white Citroen. The law had arrived.

Chapter 5

There are several police forces in France. The two principal organizations are the Police Nationale and the Gendarmerie. Both were represented in the two men who got out of the two vehicles and stood with us, looking at the body of poor Emil Laplace.

The man from the Police Nationale was a strapping young fellow who surely had to be a rugby player. He introduced himself as Carl Nevernois and after he had ascertained all our names, he explained the setup, mainly, I supposed, for my benefit as a foreigner.

The Police Nationale handle all civil matters—domestic strife, land disputes, and, the most time-consuming, traffic offenses. The Gendarmes handle any criminal matters, but as the Saint Symphorien region was not large enough (or perhaps not unlawful enough) to justify a gendarmerie, it was customary for crimes to be reported to the Police Nationale who then call in gendarme assistance from a neighboring region.

However—and in France there are always a great many "howevers"—it just so happened that a Poste Provisoire de Gendarmerie had recently been established locally. I knew that this meant a temporary office but I wondered why it had been necessary to open one here. It wasn't the time to ask so I politely shook the hand of the gendarme.

His name was Aristide Pertois and he didn't inspire confidence in the least. He was about six feet tall, with a slim build, bristly black hair cropped close to his bullet-shaped head and a small black mustache. He had a look of perpetual surprise on his face, caused partly by his thick black eyebrows, which always seemed to be raised, and partly by the circular lenses in his wire-framed glasses. He might have nodded minute acknowledgment of meeting me, but more likely it was a reflex action caused by a fly buzzing across his face.

The two policemen soon had Jean-Jacques's story. "There was no one outside," Jean-Jacques concluded. "I shouted but no one came. I went in to the office and phoned for the ambulance."

I told my story, keeping it very simple. Simone confirmed that she had found me standing over the body.

The two ambulance men were examining the body while we were talking. The Police Nationale man, Carl Nevernois, had told them sternly not to touch it but their professional curiosity got the better of them. Disdain for authority is an essential component of the French temperament and the greatest disdain is expressed by one branch of authority for another. One of the ambulance men explained that they weren't touching, just looking.

The gendarme asked them what they thought had happened to Emil. The senior of the two answered promptly: "Sangliers." There was a silence.

Sangliers are wild boars and are found scattered in various parts of Provence. They are hunted enthusiastically for their highly prized meat. They weigh up to a quarter of a ton, hunt in packs, and can be very dangerous.

"Do these wounds look like they were made by sangliers?" the gendarme wanted to know.

The ambulance man hesitated.

"Well?" pressed the gendarme.

The wounds looked as if they had been made by the tusks of a sanglier, the ambulance man said, but admitted that he had never before seen a person so mutilated.

"We've never seen any sangliers near here," Simone said sharply.

"But hunters go out after them," Lewis pointed out. "They must expect to find some."

"I've lived in these parts for thirty years," Marcel contributed. He had identified himself to the police as Marcel Delorme, wine master. "I hunt all the time. I've never seen a sanglier, but there may be some."

"If this was one sanglier," said the senior ambulance man, "it was a monster."

There was a chilly pause. Each of us was no doubt picturing a huge, slavering wild beast with tusks like an elephant and teeth like a crocodile.

"We will want statements from all of you," the Police Nationale man said. "We can take them in the office here. Later, you may be asked to come to Police headquarters for further questioning."

"Or to the Gendarmerie," put in the gendarme.

"Then," the other policeman went on, ignoring him and turning to Jean-Jacques, "you will take us to the place where you found the body."

Jean-Jacques nodded, now beginning to feel grief at the loss of his colleague as the realization finally sank in.

The policeman pointed to the two ambulance men. "You can take the body to the hospital."

"The hospital?" repeated one of them. "But he is dead."

"That's right," said the other. "He should go to the morgue."

"He cannot go to the morgue until he is pronounced dead by the police surgeon," said the policeman firmly. He used the term *médecin légiste,* which neatly describes the profession as legal doctor.

"Then send for the police surgeon."

"It is simpler for you to take the body to the hospital. The police surgeon can go there."

"Living people have to be taken to the hospital, dead people to the morgue." The ambulance man was digging in his heels. "I can show you in the manual where it says that—"

"Sometimes it is necessary to use one's judgment," said Nevernois, and there was a hushed silence at such an heretical pronouncement.

It was broken by the gendarme, Pertois.

"The body cannot be moved until the *médecin légiste* has examined it," he said. His tone was flat and expressionless but it had an underlying ring of authority.

"I'll have to phone in for instructions." The ambulance man was falling back on his standard means of existing from a difficult situation—get someone else to take responsibility for the decision.

"Tell them that you are under orders." The policeman was determined to have the last word. He turned to us. "If you will all go inside, we will take your statements as soon as the body has been taken to the hospital."

The ambulance man gave him a glare and went to his vehicle. We all went inside.

Chapter 6

*I*t was after seven o'clock when I arrived back at the auberge. The sun was dropping but it was still warm and the pool looked so inviting that I changed quickly and dived in. It was refreshing after such an eventful day and I could thrash away to my heart's content, unloading all the tension. Most of this was from waiting, as taking statements was clearly not a subject taught in any detail at the police academy. After the swim, I dressed and picked up the phone and dialed one of the numbers Sir Charles had given me.

No, he assured me, I was not interrupting his dinner. He didn't attempt to conceal his surprise at hearing from me so soon. Had I learned something already? he asked eagerly.

He took the news quite well after a hollow repetition of "You found a dead body!" Latching on to the sanglier aspect of Emil's death, he told me about being unhorsed by a wild boar in the Punjab when a young officer.

"So I know what ferocious beasts they are," he continued. "Still, an unsettling thing to happen on the first day. Don't let it upset you. I'll look for your report in two weeks as agreed." I took that to mean that he wasn't interested in local gossip, just facts on the case in hand.

We ended the conversation and I went down to the "library" where I ordered a much-needed glass of champagne. The shelves held a large number of volumes, all in French and mostly paperback novels. Maigret and Arsene Lupin dominated but Poirot and Hanaud were there too in translation. The book-lined walls, the thick well-worn carpet, the heavy drapes at the tall windows, and the pieces of period furniture gave the room a peaceful atmosphere. Ten minutes later, I went into the dining room and looked through the menu with eager anticipation.

A universal piece of eating advice is to savor the cuisine of the region, and in Provence this is no hardship. The region has its own world-renowned cooking styles and ingredients. Between this and Madame's helpful suggestions, I selected the Pâté de Grives followed by the trout with mushrooms. For the first course, three of the small thrushes are needed for each diner and only the gizzards are discarded as they make the pâté bitter. Everything else goes in including the bones, and the only unusual addition is juniper berries. Madame said that this was the recipe of the famous Troisgros Brothers whose restaurant in Roanne is well known throughout France.

Served with triangles of hot, thin toast, it was superb, and the trout, although a more conventional dish, was equal to it. A plump fish, fresh from local waters, made a fine main course. It was cooked in butter, meunière style, then covered with mushrooms and baked in the oven for a few minutes at the end and served accompanied by a sauce noisette and some steamed parsley-strewn potatoes.

I had asked for a wine from the local Peregrine vineyard but Madame shook her head. They did not carry any Peregrine wines. The vineyard was so near, I protested, surely the auberge should have them. No, it didn't, said Madame. It was not that extraordinary—I have stayed in the village of Chablis and been unable to buy the local wine, renowned as it is. Instead, I drank with my dinner a half bottle of Willesford wine, labeled Bellecoste. It was pleasant without being extraordinary. I took a bottle of Perrier up to the room, firmly resisting the temptation to have a dessert, despite Madame's entreaties.

The next morning, I had planned a tour of the Willesford vineyard and hopefully a beginning to an exposé of the mystery of the excessive offers. The death of the unfortunate Emil put a question mark against that. I decided to drive out there and decide what to do.

It was another beautiful day, warm and sunny but not hot. A gentle breeze ruffled the sunflowers as I drove past a field of them, peering anxiously up at their celestial benefactor. Two police cars stood in front of the Willesford vineyard buildings. The investigation continued, it seemed, so I drove out and went to my secondary destination, the Peregrine vineyard. I had planned on coming here anyway, though I would have preferred to get the story on Willesford first.

I drove past neat rows of vines which looked healthy and productive in the black soil. There was only one building at the end of the well-kept dirt road. Near it stood some gleaming stainless steel barrels and a minitractor, fairly new. I found a door and knocked. There was no reply and I had to knock again. A man opened it.

He was a pleasant-looking fellow in his late thirties and he greeted me with a half smile. I gave him my cover story about articles for a magazine. He nodded and invited me in to a small office with windows looking through into the winery. Schedules hung neatly in a row on the wall and a large bulletin board showed fermentation times, bottling dates, and shipping details. What looked like a decorative painting under glass was actually an enlarged wine label, and there were several framed photographs.

"Gerard Girardet," he introduced himself. "I am the manager." He switched to English, which he spoke extremely well. "You are writing articles on vineyards owned by English, you say? The vineyard you want is, of course, next door."

"I know," I told him, "but I want to get other viewpoints as well as talking to them directly. Unfortunately, there was a sad accident there yesterday and the police are still investigating."

He nodded and motioned me to sit at the small desk with him. "I heard about poor Emil. Gored to death by a sanglier . . . it's hard to believe."

He noted my surprise. "Oh, yes, I know all about it. This is Provence—village gossip is like native drums. Everyone knows everything that is going on."

"Then you probably know a lot about the Willesford vineyard?"

"Impossible not to—we are practically surrounded by it."

"It seems to be much larger than you."

"It is. Very much larger."

"Doesn't that intimidate you?"

He waved his hands in typically French gesture of dismissal. "Certainly not. Why should it? Willesford has its wines, we have ours. It has its markets and we have ours."

That was a good opening for the question that had puzzled me from the night before.

"Do you sell locally?"

"No. Willesford has the market—what is the expression . . . 'sewed up'?" I nodded. "Yes, sewed up, so we sell elsewhere—Paris, Lyon, Marseille—and the higher price we can charge pays the freight."

"There are rumors in London that Willesford wants to buy you out," I told him, employing the principle that it sometimes pays off to appear obtuse.

His smile broadened. "The rumors I've heard are the other way around."

I looked amazed.

He seemed pleased with the reaction he had generated. "And it's not all rumors," he said. "Peregrine has made offers for Willesford. So far, Willesford's turned them down."

"Why does Peregrine want to buy?"

"To enlarge, to expand. We are very limited here. I will show you around. You will see."

He certainly was open. Whatever was going on, he either wasn't a part of it or he was a fine actor.

"Peregrine is a Paris-based company, isn't it?" I asked casually.

"It's a conglomerate. It has offices and operations in many cities and is involved in many businesses."

"And it wants to expand in the wine business?" I said to encourage him. "That would be good for you, I suppose. You'd get to run the entire operation."

"I would hope so, of course. I have done a very good job here. It would not mean the loss of any people at Willesford, either. Combined, the two vineyards would be very strong and we would want to keep all the team."

"You know Simone Ballard, Lewis Arundel . . ."

"Certainly. Marcel, *the maître de vin,* too. Oh, we are rivals, you might say, in as far as we both make wine—but nothing more."

I wasn't getting anywhere on this tack. Time to try another one.

"This unfortunate death . . . will it affect Willesford's business, do you think?"

He shook his head firmly. "No, why should it? Nothing to do with wine."

"I hadn't realized that such dangerous animals roamed this part of Provence."

"You find sanglier on the menu at many restaurants so they must be in this area. It is true that people don't usually see them—only hunters."

"But they are not usually this big and dangerous," I said.

He frowned. "Does anyone know how big this one is?"

"Well, no, but if it attacks men, it must be big . . ."

"Hmm," he said noncommittally. "Anyway, it is wine you are interested in. Would you like to see our vineyard?"

* * *

Traces of morning dew still clung to some of the vines. The sun was still climbing and throwing shadows across the rows. The grapes looked healthy, still small for they had some months to grow before being picked. Gerard looked at them proudly.

"Do you expect a good vintage this year?" I asked him.

"So far, it looks that way. We have the promise of plenty of sun and if, like last year, we have some rain late in the season, it will be an excellent vintage."

From here, the cliffs behind both vineyards stood tall and forbidding against the light blue sky. There were chalky patches but mostly they were scrubby low growth with a row of pines along the ridge. I noticed what I had not seen before: occasional dark holes in the cliffside.

"What are those?" I asked.

Gerard followed my finger. "Caves."

"Are they old?"

"Troglodyte tribes lived in them a very long time ago. When the Romans came here, they used the caves to store grain and wine. They have been used many times since. The Cathars hid in them during the religious persecutions. The Maquis used them as hideouts during the Nazi occupation. The Provençal temperament is obstinate and independent. The locals did not like the Germans, and the caves made ideal places to store weapons, to hide when the Germans came looking to make reprisals."

"What's in them now?"

"They are empty. Mam'selle Ruche, the schoolteacher in Saint Symphorien, takes tours through every Saturday afternoon, when the school is closed. It is risky to go except on the tour—it is said that the caves go very deep inside the hills and a person could easily get lost and never come out."

He turned to go back into the building. I was still looking at the cliffs.

"Something wrong?" he asked.

"No, no," I said. "It's very pleasant out here in the sun."

The building was efficiently utilized, not a square meter wasted. The vats were all stainless steel, like the ones outside. Valves and pipes were all stainless steel or shiny copper. Temperature controls were fitted—a feature not usually found in such small vineyards. The control booth had an electronic scale and a digital readout. Bottling was automatic, even though it was the smallest automatic bottling unit I had ever seen.

It was all a far cry from most wine operations. No dirty floors and smelly wooden casks, no cracked and patched green plastic hose littering the aisles, no boxes and barrels and miscellaneous paraphernalia that was no longer wanted but left lying around on the chance that it might be useful one day.

It was the cleanest, smartest, tidiest operation I remembered seeing for a long time and I told Gerard so. He looked satisfied..

"And it's the vineyard with the smallest staff," I added.

"It's mostly me," he said with just a touch of pardonable smugness. "The equipment is almost entirely automatic, so I can handle the operation alone. Oh, at harvest time we have Spanish labor to do the picking. Numbers of them come through this area every year—they can make more money here than at home. I can always get a man or two in from the village if I need them for loading or unloading. Otherwise, it's just me."

"Your winepresses look large for your throughput," I said. "Why is that?"

"I don't like to subject wine to any unnecessary manipulation. I don't like to fine or filter it, so what we do here is make the most use of whole-cluster pressing. The hoppers are built to our own specifications so that they keep the grapes whole as long as possible. Then, with the oversized presses, we get more free-run juice and very little sediment to filter out."

"But picking the grapes as whole clusters means that you get more leaves, doesn't it?"

"Yes. We use a simple air blast on the feed hoppers to get rid of them."

It was certainly a highly efficient little wine factory but . . . little, that was the operative word. Did the small output of wine justify such sophistication? The use of an air blast to remove leaves was usually seen in only large, high-output vineyards. Gerard beckoned me to follow him. We went into a compact but fully equipped laboratory. He opened a cabinet and took out a bottle and two glasses. He pulled the cork and poured.

He handed me one of the glasses, took the other, and held it up to the light. He appeared content with his examination, toasted me with a nod, and we drank.

It was a distinctive white wine, starting with a spicy aroma then continuing through a lush texture, floral yet buttery at the same time. It was full bodied but smooth with a lingering finish, hinting of pear. I congratulated Gerard and told him, "Reminds me of one of the better white wines from the northern Rhône—say, a Condrieu."

"I am glad you like it," he said politely.

It was, in fact, considerably better than I had expected. If he made wine of this quality, it wasn't surprising that it could be sold in Paris or Marseille for good prices—certainly better prices than the local auberges would want to pay.

We drank again and somewhere a door banged. Footsteps could be heard and then the door to the laboratory opened. A man peered in. When he saw me, he said quickly, "Sorry. See you later, Gerard." He closed the door and was gone before I realized that he had spoken in English.

In the glimpse that I had of him, the man was very heavily built and carried himself in a slight crouch. He had a mass of unruly, curly hair and a face that was dark, almost swarthy. His complexion was uneven, with small growths on the nose and one cheek.

"It has been compared to a white Chateauneuf," Gerard said as if there had been no interruption.

"I would say this is better," I told him. I could ignore interruptions too.

"Another glass?" he offered.

"No, thank you. It really is excellent but I must go."

"Stop in again anytime," he said as we came out into the neat courtyard. "I am always glad to be of help."

I stopped as I reached my car and made a show of going through my pockets for the car keys. In truth, I was scanning the cave entrances—those dark, mysterious holes in the chalky cliffside—and trying not to be obvious about it.

I could see nothing now, but when we had been outside before, I had distinctly seen a figure come out of one of the caves, then hastily duck back out of sight. And this was Friday—not Saturday, the day of the schoolteacher's tour.

Chapter 7

The Willesford vineyard was just as deserted as the last time I had been here but this time Annabel came bouncing toward me as soon as I got out of the car. I said a few soothing words which amounted to "I come in peace" and this, surprisingly, prevented her from barking, though she stood poised and quivering, regarding me with a reproachful look that I couldn't avoid interpreting as "You—last time you were here there was a dead body."

Simone was in one of the offices, encased in glass and surrounded by paper. I rapped on the door and went in.

"Ah, *c'est vous*," she said. Her tone would have been appropriate four hundred years ago when a messenger announced the approach of the Black Plague.

"Yes, it is," I agreed. "I'm sorry I didn't get to talk with you before but it was not the right moment. Now that the police have gone, however, I wonder if I might have a few minutes of your time?"

She mentally reviewed several good excuses but evidently rejected them all on the grounds that she would have to do this sooner or later so better get it over with. She sighed, put down her pen, and said, "Very well. What do you want to know?"

I eased her into it gradually with questions about the area, the yield, the type of grape, the quality of wine, the market . . . all the routine questions that anyone would ask. They were also the questions to which she had answers right on the tip of her tongue and this gave her confidence, so when I hit her with my next question, she was taken aback.

"Why does the Peregrine vineyard want to buy you out?"

She straightened in her chair. "Who told you that?"

I gave her my look of surprise. "Everybody. It's common gossip."

She said nothing so I asked quickly, "Why? It's true, isn't it?"

"There—there have been offers," she admitted slowly.

"I can see they might want to expand—they don't have much land."

"You've been over there?"

"Yes. You were tied up with the police so I went and talked to them first."

"You talked to Gerard?"

"Yes. Nice fellow. Very helpful."

"What did he tell you?" she asked.

"He said Peregrine is seeking expansion. He thought your two vineyards together would be a powerful force in the wine business." I was overstating a little but it might stimulate her into telling me something. She didn't.

"He pointed out that the two of you don't compete so there would be every reason to combine."

"Don't compete?" Her voice rose.

I brought back my surprised look. "That's what he said. You mean you do?"

She shrugged. "Maybe not." She eyed me suspiciously. "Is this what you want to talk about? Merger? Takeover? I thought you were interested in how we run the vineyard?"

Whoops. She was sharper than I had thought. "I am," I said promptly. "But the emphasis of the articles will be how English companies run vineyards in France. If you're going to be bought out by a French conglomerate, then I may have to do some rewriting before we go to press." I hoped that was the right expression.

She stood up suddenly. She was wearing a light gray sweater and a light green skirt. "If you want to look through the operation, come along. I'll show you."

The Willesford vineyard was quite a contrast to the pristine neatness and sparkling cleanliness of the Peregrine operation. Not that it was dirty or untidy, but it didn't have that shiny look of constant care and attention. The copper and stainless steel at Peregrine made a big difference, of course. Their metallic glitter conveyed a naturally immaculate appearance whereas the oak vats and barrels at Willesford looked brown and dull and lifeless.

The floors here were well swept, though. That was one of the first things I looked for. There were no dropped grape skins, stems, or leaves. Nor were any pieces of equipment in need of cleaning or repair. The place appeared to be operating at an optimum level of production.

Simone led the way on to a catwalk above a row of presses. A dozen enormous vats stood open on either side. The air was sweet and cloying; motors rumbled and the catwalk vibrated. Simone explained that the grapes were crushed and destemmed in the bins outside. The red grapes were pumped into the big vats to steep, skins and seeds too. The natural yeasts clinging to the skins would kick off the fermentation and the juice would turn deep red.

"White wines are in the next building," Simone said, having to raise her voice to be heard over the din of machinery. "Their juice has to be pressed from the grapes first and allowed to ferment by itself. That's called the must. It's more sensitive and has to be kept cleaner—at a lower temperature, too, to protect the aroma."

She hadn't asked me how much I knew about wine making and I didn't volunteer any information. Better to let her think I didn't know much— that way she might talk more.

In the bottling room, metal conveyor lines clanked and bottles rattled as they were filled, six at a time. Corks were rammed home and foil slipped into place, all mechanically. The next stage was labeling and although none of the equipment was new, it was all running smoothly. Bottles were slid into cardboard cases and automatic folding and sealing completed the operation.

It was a sketchy tour—American friends would call it a ten-cent tour—and Simone didn't describe any of the departments. We went to the tasting room, which was open though none of the public was here yet.

"Try this one," Simone said and I wondered if she thought that plying me with wine was a way of shutting me up.

It was a white, the Pont Vieux. I recalled that Sir Charles had told me this was one of their table wines and that their best white was Sainte Marguerite. Simone wasn't doing me any favors, that was clear, though when I had drunk half the glass, she immediately filled it.

"Very pleasant," I said, trying not to sound like a patronizing tourist.

"It's a very popular wine," she said matter-of-factly.

"In England?" I asked.

"Yes, but here too."

"In this region?"

"Oh, yes. Almost all the local restaurants and markets sell it."

"How many different wines do you make?" I knew the answer but I didn't want her to know I knew. She told me their names and identified which were red, white, and rosé but didn't describe them further.

"Like to try another?" she asked without any great persuasiveness.

"I don't think so, thanks. It's supposed to be bad to mix different wines, isn't it?"

She shrugged. I was relieved that at least she hadn't poured me the rosé.

While we were walking back to the office, I asked, "Have the police come up with anything new?"

"No. I don't believe there is anything for them to find. Poor Emil ran into a pack of wild boars while he was mushrooming. They can be very vicious animals."

I sneaked a sidelong look at her as we walked. Her expression suited her words and there was no hint of her hiding anything. At the same time, I noticed that she was more attractive than I had thought. She had high cheekbones and good features—if she had worn any makeup, particularly on her eyes, she would have been stunning.

"I may find some questions arising as I get further into the story," I told her. "I hope I can come and ask them?"

She shrugged carelessly. "All right. If you have to." She even condescended to give me what might have been the ghost of a smile.

I felt I had made real progress.

Chapter 8

Narrow trails led off from the vineyard road but the map didn't show them. I drove near to the foot of the cliffs and looked for a footpath. It was easier than I expected. After all, the cliffs and the caves had been here for hundreds of thousands of years and lots of people and animals had been up and down. It wasn't surprising that a lot of paths remained.

The sun was higher now in a cloudless sky and the temperature was rising. Birds soared in the currents of warm air. Soon I was high enough to come out on to a narrow path that ran past the cave mouths. I had to tread carefully but it was just wide enough for one person.

After two or three dozen paces, the mouth of a cave came into sight. I stopped and listened. I could hear nothing but the soft sigh of an occasional breeze and the background music of nature's Muzak—the cicadas. I went on and paused at the mouth of the cave. I could still hear nothing and it was black inside. I took a few tentative steps in and stopped.

When my eyes adjusted to the gloom, all I could see were bare walls. I looked over the ground but it too was bare. I went back out and walked cautiously to the next cave.

It was pitch-black too and I was about to go on along the path when I heard the faintest of rustles. The back of my neck tingled and I had a mental image of a massive hound of the Baskervilles (porcine variant) leaping out at me.

A fly buzzed noisily by, then another. Several were buzzing around and they seemed to be coming out of the cave. I was aware of something else coming out of the cave too—a very strong smell. It was the smell of pigs . . .

P. G. Wodehouse said, "Pigs is pigs" and I hoped that was all they were, not wild boars. I had an urge to go inside the cave and have a look but I was able to fight that urge without any trouble. . . .

I stood frozen, staring.

A shiny revolver had emerged from the dim interior of the cave and was pointed right at my middle.

"Who are you? What are you doing here?" The voice was that of a woman, but women can pull triggers as easily as men.

I tried to answer but my mouth was too dry. The revolver jerked impatiently and that brought words rapidly. I gave my cover story about being a journalist from England doing a story on the Willesford vineyard. By the time I was finishing, I was getting a little nerve back. I waved my arms in exaggerated accentuation of my words, hoping that if there were people below, they might be able to see me and know that there was someone up here. I could still see nothing of the woman except fingers around the gun but she was perceptive and realized instantly what I was doing.

"Come inside!" she ordered. The gun backed slowly away and I followed.

The cave widened into a sort of antechamber. Two other caves led away from it and the area we were in was roughly circular and the size of a large room. There was nothing in it although the smell of pigs was much stronger despite the slight chill of air that had never known sun.

"I don't believe you," the woman said in an unpleasant tone of voice. "Tell the truth—what are you looking for?"

"I've told you the truth," I insisted.

I was becoming accustomed to the light now and I could see her clearly. She was slim, dark, and attractive with a brisk, businesslike aspect to her appearance. She held the gun as if she knew how to handle it, and the way she carried herself suggested that she was determined and decisive.

"You killed my husband, didn't you?" The gun moved menacingly.

"No, I didn't," I said quickly. "He was dead when I found him."

"What?" She snapped out the word and took a step toward me.

"He was already dead. I—"

"What are you talking about? Where did you find him?"

"In front of the Willesford vineyard," I said.

I could see her eyes now. They were dark and beautifully shaped but they were staring. "What are you talking about?" she asked again. "Who did you find?"

"Emil Laplace, he—"

"I'm not talking about him. He's not my husband."

Now there was another body and it seemed as if I was under suspicion for it too. "Who is your husband?" I asked. It was time for some clarification. She ignored my question.

"Stand over there," she ordered. I did so and it enabled light from outside to fall on my face. I hoped she was a good judge of character and would immediately observe my complete innocence.

"Show me your passport," she ordered.

I took it out slowly and handed it to her. She held it up so that she could see it in the diminished light and keep me in view at the same time.

"This does not say you're a journalist."

"Sometimes that's an advantage. Gets me into more places."

She studied the passport further, then closed it and handed it back to me.

"Can you put that gun away?" I asked. "We could talk better without it."

She had a black shoulder bag that matched her black slacks and light sweater. She snapped it open and put the gun into it, though I noticed that she didn't close it and her hand didn't stray far away from it.

"Who is your husband?" I asked again.

"Edouard Morel," she said.

"Private detective, office in Nice. Hired by Willesford Wine Group to find out why Peregrine wants to buy them out at a ridiculously high price."

She said nothing. She had gained more from me than if she had used thumbscrews and an iron maiden.

"How do you know this?" she asked.

My mission was supposed to be confidential. The conventional investigator would suffer all manner of torture rather than divulge who employed him but I wasn't conventional. Furthermore, it looked as if I could learn more by being honest—an unusual state of affairs but one that had to be faced. If I were to tell anyone what I was really doing here, Edouard Morel's wife was surely that one.

"I had intended contacting your husband," I told her. "Are you saying he's dead? When did he die and how?"

"Sir Charles hired my husband to find out, as you say, why Peregrine wants to buy out Willeford's vineyard. He was not able to find out anything of value—or so his reports indicated—and Sir Charles terminated his contract. It would be reasonable if Sir Charles hired someone else to investigate." She eyed me critically. "That is probably you."

I made up my mind. It was my decision, and facing a determined-looking woman with a pistol inches from her hand, I felt justified in telling all.

"You're right. I'm not supposed to tell anyone—that's why I'm using the cover of a journalist. I arrived yesterday. I found Emil Laplace when I went to the vineyard—he was already dead. I didn't know that your husband was dead too," I went on.

"I don't know for sure that he is. I haven't heard from him for two weeks and he hasn't been near his office. And I have a feeling . . ."

"You said 'or so his reports indicated.' Does that mean he really had found out something of value?"

"I don't know."

Perhaps I had been too hasty in being truthful with her. Maybe honesty wasn't always the best policy after all. Was she holding out on me now?

"You say you don't know. Do you suspect?"

"I didn't work with him. I don't know a lot about his investigation."

"You know enough to think he had found out more than he told Sir Charles."

She was hesitant now and I wondered why. When she finally answered, she said, "When I hadn't seen him for several days, I took the duplicate key to his office. I went there and looked through his files."

"And what did you find?"

"He was researching the backgrounds of several aristocratic families in Provence. I don't know why. Then on two occasions, I saw his car outside the newspaper office. He once said he found back copies of the paper very useful."

"What are you doing here in the caves?"

"I noticed chalk on Edouard's shoes on two occasions. These caves are the only place I knew it could have come from."

"What have you found here?"

She shook her head. "Nothing. I think someone has been here but I'm not sure."

"You smell the pigs?"

"Yes." Her eyes searched my face. "What about it?"

"Emil Laplace was gored by sanglier."

She shivered. "You think they are in these caves?"

"They may be."

She snapped her bag shut. I felt relieved and motioned outside. "Shall we go?"

We went out into the warm air, which was like a blanket after the chill of the cave. She followed me along the path and down the cliffside.

"Where is your car?" she asked when we reached the bottom. I pointed.

"Mine's over here."

"I think we should cooperate," I said. "We'd both like to find your husband. We have a better chance of doing it if we pool our information."

She seemed hesitant again. I felt she was holding back, but she nodded. "Very well."

"We could start by having lunch."

She hesitated but then she said, "No, I can't," adding quickly, "perhaps another time. Where are you staying?"

I told her. She took a card and a pen from her bag, crossed out the name, which was that of her hairdresser she said, and wrote her name and phone number on the back.

"I'm Veronique," she said, and the faintest of smiles crinkled her mouth.

"Let's keep in touch," I said. She nodded and walked off. I watched her trim figure as she picked her way through the scrubby undergrowth. I had gained an ally at least, I thought, but she wasn't telling me all she knew and probably little of what she suspected.

Did she really believe that Edouard Morel might be dead? Or suspect?

Or know?

Chapter 9

❧

I drove into Saint Symphorien and parked in the busy main square. A solitary official was engaged in a casual endeavor to see that shoppers and visitors did not park in impossible places but he was spending more time in public relations, chatting with mothers about their children and debating with three grizzled old-timers Olympic Marseille's chances in the European Soccer Cup.

It was a typically Provençal scene. The Romanesque church had a severe front and pock-marked walls from countless sieges and battles. Behind it, the ruins of the old castle thrust jagged stone teeth into the air. Shops and stores surrounded the square and busy bargain hunters sought out the plumpest chickens, the most glistening tomatoes, and cheeses so powerfully endowed that they overcame all the other smells—of which Saint Symphorien had its full complement.

On one corner of the square, the pharmacy had a massive chart in the window showing color pictures of mushrooms and carefully identifying the poisonous ones. Next door was a patisserie with a toothsome array of chocolate cakes, pies, and biscuits in the small window. Next to it was a bar-restaurant,

La Colombe, and the menu outside promised a modestly priced meal prepared with all fresh ingredients, so I went in.

On one side was a bar, a "zinc" as they are still known, though no longer covered with a galvanized sheet. Behind it, the wall was covered with gaily labeled bottles and a mirror that was yellowing with age. Three elderly men in working clothes were drinking an early lunch and arguing loudly about a television soap. Farther along, a man sat at the bar alone, hunched over his drink.

A dozen tables, mostly empty, were covered with red and white tablecloths and set for meals. I chose one and studied the menu. It offered a good selection of simple and popular country-style dishes and I decided on the grilled red and green peppers with anchovies to start and the gambas flambéd with cognac as the main course. Provence wines are nonvintage and many are of mediocre quality, but most are very drinkable. I chose a white wine that I knew, the Château Sainte Roseline from a vineyard in Les Arcs-sur-Argens, as there were no wines from Willesford or Peregrine listed.

As the waitress took my order I noticed the man at the end of the bar looking at me as if he knew me. There was something vaguely familiar about him. I could see him better now and I remembered him from Gerard's office.

Anyone connected with either vineyard in any way was a potential source of information and I gave the man a nod and a smile by way of encouragement. He nodded back and I waved a hand to the other place setting at my table.

After the briefest of hesitations, he picked up his stein of beer and came over. I introduced myself.

"Elwyn Fox," he said. "Didn't I see you at the vineyard?"

He spoke in English and I replied in the same language. "You did. Have a seat."

He put down his stein and settled himself carefully into the chair. He was a big man, and he had a ponderous way of moving that made him seem even bigger. The dark brown leather windbreaker added to the effect of size just as his puffy, weather-beaten face and unruly brown hair probably made him look older than he was.

"I'm writing a series of articles on vineyards in the south of France under British ownership," I said to get the conversational ball rolling. "The Willesford vineyard is one of the first and I went to talk to Gerard to get his viewpoint on his neighbors."

"Is that a fact," he murmured. "Well, now, ye couldn't have chosen a better man to do that. Gerard is a very nice chap and knows as much about wine and how to make it as anybody in the district."

He had a singsong accent and a soft-spoken voice.

"You're Welsh," I said.

"That I am," he agreed. "Born in Llangollen. My mother was born there too. My father was a Cherokee Indian. His name was Running Fox but he changed it to Ronald Fox to suit the purposes of civilized bureaucracy."

He had the singsong intonation typical of Wales. "So ye're writing about the vineyard here." He said it as if he didn't believe it for a second.

I tried to ignore that impression as I said promptly, "Yes and I must say I didn't expect to find a dead body as soon as I got here."

"Emil." He said the name without emphasis.

"Yes, poor chap," he went on, "many's the drink I've had with him in here . . . and other places."

He drained his stein as the waitress approached with my bottle of wine and I invited him to have another beer. The waitress took his glass almost before he had nodded agreement. She evidently knew his habits.

"Cherokee and Welsh—that's an unusual heritage."

"It is indeed. My father was with the Wild West part of a traveling circus. He was getting tired of the continual moving and Llangollen struck him as a place to settle. He met my mother and they were married in a month."

"You work at the vineyard?"

"Not exactly."

"What does that mean?" I asked.

The waitress set another liter stein of beer in front of him and he took a few swallows from it before answering. "I'm a dowser."

"A what?"

"A dowser. It's a sort of gift really. You see, my father was the son of a medicine man, a shaman they call them. He had some gifts himself but he didn't like to use them. They made him feel different and he didn't like that. That's why he joined the circus and confined his tricks to riding horses bareback, shooting a bow and arrow, that kind of thing. My mother—now she was the real thing. . . ."

This was a strange man with a strange story. Why on earth did a vineyard want a dowser?

"You say you have these gifts. Do you have any thoughts about Emil's death?"

He shifted his bulk in the chair. He was like a big shaggy brown bear.

"I don't know a thing about it," he said softly. "Anyway, you came here to write about vineyards, didn't you?"

"I found the body," I said defensively. "That's why I'm interested. My first day here and I find a dead body."

"He wasn't dead when you found him," he said quietly.

"Yes, he was. Jean-Jacques said Emil wasn't dead when *he* found him."

"Ah," he said without expression.

The waitress evidently knew the timing of his drinking and came over with an inviting look. He nodded and she went back to the bar.

"How long do you expect to be here?" I asked conversationally.

"Don't know. Till the job's finished, I suppose."

"At least Gerard must be a nice guy to work for." I was probing and not with any success.

"Don't have a lot to do with him. We have a little chat now and then, that's about all."

Now that he had started, he didn't seem reluctant to talk, and I watched him take another swig from the stein before he continued.

"My mother was the seventh daughter of a seventh daughter. She was a seer just as her mother was a seer."

"It's a person who has second sight, isn't it?"

"Aye, some people call it that. She could see things that others couldn't—she knew things . . . she warned about the fire in the colliery at Festiniog a week before it happened. Fools wouldn't listen to her and thirty men died. They listened to her afterwards though. People would come and ask her things . . . when little Megan Evans wandered off and got lost, my mother could *see* what Meg was seeing and it was from that that they found her."

He paused to drain the stein and I asked, "And you've inherited these gifts from both your parents?"

He nodded. "That's why I'm a dowser."

I couldn't keep the querying note out of my voice as I said, "You're dowsing at the Peregrine vineyard?"

"That's right."

I drank some wine. It was light and fresh, just the way I remembered it.

"That's the truth. The last job was in Spain—a godforsaken spot in the south. It was too far away from the Mediterranean coast and not near any cities. Some German builders wanted to put up a big housing development but they were fighting with the authorities—not greasing the right palms, I imagine. There was no early prospect of running in water mains so they wanted me to find out where they had to dig wells and see how deep they'd have to be." He shuddered. "Terrible job that was."

"Did you find water?"

"I always find it if it's there."

"Having any luck here?"

The waitress came, his beer in one hand and my peppers and anchovies in the other. He took a long draft. "It takes a while sometimes."

Red and green peppers with anchovies is a dish that is particularly Provençal. It carries the flavor of the terrain, full of light and sunshine.

"Care to join me in some lunch?" I invited.

He looked dubiously at my plate. "No, thanks, not now. Might eat later."

I was aware of someone at my shoulder and looked up.

It was Lewis Arundel, the sardonic Englishman from the Willesford vineyard. He smiled a wry, lop-sided half smile at both of us. The nod that he and Elwyn Fox exchanged suggested that they knew each other well. The waitress came with a stein of beer for him. I motioned to a chair and he sat down with us. Apparently the two of them were regular drinking partners.

"How's the investigation going?" Arundel asked me.

Chapter 10

"You'd know more about that than I would," I told him. "I believe the police have spent a lot of time there at the vineyard."

"Poking and prying. Asking silly and unnecessary questions."

"Have they reached any conclusions?"

"The wild boar theory seems to be holding."

I decided that his bored tone was normal and natural to him, not confined to this conversation.

He glanced slyly at the Welshman. "Pity your supernatural powers don't stretch beyond dowsing. You might be able to help the police find out exactly what happened."

"Emil was gored by a wild boar," Fox said and took another large swallow of beer.

"I knew that there are sangliers here in Provence but I didn't realize they were this dangerous," I said, keeping the conversational focus on this point.

I looked at Arundel. "You've been here a long time, haven't you?"

"Two and a half years."

"Heard of any sanglier deaths in that time?"

"You hear warnings on Riviera Radio when it's

the mating season. Somebody must think they're dangerous."

"But they don't usually come so close to human habitation, do they?"

Arundel gave me one of his supercilious looks. "Going to write an article on sangliers too, are you?"

I hadn't thought of that as an additional cover story but I accepted the contribution gratefully. "I was thinking one of the English sporting magazines might be able to use it. There's a hazardous angle that would be novel to readers in the UK."

Arundel grunted. "Better be careful asking questions. You're under suspicion already, you know."

Fox looked at him sharply. So did I.

"Suspicion?" I said. "Of what?"

Arundel drank beer, slowly, savoring the moment. "Some people believe that you are not what you seem."

I laughed nonchalantly. I hoped it came out that way. "Me? Not a journalist? Then what am I?"

Fox was taking all this in, his eyes flickering from Arundel to me and back like a spectator at a tennis match.

"There are those . . ."—Arundel said slowly and with a deliberate pause—"who think that you're here to scout out the land for the homes."

"Homes?" I certainly must have looked innocent of this charge. "What homes?"

Arundel drank more beer, keeping me in suspense as long as he could. It was Fox who answered. "There's a story going through the village that a colony of retirement homes is going to be built somewhere near here."

"And they think I'm connected? That's ridiculous," I said firmly. "I came here to do a story, that's all. Naturally, I'm always looking for new ideas."

Arundel looked at me with that same arrogant stare. Fox said nothing.

The waitress came with my gambas at that moment and the flambéing operation at the table proved to be a convenient hiatus. We all watched the flames flicker and die.

"Bon appetit," said Fox ritually.

"I must be off," Arundel said. He threw some coins on the table, drained his beer, and left.

Fox watched me start eating. "Okay are they?"

"The gambas? Yes, fine."

"They're pretty good here," he said conversationally. "They use fresh stuff—well, not all the time but mostly."

"No excuse with gambas," I commented. "With the Med only a few miles away."

"Aye, but that doesn't bother some of the places. They'll still serve frozen fish."

"I'm surprised that water's a problem here though. Are you having any luck?"

He didn't answer right away, then he said abruptly, "It's that film."

"What film?"

"Two of them really—that *Manon des Sources* and . . . what was that other one?"

"Oh, *Jean de Florette,* you mean? Yes, they were about Depardieu's flower gardens, weren't they? And Yves Montand, the villain, blocked off his water supply so all his flowers died."

"Yes, well, everybody thinks it's like that down here."

"And it's not?"

"No—I mean, not that dramatic, anyway."

"So there's plenty of water?"

"The water table's fairly high. After all, Provence borders on the Mediterranean. But it doesn't always come up to ground level exactly where you want it."

"But there's plenty of irrigation, isn't there?" I didn't understand what he was telling me. What I wanted to know was, why was he dowsing?

"Oh, there's irrigation, of course."

"Then there must be plenty of water; people have been growing grapes here for centuries." I was going to give up but he wasn't making it easy for me.

"They still get droughts occasionally," he said doggedly.

"Well, water's a valuable commodity," I admitted, "and I suppose with the accountants always looking for lower costs, it's vital to have it available at the right place at the right time."

"That's it exactly," he said, pleased.

Except that wasn't it and there was something he wasn't telling me, something he was hiding. I returned to the gambas and he seemed relieved that I had let him off the hook. I hadn't though—not completely.

"As I get into this article, perhaps we can talk about this some more. Readers will be fascinated to hear about how you find water under the ground."

"It's a hard thing to explain. It's a gift, ye know, and I don't know how it works. I just know it does." He sounded earnest.

"A lot of people believe that there are earth currents, don't they? Magnetic currents of some kind that can be tapped?"

"Yes. Dowsing probably originated here, you know."

"Here?" I said, surprised.

"In ancient times, but the art was lost for years. Then a French abbott, Abbe Paramelle, spent much of his life seeking underground springs here in this region. At first, he wanted to help poor peasants who couldn't grow crops in arid soil."

"The church must have frowned on it, surely. Didn't it smack of witchcraft and magic?"

"Aye, some church authorities wanted the abbott burned for sorcery, but others said it was a gift of God. He was successful and the people of the district loved him when he found many springs that brought them their much-needed water."

"Do you use a twig or a metal rod or something else?"

"It depends. I have used lots of different shapes and materials. I get results with most of them but they can vary with conditions, terrain, even weather."

"I suppose some dowsers like specific tools?"

"Oh, I know dowsers who use only copper rods. Some use twigs. I know one who even uses a forked shape that he designed himself—he had it made in plastic. It works, for him, anyway. In earlier days, a silk thread was popular. Some dowsers dangled a coin or a disk from it. The material needn't be important—every dowser has to find out what works best for him."

He was talking freely enough now. Was he glad to be off a subject he wanted to avoid? It was time to throw him off balance. . . .

"So, when you've found water, your job here is finished?"

"Perhaps . . . perhaps not." He was being evasive again but he didn't seem disconcerted. "The abbot Paramelle found dozens of springs. He kept on and on. Perhaps, they'll want me to keep on."

"The Peregrine vineyard is small. You'll soon have covered all of it, won't you?"

"Eventually. Sometimes, I have to go over the ground more than once."

He finished his beer.

"Another?" I invited, and I thought he gave it serious consideration but maybe my questioning told him it was time to end the session.

"No. Thanks anyway."

He went out into the square. I finished my gambas and had a small cup of powerful black coffee. I had a lot to think about. A whole new dimension of the investigation was opening up before me. Why were the Peregrine people looking so desperately for water? The vineyard looked as if it had ample irrigation; the grapes appeared healthy enough. If they weren't getting plenty of water, couldn't they put in larger pipes? Of course, that would cost money—maybe the vineyard didn't have a high enough grape yield to justify that?

Well, I could check on those points right now. I paid the bill and asked directions to the *mairie*.

Chapter 11

*I*n a French village, the *mairie* is the seat of all power and the center of all authority. When the village is in Provence, Paris is merely the name of a city far away, and no local would accept for a moment any edict issued from it unless it was endorsed by the local *mairie*.

The *mairie* in Saint Symphorien was two streets from the main square and occupied an ancient building in a narrow cobbled street. A pretty fountain tinkled merrily in front of it but the stone steps leading up to the battered wooden door showed the wear of thousands of feet, from hopeful brides and proud parents to indignant taxpayers, furious homemakers, and angry motorists.

The massive iron handle creaked as I turned it but the door swung open easily and led into a chilly, dark hall. More stone steps led upward to a large friendly woman at a high wooden counter in a large busy room. I explained that I was a journalist from England, that I was writing an article on local vineyards and wondered about the question of water supplies. "So many English love to visit this beautiful area," I explained. "But it is a dry climate and readers will wonder how grapes can grow here. They are used to a lot of rain there, you know."

She nodded vigorously. All the French know of the atrocious English weather. She went to a rack of thin shelves and pulled out a crinkled map. Her long brown finger wandered over it then stopped at some broken lines. Those were the water pipes, she said, 150 and 250 millimeter, that supplied the two vineyards. The water came from the Gorges de Verdon reservoir.

There was plenty of water, she assured me. I asked about drought years and she shook her head firmly. "Emergency plans exist: cuts at certain hours, limited supply to nonessential businesses—"

"And the vineyards?" I asked. Her eyes widened at this foolish question.

"Oh, no, m'sieu. Their supplies are never affected. Wine is the most important product of Provence."

While I was here, I raised the subject of the A8b, for the specter of that new autoroute slashing its band of devastation through Provence haunts even those not likely to be affected. It appeared that it would not be authorized for some years, and even then it would pass nowhere near the vineyards. No, she said in answer to my next question—no other projects had been approved or even contemplated that would affect the vineyards. Retirement homes? She shrugged off the idea. Down on the coast perhaps, she said derisively, as if referring to another world.

At Le Relais du Moulin, I had the pool to myself and when I went into the lounge for a Kir before dinner, Madame was eager to tell me of the day's

specialties. I selected the escargots in garlic, assured
by Madame that these were the species known as
"vigneron" as they are fed exclusively on vine
leaves in the Burgundy region, and followed these
with a fish casserole containing turbot, prawns,
crayfish, mussels, clams, and rascasse. This latter is
translated unfortunately as scorpion fish. It is tasty
though short on meat, but ideal for a stew, bouil-
labaisse, or casserole.

A bottle of Willesford's Sainte Marguerite went
very well with it, and the chef's use of bay leaves,
saffron, onions, lemon juice, tomatoes, and marjoram was neatly done. He had, I was sure, added
some Banyuls, a sweetish dessert wine, to balance
the lemon juice.

I had a mandarine mousse that was light and
fluffy as air—almost—and a cup of coffee. I was
still enjoying this when Madame came hurrying
over with an envelope that she said had been left at
the desk.

Inside was a sheet of the squared paper that the
French inexplicably prefer for writing notes. The
message on it was in English. It was printed in large,
blocky capitals and it was unsigned. It read:

IF YOU WANT TO KNOW MORE ABOUT THE DEATH OF
EMIL LAPLACE, COME TO THE PLACE DES ARMES IN
COLCROZE TOMORROW AT 11:00 A.M.

Chapter 12

Breakfast the next morning was served on the terrace at Le Relais. It was a spectacularly beautiful Provence day. The sky was cloudless and a freshly washed blue. Long-tailed birds reveled in the gentle breezes, soaring and wheeling, raucously applauding one another's aeronautical skills.

By the standards of many other countries, a glass of orange juice, a cup of steaming black coffee, and two croissants, crisp and hot though they may be, do not constitute any kind of breakfast. There was fresh butter, which helped, and, as a concession to English and American visitors, a bowl each of raspberry jam and marmalade. It wasn't much of a meal on which to go out and confront an informer who professed to have information on a suspicious death, but I resolved to have a good lunch in Colcroze and make up for it.

I had brought my Michelin map to the table and soon found that the map did not show Colcroze. *Col* means "hill" and *croze* is an old Provençal word for "cross." Many villages in Provence have names with 'croze' as part of them, bestowed in the eleventh to fourteenth centuries by returning Crusaders.

The waiter had never heard of it, he said, adding

that he was from Montpellier anyway and a "foreigner" to Provence. Madame was in the village on a buying mission and I was passed on to Henri, the headwaiter. He tried to explain where it was and eventually put an X on the map. When I asked him why it wasn't marked, he shrugged as if that were a strange question. I thanked him and went out to the car. I was early, but indications were that finding Colcroze might not be easy.

An hour later, I was able to confirm that. I was in delightful Provençal countryside, fields of heather and lavender on all sides. I was also at a crossroads with no signpost. I made a guess and turned left.

The terrain was getting more hilly and I guessed I must be approaching two thousand feet in altitude. The air was fractionally cooler but the temperature was still very pleasant. I kept climbing. I hadn't seen a car or any sign of habitation for some time but I continued. Then the ground fell away to my left, giving a clear vista that allowed me to see a village a few miles ahead.

It looked like most Provençal villages, an untidy sprawl of houses huddled together behind massive, towering stone walls. The ruins of a castle struggled to reach above the rooftops . . . but I could see no more and drove on slowly, hoping that Colcroze was not like Brigadoon, appearing only once a century. I was experiencing doubt when a huge stone arch appeared ahead. It was set into massive walls and the entrance to the village.

It was so dark I was tempted to turn on lights. Houses on both sides reached up four and five stories, with irregular fronts, tiny windows, and large forbidding doors. The street narrowed and if a vehi-

cle came in the opposite direction, one of us would
have to back up.

At an intersection, an old church looked gray
and forlorn. My eyes were adjusting to the gloom
and it seemed I was in one of the less desirable
parts of the village. Shops were either closed or
out of business and—I suddenly realized—I had
not yet seen a person. I went on slowly and came
out into the dazzling brightness of the main
square.

It was deserted.

There was not a car, not a human being in sight.

I didn't have to park the car, I just left it and
walked across the square.

The village was abandoned and had been for
some time. How long, it was hard to tell. In this dry
climate and at this altitude, it must have been many
years. It could have been decades . . . could it have
been centuries?

I felt a shiver of apprehension.

It was not a good place for a meeting. It was ten
minutes before the appointed time. I made a tour of
the square, silent in the drowsing sunshine. Shop
fronts were boarded up, the beams cracked and turning to powder, nails rusted till no metal remained.

There are a number of ghost villages in Provence.
The oldest date back to the years of the Plague when
a third of Europe's population was wiped out. During the following years, other pestilences and epi-
demics swept through weakened communities.
Towns and villages were desolated. Biot, near Antibes, is an example of a village brought back to life
after more than a hundred years when the bishop of
Genoa sent fifty families there to regenerate it.
Some villages were bypassed by new roads, others

"died" as the industries that had sustained them were rendered obsolete.

Colcroze had a brooding air of mystery as if it might spring back to life at any moment. I looked uneasily around the square. Was my informant here already, waiting for me?

The inference of the note was that there was more to Emil's death than appeared. If he had not been gored by wild boars . . . the lurking suggestion was that he had been murdered. By whom and why were the inevitable questions. Was there a connection between Emil's death and the puzzle of the Willesford/Peregrine buyout offer?

The faintest of breezes brought up tiny swirls of dust from the cobbled square. A sharp noise startled me but it was a damaged shutter, slamming open and shut. An open space had a few stone benches under ancient plane trees.

The possibility that I was in danger had to be faced but it didn't seem too likely. If an unknown assailant wanted to dispose of me, it surely could have been done sooner and without the need to bring me out here. On the other hand . . . I pushed away all the thoughts that were on the other hand.

It was a minute or two before eleven, the witching hour. The breeze had died and it was utterly still and quiet again. I walked across the square and sat on one of the stone benches. It was warm and I felt drowsy. I thought I could hear the hum of a large insect but then it was gone and the silence spread like a cloak. I stretched out and must have closed my eyes and dozed.

I awoke, suddenly aware of a dull, low-pitched buzzing. A shadow passed across the sun and I looked up but could see nothing. I must have been dreaming. The buzzing noise was louder and the sky darkened by a shape above me. It was a monstrous insect—no, that was impossible . . . it was too enormous, too gigantic. It had green and brown wings and a beaklike nose—it was peering down, searching for prey.

I awoke—or thought I did. I stood up in alarm— or thought I did. Was I awake or still dreaming? A black dot materialized and grew larger, larger . . . it was blotting out the sun. Was the terrifying creature diving down at me? The only thought in my mind was to escape from this haunted place but I felt the terrifying certainty that it was too late.

Chapter 13

I couldn't tell when the transition from dreaming to waking occurred. It was probably when the black shape, growing larger by the second, hit the cobbled square and burst into a thousand fragments. From inside it, a thick cloud of black gas emerged and spread instantly. Then it seemed that the cloud separated into individual particles as it spread further. I was certainly fully awake by this time. The pulsating black mass came toward me and I realized that the object that had fallen was a beehive and the separating particles were enraged bees.

They were all around me, buzzing furiously and looking for anyone to wreak their anger on—and the only one there was me. I flailed my arms wildly, fully aware that it was the wrong thing to do as it would only make them angrier but not able to stand there like a statue. More and more came, probably sensing that they had me outnumbered. I could see only a dark blur as they surged over me and I wondered vaguely how many bee stings it took to kill a person.

It was probably only seconds, though it seemed like hours, and then a new sound penetrated the belligerent buzzing. A sort of roaring noise rose in intensity. I flailed even more madly and through a gap in the dusky cloud I saw a bright red car shoot out of one of the side streets and enter the square like a champagne cork shot from a bottle. Tires screeched as it bounced and swayed over the cobblestones and the engine rose to a high-pitched whine. Brakes screamed as it skidded to a stop beside me.

A figure jumped out holding a small cylinder, red as the convertible. Then I was drenched in a cooling white gas and the bees were melting away magically. In seconds, almost all of them were gone. I was beating frantically at a few diehards that were reluctant to retreat and I saw that the red cylinder was a fire extinguisher and it was wielded by a girl.

All the salient features of young good-looking girls usually register with me very quickly, but I must admit that this was one occasion when it took longer. A few bees still persisted though their cause was lost and I slapped at them to encourage them to join their smarter comrades who knew when the contest was over.

"Are you hurt?" the girl asked in French. "Did they sting you?"

I was out of breath but I managed to gasp an answer.

"I think I'm all right, I—ow! there's a sting, on my neck. And—ow, there's another . . ."

In the tension of the moment, I had spoken in English but I didn't realize it until she replied in the same language, almost without an accent.

"Do you know if you're allergic to bee stings?" she asked anxiously.

"Not as far as I know, but then I've never needed to find out."

"Better get in the car. I'll take you to a doctor."

She tossed the extinguisher behind the seat, revved the engine, and raced out of the square as if all the bees in Provence were after us. I was beginning to calm down and was able to take stock of the situation. The girl first, of course . . .

She had hair the color of corn and it was cut in a seemingly careless manner that had probably taken hours. It draped down almost to her shoulders and fluttered gently in the breeze as I noticed too that this was a convertible. Her eyes were blue but a strong, almost dark shade. She had lovely features, mobile and full of character. She handled the car—I saw it was a Maserati—like a race driver, shifting expertly as we swept out through the stone arch and onto the road. She was wearing a tight-fitting jump suit in immaculate white. It had metal buttons and a wide brown leather belt. A forest green shirt in a silklike material peeked out at the neck.

"I have to thank you for saving my life," I said, speaking loud enough to be heard over the thunder of the engine, which sounded as if it had enough horsepower for a jet bomber.

She smiled charmingly. "I was going to say 'It was nothing' but that would be an insult in English, wouldn't it?"

I introduced myself, using my cover story.

"Monika Geisler. I am from Stuttgart." I noticed now the slightest of German accents as she went on, "I am a magazine photographer. I am doing a piece on hilltop villages and I heard about this one."

"It's off my list," I said. "Too dangerous."

"Where did all those bees come from?" she asked, paraphrasing George Custer.

I hesitated. It sounded silly to talk about giant insects dropping beehives on me—silly even to me. "I fell asleep and the next thing I knew, I was surrounded by them."

She darted me a sympathetic glance. "Do the stings hurt?"

"Not if I don't move."

"There's a village just here. We can have those stings examined."

"Oh, I don't think they're serious—"

She gave a dismissive wave of one hand. "Ah, you English! So stoic!"

She didn't bother to put her hand back on to the wheel, steering expertly with one hand around a sharp bend in the narrow road without slackening speed.

"If you hadn't told me you're a photographer, I would have thought you were a race driver," I told her.

"I am," she said matter-of-factly. "I was second in the Formula Two at Monte Carlo last year and winner of the Mercedes Cup at Nuremberg the year before."

A handful of ancient cottages heralded our arrival in a village with a sign announcing its name as Beauvallier. It turned out to be more sophisticated than it first appeared and there was a row of modern shops and stores. Monika stopped in front of a *pharmacie* with its green on white plaque depicting a serpent coiled around a staff.

"The pharmacist can advise how serious your stings are," she said.

I was aware that in France the course of studies to become a pharmacist is lengthy and difficult. The pharmacist is highly regarded in the community and many smaller villages do not have a doctor as the pharmacist can handle most medical problems.

Monika's imperious manner brought prompt attention and two of the staff, a man and a woman, examined me inside the shop. A few dabs with an ammonia-smelling fluid and they pronounced me in no need of a doctor. It seemed much ado about nothing now, but a while ago, when I had been smothered in a cloud of angry bees . . .

As we went outside, Monika asked, "How did you get to Colcroze?"

"I had a car."

"I didn't see it there."

"I forgot about it," I said. "I was so glad to be able to get away with you, I didn't think of anything else."

"How do you feel now? Do you want to go back and get it?"

"What I want to do is buy you the best meal in France as a way of saying thank you for saving my life."

She smiled delightfully. "I would be happy to accept although I think you overstate it. In any case, I have another assignment today. Suppose I take you back to get your car and we have lunch tomorrow?"

"Excellent," I said enthusiastically. "If you could choose anywhere to eat, where would it be?"

She shook her head reprovingly. Her blond hair danced as she did so.

"You don't mean that!"

"Certainly I do."

"I have always wanted to eat at—but, no, it's not fair to ask you . . ."

"Yes, it is. Ask me."

She eyed me mischievously for a moment. Then she said, "Very well. The Louis Quinze in Monte Carlo."

I had to admit I had asked for it. Probably the most illustrious and famous restaurant on the Riviera. As for cost . . . well, never mind that. After all, hadn't my life been saved?

"Okay," I said casually. "The Louis Quinze. Tomorrow."

Chapter 14

I drove back to Saint Symphorien, choosing the wider roads over lesser ones and with more than one nervous glance at the sky. One of those terrifying insects was enough—a horde of them would be like a scene from a John Carpenter version of *Food of the Gods.*

The busy center of the village was a welcome refuge. I parked and strolled around, not leaving the crowded pavements, but then I realized that I was hungry and the dilemma of where to eat took priority. As a change of pace, I chose Timgad, a restaurant serving north African food.

The south of France has a large population of *"pieds noirs,"* French who were forced to leave their farms and plantations in north Africa when the former colonies became independent. Another large group is the "Maghreb," natives from those same countries who retained their French citizenship and could come to France to live and work.

Inside the restaurant, it smelled wonderful. Chilies, coriander, curry, and mint aromas floated in air that was without the "advantage" of air-conditioning. Colorful banners and posters covered the walls, basket chairs and tables had pale blue cushions and covers, and the blue and white tiled floor suited perfectly.

A smiling Arab girl brought me a menu. It was in both Arabic and French and I concentrated on the French side. I have had amusing experiences in Asian restaurants in France attempting to translate the French-named dishes into English when the original translation already left a lot to be desired. I had eaten in Arabic restaurants and was familiar with many of the main dishes. Foods there are naturally low in fat and lively on the palate due to the spices I had smelled in addition to garlic, cumin, and caraway. Cooking styles are generally simple. Whereas in the West, we cook aromatics such as onion and garlic first in either oil or butter before adding any other ingredients, in north African cuisine it is customary to put all the ingredients into one pot at the beginning.

I chose the fennel marinated in lemon and served with feta cheese as the first course. It is simple and very refreshing. The other diners were about half French and half Maghreb and I watched the latter to see if they were eating in true Moslem style. They were not—this requires that the diner eat only from around the edge of the dish, leaving the middle so that the blessing of Heaven can descend upon it. I ate all of my salad.

I followed it with a tiny bowl of "Lablabi," a thick soup of garbanzo beans, a widely used vegetable. The Koran forbids the drinking of alcohol, but for nonbelievers the restaurant had a very acceptable rosé wine from Carthage. The main course offered several lamb and fish specialties but I chose the Chicken Tagine. A tagine is a stew and this one was strongly flavored with saffron, which also gave

it a rich yellow color. Garlic, almonds, lemon, and
cinnamon added a variety of tastes. The girl brought
me a small silver dish of rice and honey cakes in
place of a dessert.

As I stepped out into the dazzling afternoon sunshine, I was greeted by name. It was Aristide Pertois, the gendarme.

"Any progress on the case, m'sieu?" I asked.

"Ah, that is what I wanted to talk to you about."

"How did you know where to find me?"

"Your car."

"It's a Citroen C2V, black, no distinguishing features."

"Its license plate is unique," he said suavely, mo-
tioning to a disreputable-looking bar a couple of
doors away. The tables outside were dirty and piled
with unwashed glasses and plates. A television was
loud inside and from a small crowd of workmen
came noisy arguments. A tough-looking man was
waiting on tables.

"There?"

"Certainly," he said. "We won't be disturbed."

He was right. We went in and sat at a table farther down the room and no one threw us as much
as a second glance, not even the waiter. Aristide
took off his cap and set it on the none-too-clean
tabletop.

"Pastis?"

"Are you having one?" I asked in surprise.

His eyebrows had that perpetually raised look I
had noticed before. If it were possible, they went a
fraction higher now.

"Of course," he said. "I like pastis."

"It's not the pastis. It's just that in England, policemen don't drink on duty."

"They don't?" He sounded disbelieving. "Why not?"

"I don't know—I think it's something to do with alcohol affecting their judgment."

He stared at me, then shook his head.

"You have some strange ideas in your country," he told me, waving imperiously and calling loudly for two pastis.

"So what progress on the investigation?" I asked.

"The investigation . . . ah, yes." The round lenses and his round black eyes made it hard to tell what he was thinking. "The wounds and injuries to Emil Laplace are all consistent with being gored to death by a sanglier," he said carefully.

This gendarme wasn't as dumb as he looked. There was certainly more to him than I had previously thought. So much for first impressions.

"Do you know something that makes you think Emil's death wasn't caused by being gored by a sanglier?" I asked him outright.

He didn't answer for a moment, then he said, "I intend to investigate further. What can you tell me that might help?"

"I've told you all I know. I've only just arrived here. I'd never seen Emil before, or any of the others at both the vineyards."

The bouncer came and set down a glass of pastis in front of each of us and a carafe of water. The gendarme poured a little water into his glass and I did likewise. The liquid turned milky. Aristide eyed his for a couple of seconds, then drained the glass. I drank part of mine.

"You know much about wine?" he asked me.

"Enough to be able to write about it."

"It should be an interesting article," he said in a neutral voice.

"I hope so," I said, trying to be just as neutral.

"You knew none of the people at the vineyards?"

"None of them."

"What about Andre Chantier?" He shot out the name as if hoping to catch me unawares.

I shook my head. "I've never heard the name."

He tried to drain his glass again but there was nothing in it. He half turned as if about to order another but he didn't.

"Who is he?" I asked.

"Andre Chantier? He used to work at the Willesford vineyard."

"Used to?"

"He left a few months ago."

I finished my pastis. "Does this have some meaning?"

"I would like you to inform me if you run across the name."

"Certainly."

"Or any other information that might be of use."

"Of course."

He put his cap back on and stood up. I reached into my pocket to pay for the pastis but Aristide shook his head. "There is no need. I have an arrangement." He gave the bouncer a nod and walked out.

He was a very unusual gendarme.

Chapter 15

The Casino at Monte Carlo has a worldwide fame that stems from its patrons of an earlier era—from most of the crowned heads of Europe to Mata Hari and inveterate gamblers like Harpo Marx and King Farouk. "The Cheese," as the Casino is called locally, is adjacent to the Hôtel de Paris, and inside the hotel is what many consider to be the finest restaurant in the Western world. It was here that I was bringing to lunch the girl who had saved my life in Colcroze.

The first impression of the interior of the Louis XV restaurant is that it is all gold. Ceiling, walls, curtains, carpets are all various shades of gold and the feeling of opulence is almost overwhelming. Only the four gleaming crystal chandeliers tone down the golden vista.

I would have thought a table reservation at such short notice to be out of the question but Monika had insisted that she undertake the task and to my surprise, she succeeded. When we were greeted effusively by Benoit Peeters, the maître d'hôtel of the Louis XV, I assumed it was due to her racing feats in the Grand Prix.

A smiling young man placed a small footstool at

Monika's side for her to put her handbag—a thoughtful touch and made easier by the wide spacing between the tables. We asked what the house aperitif was and we both ordered it, a version of a Bellini but added to the champagne, rather than the usual peach juice, was a Provence liqueur with a dry peach flavor.

A bread cart arrived with more than two dozen unusual kinds of bread, all the product of the Louis XV's own bakery. Some contained olives, some walnuts, some orange zest. There was Viennese bread, Swedish bread, Milanese bread, German pumpernickel, bread leavened and unleavened . . .

"I understand that one baker makes all of this bread fresh every day," said Monika.

"Only one?"

"Yes, although there are over ninety cooks in total in the kitchen."

She looked ravishing in a clinging beige silk jersey dress with chunky gold earrings. Her blond hair was lustrous, dancing freely every time she moved her head, and I still had a difficult—if enjoyable—time trying to decide just what shade of blue her eyes were.

"I have been wanting to ask you . . . ," said Monika. "What were you doing in Colcroze?"

We both nibbled on the irresistible breads.

"As I told you, I'm doing a story on vineyards in the south of France that are owned by English. I remembered that when I was here some years ago, I was taken to visit a couple of ghost villages, and I thought that if I could gather material on a few of them, it would make a good story too. Someone in the auberge mentioned Colcroze."

"Where are you staying?" she asked.

"The Relais du Moulin near Saint Symphorien."

"Why there? I mean, any particular reason?"

"I'm covering a vineyard nearby. It's the first in the series."

"How long are you going to be there?" she asked casually.

"Well, this assignment may take longer than I had planned if the local population is all as unfriendly as the bees."

The maître d' returned and after some discussion we elected to accept most of his recommendations, which is usually a good idea in a restaurant as renowned as the Louis XV. Chef Alain Ducasse's celebrated cuisine straddles two nations, France and Italy, taking the best from each. He uses humble ingredients and his emphasis is on vegetables—a choice that fits admirably with the modern trend toward a healthier diet.

First, we had large green raviolis on a bed of wilted arugula and baby violet artichokes. After the plates had been placed in front of us, the waiter crushed lumps of soft goat's milk cheese with olive oil in a small bowl, sprinkled it with black pepper, and scattered it over our plates.

"Was your photographic assignment yesterday here in Monaco?" I asked Monika.

She shook her head and the shiny blond hair shimmered.

"It wasn't a photographic assignment," she said. "I was modeling for Benetton."

"You model, too?"

She nodded. "This is superb, isn't it? Just the right amount of pepper."

"You're a photographer, a race driver, and you

model?" I was amazed. "Is there anything you can't do?"

"I can't cook," she said with a tiny smile. "That's why I'm enjoying this so much."

We had been offered the choice of pigeon grilled over hot coals and served with foie gras or *cochon de lait,* suckling pig, roasted and served with gnocchi as the next course, but we both went for the *"loup,"* the Mediterranean sea bass baked in the oven and accompanied by wafer-thin potato chips. The wine waiter recommended three possible choices of a white wine with it and after a quick mental review, I tried to sound as if I were making a stab in the dark by ordering a Rhône white, a St.-Joseph from the Domaine Cheze.

Saddle of rabbit wrapped in bacon and roasted over fennel was the main course and another reminder that the chef makes the maximum use of local ingredients, even those that might once have been considered peasant fare. Once again, it was ideally prepared, and the fennel with that hint of aniseed lurking behind its flavor enhanced the succulent rabbit. With this, we drank a Bordeaux, a Pauillac from the Pinchon-Lalande château, also a suggestion by the wine waiter.

We topped the meal with a delicious mascarpone sorbet with wild strawberries, although the small tarts filled with orange cream and the rightly famous Ducasse-made chocolates that were served in complementary fashion afterward made a dessert a questionable indulgence.

"No more meals like that for a month," said Monika firmly, "or my modeling career will come to a sudden stop. Let's take a stroll around the port and tell ourselves we're working off all that food."

It was warm and pleasant, and gentle breezes off the Mediterranean were ruffling the gaily colored flags on the pleasure boats as we walked. A host of nations were represented and vessels from as far afield as South Africa, Panama, Turkey, Indonesia, and Hong Kong were lined up. Tall-masted sailing schooners were side by side sleek powerboats.

"Boat watching" is one of the most popular forms of free entertainment on the Riviera. Antibes and Saint Tropez are the best ports to indulge in it, but whereas in Saint Tropez it would be unusual during the season to find a yacht without its display of people, in Monaco it is unusual to find one engaged in such indecorum. Today seemed to be the day for the unusual . . . sounds of merriment came from ahead of us.

"Sounds like a party," Monika murmured.

The vessel from which the noise was coming was a spectacular sight. I know nothing about boats but this one was well over a hundred feet long and pristine white with sparkling chrome rails that looked as if they were polished three times a day. Deck after deck climbed up to a streamlined funnel mounted in a superstructure that belonged in a James Bond movie.

People seemed to be all over the vessel and figures could be seen in the staterooms, though the aft deck near the dock was the busiest area. Waiters in dazzling uniforms moved swiftly through the knots of people, dispensing food and drink. Monika and I stopped and gazed at the sight of such magnificence and luxury.

A voice called down from the rail. "Monika! Hey there! Come on up—both of you!"

Chapter 16

On board the floating palace, Monika introduced me to Grant Masterson, the man who had hailed her. He was tall, had a husky build, and looked to be in his late forties. His face was strong and well tanned and he wore a T-shirt and white pants. I assumed he was one of the crew until Monika murmured, "This is Grant's boat."

"It's a beauty," I said, hoping that was the way you complimented boats.

"Two twenty-five-hundred-horsepower Rolls Royce Marine Merlins," he said. "Can cruise two thousand miles and sleeps twenty. Every modern device from radar, sonar, radio, and direction finders to satellite navigation." He gave a boyish grin. "At least that's what the crew tell me. I really don't know anything about boats from the technical viewpoint, but I do know I love this vessel."

"So you should," I said, mustering up a little more enthusiasm this time, "it really is magnificent."

"She."

He stopped and it was a second before I caught on. "Oh, yes, the crew call her 'she,' you mean?" He nodded and I turned to Monika. "Why are all boats feminine?"

"Because they're charming, beautiful, and un-complaining?" she suggested with a wicked smile.

"Or is it because they're difficult to control and expensive to maintain?" said Grant with a straight face.

We laughed together, then Grant said, "Let me get you a drink and introduce you to some people."

A waiter responded promptly to Grant's wave and handed us glasses of champagne. A tray of appetizing-looking hors d'oeuvres was sailing above our heads when Grant stopped the man underneath it. Monika and I exchanged amused glances. She explained to Grant that we had just dined at the Louis XV and might not eat again for a week. Grant nodded and was about to release the waiter when Monika said, "But it would be an insult to your chef . . . ," so we both ate one of the small pastries filled with foie gras and topped with a slice of smoked salmon.

"Ah, here's a fellow countryman," Grant Masterson said. "You must meet him," he said, winking, "—bankers are always useful to know."

His name was Terence McGill and he was manager of the Monaco branch of the Bank of Belgravia. He had been here three years, he told me as Monika excused herself to go talk to a buxom redhead she was acquainted with from the racing circuit, although she looked as if she might be on the modeling circuit too.

"Grant Masterson is one of your customers, I take it?"

"Yes, for some time."

"I hadn't met him before today," I said. "What line of business is he in?"

"Many. He owns property in a dozen countries, a freight company, a couple of golf courses, a cinema chain, some farms, processing plants for food products—"

My attention focused sharply. "Food? He's in the food line?"

"Yes. He's opening a new line of delicatessen-type shops, selling specialty foods. Some will be independent, some will be in supermarkets."

He frowned slightly, noting my interest. "What's your line of work?"

"Me? Oh, I'm writing a series of articles on vineyards in the South of France."

"A journalist." He sounded disappointed and there was something else too—was it apprehension? Perhaps alarm at being quoted was normal for a banker.

"My theme is vineyards in the South of France under English ownership." I hastened to add, "Don't worry, I'm not concerned about Grant Masterson or his plans."

He looked relieved, although he said, "The information's not exactly secret—in fact, it's been mentioned in some of the magazines already."

In my cloak-and-dagger persona as a journalist writing about wine and vineyards it was true that the information about Masterson's plans was not of interest. As the Gourmet Detective, it had aroused my professional curiosity. Fortunately, McGill didn't seem worried and I tossed in a remark about wine being sold in many delicatessens to placate him further. Nevertheless, he excused himself and moved on through the throng, seeking safer conversational companions than a journalist.

Circulating, I ran into Monika, who was in between groups. "How did you come to meet Masterson?" I asked.

"Oh, I met him at a party at the palace that

Princess Caroline gave," she said offhandedly. "Since then he's sponsored me in the Grand Prix and a few other races."

As she left me to greet an Asian couple, I had an opportunity to scan the people on deck. The majority were men but the women were mostly young and good-looking. There was a handful of both sexes in crisp white uniforms, obviously officers of the vessel. A dark-haired, trim man of young to middle age detached himself from them and introduced himself as the captain, George Gregali. He was a Greek who promptly disclaimed any knowledge of Masterson's businesses. "I run this boat," he told me. "I take him anywhere he wants to go, anytime he wants. That is my role."

"Does he spend much time on the boat?"

"Alas, not a lot. His activities take him all over Europe and often to the USA and he flies mostly. But he loves to spend time here on *Windsong*." He waved a hand invitingly. "Have you looked over her?" I admitted that I hadn't. "Let me show you through," he offered.

The chance to see such luxury is rare. The main salon had enormous round windows reflected by floor-to-ceiling columns of mirror. The next deck was the entertainment area where TV programs from all over the world were received by satellite and shown on giant screens and pulsating disco lights accompanied a laser show. The carpet was fiber-optic material and vibrated with different colors as dictated by the music. From controls at your bedside, underwater color TV cameras relayed pictures to monitors on the walls and ceiling of your stateroom.

The luxury was unrelenting. All the bathroom

fixtures were cut from solid lapis lazuli and the knobs were of gold. A helicopter crouched on the aft deck and, Gregali told me, could be airborne at five minutes' notice.

"Stupendous," I said as we left the mind-boggling technological wizardry of the control room.

Gregali smiled, proud of his domain. "It is impressive, is it not?"

I thanked him and wandered away, leaned on the mirror-polished rail, and looked at the Royal Palace, all pink and white, up on top of "the Rock."

Voices nearby attracted my attention. They came from a group where a tall, ungainly man with a shock of unruly hair was talking loudly. Two men and a woman were listening and I strolled over and joined them.

". . . is well accepted that the planetary bodies influence Earth and everything on it," he was saying. "The moon affects Earth's oceans and controls the tides—the Romans knew about that—so naturally it affects all that happens on the solid portion too. The giant planets, Jupiter and Saturn, are farther away but they are so huge, they still affect us. Jupiter has thirteen hundred times the volume of Earth and Saturn is almost as big, so how can there be any doubt that they influence us?"

"By us, you mean people?" asked the woman.

"Yes, although my current studies concern plants," the man with the unruly hair replied.

"All plants?" asked the Italian.

"Principally grapes at the present time."

The ungainly man speaking had an awkward way of moving, almost like a puppet. His arms and hands seemed to be uncoordinated and he gesticulated wildly to emphasize his words. His accent evaded me. Mention of his study of grapes did not, though.

"What influences have you found to be exerted by planetary bodies on grapes?" I asked.

He turned his gaze in my direction and stared at me. Then he held out his hand. "Professor Rahmani," he said and went on:

"Grapes have a close association with man and respond more readily to the influences of the universe. I chart the orbits of the planets and use them to define the best times to plant, to prune, to harvest, and to ferment. I can counsel which grape varieties respond best and I can advise which soil components yield the best results."

I was fascinated by the professor's exposition and so were the others.

"Professor, are you saying that you can produce better grapes this way?"

"Much better!" he said enthusiastically. "I can grow grapes that are twice as large and contain three times as much juice. The juice is tastier and fuller bodied."

"Are you being supported by the wine industry?" I asked him.

"No." He shook his voluminous head of hair. "They are reactionaries. They don't want to see any change, not even if it's progress that can be proved. The wine industry is stuck in the mud of centuries."

It wasn't an appropriate metaphor but it reflected his ire. I pursued my line of questioning now that it had a definite destination.

"Perhaps individual vineyards would see an advantage in being involved in your work?"

The professor looked at me without answering

immediately. Before he could do so, a short Italian with the pragmatic viewpoint of a businessman said, "Perhaps our host, Grant Masterson, might want to invest in your ideas?"

The professor took out cards and handed one to each of us. They were impressively and expensively embossed. They displayed the name "Institute for the Study of Planetary Influences" and had an address in Provence.

"Please feel free to visit whenever you wish to see what we are doing," he said. "We have excellent facilities and you can witness some fascinating experimentation. We always welcome visitors."

The Italian saw an old acquaintance and turned away to chat. Professor Rahmani gave me a nod of dismissal as if to say that his presentation was over and stalked away.

Chapter 17

I leaned on the rail of *Windsong* and looked out into the gentle blue Mediterranean through the gap in the harbor wall. I declined another hors d'oeuvre and thought about Professor Rahmani. Research into ways of growing bigger and tastier grapes went on all the time, although the professor's approach was decidedly less orthodox than most.

A voluptuous blonde swayed in my direction. She looked like a weight lifter but said she was a member of the Swedish women's soccer team that was here to play in Monaco's magnificent stadium. When she learned I was a journalist, she made sure that I would spell her name right, but then was gone when she learned that I wasn't here to cover that event. I caught a glimpse of Monika with Masterson. He had his arm around her in a way that suggested he was more than just her race sponsor but I lost sight of her as a new face appeared.

"We haven't met. I'm Alexis Suvarov—call me Alex."

He was a tall, well-tanned fellow in his late thirties and had flowing golden hair that gave him a look that is usually described as that of an Adonis. He had a lithe athletic build and a friendly manner.

When I commented on his Russian name, he explained enthusiastically.

His great-grandfather was one of the aristocrats who had come to the Riviera every year after the opening of the Leningrad-Nice railway in 1864. He had been acquainted with the grand dukes and duchesses and other members of the Russian royalty. Alex's grandfather had been trapped in Russia under the Communist regime but his father had come to the South of France, which he remembered from his childhood. Alex himself had been born here and was a French citizen.

He asked me what I was doing here and listened to my tale of being a journalist without showing either the dismay of bank manager Terence McGill or the indifference of the Swedish midfielder.

"Writing about vineyards owned by English, are you? We have one of them near us—Willesford own it."

"That's one of the vineyards I'm writing about." It occurred to me that if I said this many more times I would really have to write something about it.

"That Simone's a great girl, isn't she?" he grinned.

"She certainly is," I agreed. This job was leading me into a lot of prevarication.

"We delivered a case of wine for them one time," he said. "It was urgently needed at a banquet."

It was another thread of information but like most of them, it didn't seem to lead anywhere. Still . . . "You delivered it?" I asked casually. "You have a delivery service?"

"Only special stuff—high speed, emergencies— that sort of thing."

"Must be a lot of demand for that here."

"There is. We had an interesting one last week. You know they've reopened La Victorine?"

"The famous film studios in Nice? No, I didn't know that."

"Yes, well, they found that the next day's shooting script had several pages missing so we had to rush another copy to them. We did it without their losing a minute of their valuable time." He laughed and winked. "Mind you, the film's a stinker. It might have been better if they'd lost the entire script. Still, we did our share, rushing the script from the hotel in Orange to the studio in Nice in an hour and a half."

"That's incredible—you must employ race drivers," I said, amazed.

"We do when necessary. Didn't I see you come on board with one of them?"

"Monika? She drives for you?"

"Like a demon—only occasionally, though. She's usually too busy modeling or shooting photos for a magazine or leading scuba diving teams out looking for wrecks. We have a faster system than even Monika—" He broke off as Grant Masterson joined us.

"Glad to see you two got acquainted. Valuable man, Alexis," he told me. "Delivers the goods when no one else can." A thought struck him and he eyed me more keenly. "You write about wine . . . you must know something about food too."

"I—er, well, yes, I do." I saw no reason to deny it altogether.

"Know anything about truffles?"

"Yes, I wrote an article on them," I answered.

"I'm going up to Aupres in the Var day after tomorrow. How about coming with me? I'm going to the truffle market and need all the expertise I can gather. Between you and me, I'm opening a chain of delicatessens and I'm scouting a good source of truffles. It's a hit-and-miss business, as I'm sure you know. Can I count on you?"

"Yes, I'd like that. Might be another article in it— truffles are a fascinating business." I was vaguely aware that I should be concentrating on wine and vineyards, but an opportunity to get to know a man like Masterson couldn't be passed up, and besides, in my real life as the Gourmet Detective the experience would be useful.

He clapped me on the back. "Right. Pick you up then—where are you staying?"

I told him as a smart white-uniformed girl crew member came to tell him that a call from Cairo awaited. He excused himself and left. Suvarov called out to an elegant woman in a clinging flowery dress. "An old customer," he explained with a dashing Errol Flynn smile, "must take care of business— oh, and don't forget, if you need anything taken, fetched, brought, or delivered and it's really urgent—I'm your man." He whipped out a card and handed it to me. Then he was gone as fast as his reputed service.

A producer on Monte Carlo television was the next person I talked to but his interest in me waned fast when he learned I was a journalist and he escaped quickly. Monika finally reappeared with a dark-featured man in a silk suit whom she introduced as being from Iran. A car rally was being planned, she said, crossing the deserts of six nations and she was eager to participate. The way the man looked at her suggested that it was not her car-handling abilities that interested him.

I assured her I understood why she was going back to the Metropole Hotel with him to study a map of the proposed race across the deserts, agreeing that a knowledge of the route would be highly advantageous. I watched her go and with the sun sinking slowly over neighboring Spain made my lonely way back to Saint Symphorien and the Relais du Moulin, meditating on life, women, and other related and unrelated subjects.

Chapter 18

Madame Ribereau at Le Relais du Moulin could not understand why I didn't want a full meal that night even after I told her that I had lunched at the Louis XV.

"Helas," said Madame with a dismissive toss of the head, "that was lunch. Now you are ready for dinner."

My continued protestations were brushed aside and all I could do was trim down the size of the meal and tell myself that I had to eat in order to stay in Madame's good graces. I had a cup of beef consommé, a poached trout and some parsleyed potatoes, a half bottle of white wine, and a crème brûlée. A stroll around the grounds helped it to digest and I managed to stay awake through a two-hour television program extolling achievements in French literature at the turn of the century. I went to bed rather than wallow in the excitement of *Dragnet* that followed.

For once, the French breakfast of coffee and a croissant was adequate and I set off for the Willesford vineyard. The morning was bright and clear, so clear that the Alps with their sparkle of fresh snow covering were clearly visible. I drove through forests of mimosa trees and fields of red soil. A wooden hut was selling fresh milk, cheese, and yogurt and already doing a brisk trade.

The courtyard of the Willesford vineyard was again quiet. A couple of old cars were parked at one end of the buildings and I put my Citroen alongside them. Simone was once more at the desk in her office. She looked up as I went in, brushed a lock of blond hair from her cheek, and said petulantly, "Oh, it's you again."

I smiled my friendliest smile, said a cheerful "Good morning," and sat down on the one rickety chair.

She eyed me suspiciously. "You need more information?" she asked in a voice suggesting that I wouldn't get it whatever it was. The progress I thought I had made in my last visit had apparently evaporated.

"I'd like to look around a little more—if that's all right with you."

She had her mouth open to say something negative as I went on: "I can just wander round. I need to get the feeling of the place, the atmosphere—so I can pass it on to the readers," I added, as a reminder that I was writing an article.

I had another reason, too. I was curious to know if she had any objection to my going through the place on my own. If there was anything to hide, she would promptly refuse.

She shrugged. "Go ahead if you want." She returned to the files in front of her as if I had already left. I pressed on with another question.

"I was wondering . . . do you have any research going?"

"Research?" That took her attention from her files.

"Yes. You know—cloning, grafting, hybridization, that kind of thing . . . ?"

She pursed her lips. "We are too busy with production to be doing research."

"Well, you don't have to do it here. Some vineyards support programs in laboratories and research institutes; that way, it doesn't interfere with their everyday work."

"Research is kept confidential," she informed me.

"Do you know Professor Rahmani?"

She sighed and put on a pained look that said plainly, I don't have time for all these silly questions. She shook her head.

"Or the Institute for the Study of Planetary Influences?"

There was a brief hesitation, then she said, "Oh, is that what his crackpot organization is called?"

"Is that what it is?"

She shrugged again. "Astrology and wine making have nothing in common. He may have conned a few vintners to subsidize him but—"

"He has?" I interjected quickly.

"I suppose so . . . well, he must have . . . he has a lot of very expensive equipment, large modern buildings . . . it all costs money . . ."

"Yes," I murmured. She knew plenty about a man she had never heard of.

She looked away, aware of her slip, but recovered fast.

"I didn't recognize the name—your accent. . . . He approached us some time ago about research on grapes. We didn't want to have anything to do with it. Are these questions anything to do with your article?" she demanded.

"Certainly," I said before I had time to think whether they did or not. "Some vineyards believe in long-term development. Do they do it themselves, do they farm it out as a program . . . ?"

"I have a lot of work to do," she said, pulling the files a little closer. "Can you find your own way?"

"Thanks. I will."

I went through the other door, into the winery, leaving Miss Congeniality to her files. There was no one in sight. The sweet smell of fermenting grapes was powerful. Machinery buzzed softly and water was running somewhere. I walked past the rows of vats, their oaken exteriors sweating moisture. The floor was a little slippery and I trod carefully.

Farther along, I found what I was looking for. A rickety wooden desk had some papers on a clipboard, an operating manual, and a school-type exercise book. I glanced at the papers on the clipboard first. They were an hourly log of temperature readings and a record of sampling times. The manual was standard stuff and didn't appear to be much used. The exercise book was different, though—it showed grape varieties, weights, dates, and I was getting really interested when . . .

Sounds from above echoed through the cloying air—loud metallic clicks. I listened. It stopped then I heard what sounded like soft footsteps coming from the catwalk above the vats. I put the book back exactly as I had found it and stood without moving. Once more, I heard the footsteps—and while I didn't like the idea of going up myself, I liked even less the idea of a person who didn't want to be identified being above me.

I found a stairway. The metal rail was cold and clammy but I clung tightly with one hand as I climbed. One foot kicked a step and the vibrating hum sounded loud but probably wasn't. I kept on upward to the catwalk.

It seemed dizzyingly high now that I was up here. I recalled the old adage about never looking down—and promptly looked down. The catwalk ran the length of the building, branching off to run between the vats. A person could be hidden anywhere. I thought of calling out in case it was a worker engaged in the legitimate pursuit of his trade but then reflected that it was more their responsibility to challenge me as the interloper. I edged cautiously along the metal-grill flooring.

I passed two rows of vats. The lids were open to permit air to be ingested, and the contents bubbled gently. Clouds of sweet, fruity vapor swirled slowly and an insistent hiss indicated that fermentation was at a high level. A piece of cloth caught my eye. It was tied to the top of the rail and I went to inspect it. It was a scarf, once white and now stained with dark red. Wine stains, I told myself firmly . . . I was looking at it to determine why it was there when to my horror, it moved. . . .

It was too late by the time I realized that it was not only the scarf moving but the rail. Then I was moving with it as the result of a strong push in the middle of my back. My fall was like slow motion and there seemed to be ample time for the realization that the metallic sounds I had heard had been the removal of the locking pins from a detachable section of the rail.

The rail fell away and I fell after it.

The surface of dark liquid soared toward me and a thick warmth was all enveloping. . . .

Chapter 19

Saving myself from drowning was pure physical reflex. My mind was moving just as frantically, first with recriminations. I was furious at myself, falling for a lure that even the most stupid of fish would have shaken its head at in disgust. Then Edouard Morel came to mind even though he was a man I had never met. I had mentally dismissed him as simply unaccounted for, but a more sinister answer now loomed. His wife considered him missing because she hadn't had contact with him for two weeks, but he might be dead also. He might be the secret ingredient in a red wine of the current vintage—just as I would be if I didn't get out of here.

The atmosphere just above the surface of the wine was choking. Alcohol has a lower specific gravity than water so as the grapes fermented and produced alcohol, the liquid went down in gravity, meaning that I sank deeper. It was the opposite of being in the Dead Sea—I was in the Red Sea.

The "cap" of grape skins floating on the surface looked solid—especially to a drowning man—and I tried to lay my arms on top of it and get some support, but it let me sink, heedless of all the wine I had given support to through the years.

How ignominious! That was my main thought. Sent here on a wine investigation and I get drowned in a vat of red wine!

I thought about conserving my energy and floating with only my mouth above the wine. How long would it be before someone came by, though? Would I have to wait for a shift change?

I shouted for help a few times and then realized that English was the wrong language. I tried the French *Au secours* but I have always found it a silly expression and have not been able to believe that it ever brought a serious response. I tried to find a projection of some kind on the slimy wooden walls but there was not as much as a badly hammered nail.

The wine tasted awful. I wasn't deliberately drinking it, having other things on my mind, but sinking so low into it and still lower when I moved made it inevitable that I swallowed some. It was raw and vile. How could a drink taste so bad now and so good later? I hoped there would be a "later."

Time passed and I passed out. At least, I supposed I did. It was probably the fumes. When I came back to hazy life, I was still floating. People walk in their sleep—can they swim in their sleep? I called out feebly, first in French, then in English. I didn't feel up to running through the languages of the numerous nationalities likely to be represented among the migrant workers.

I was dimly aware of voices but had no idea where they were coming from or what they were saying. One of them seemed to getting more urgent, more strident, and I was dimly conscious of something moving near my head. Through a stupor that was part intoxication and part panic, I could see bars that crystallized into the shape of a ladder and I reached for it. I hung on with one hand and was slowly heaved out of the red morass. Partway up, hands grabbed me and hoisted me clear.

Simone Ballard was furious. I think she blamed me for spoiling a couple of thousand liters of what might otherwise have turned out to be perfectly good wine. The invective with which she might have bombarded me was, however, mitigated by the presence of the gendarme, Aristide Pertois.

It was his face that I saw first as I was pulled out of the vat: the flat, black eyes behind the round spectacles, the bristly black mustache, and the perpetually raised eyebrows. There seemed to be a genuine query in them now, though, and it seemed to be *What on earth are you doing in there?* I was sitting in Simone's office in a shirt and pants several sizes too big for me and I still stank of raw, fermenting wine, but my head was clearing.

"I was just wandering around when I leaned on the rail; it gave way and I fell in." Well, perhaps it wasn't *the* answer but it was *an* answer.

Aristide turned to Simone. He had been standing by the office door, saying nothing until now. "Don't you have safety checks on the rails and walkways?"

"Of course we do," she snapped.

"Then how did—"

"I don't know." Her manner was glacial.

"I'm sure the wine will be all right," I said in a placatory voice. "In the days of *pigeage,* even several monks didn't spoil it."

She regarded me in stony silence. Aristide rubbed his nose and said nothing. They both knew what I was referring to: In the Middle Ages, naked monks used to jump into the wine vats several times during the fermentation process to make sure that the skins mixed properly with the juice. The practice was known as *pigeage.* It was the only occasion throughout the year when the monks had anything approximating a bath and it was universally accepted that calls of nature were not demanding enough for the monks to climb out of the vat. There is still ribald speculation in the wine trade as to the effect on the quality of the wine.

"I was here to make a few more inquiries," said Aristide in a neutral tone. "When I got out of the car, I heard a voice shouting for help. I ran inside at once and went to where I could hear splashing."

The door opened and an arm reached in to place a clear plastic bag on the floor. It oozed red fluid inside and Simone glared at it, then at me.

"You'll want to get your clothes to the cleaners before they are ruined," she said.

"Yes. I do."

I glanced at Aristide. "Thanks," I said.

He nodded and I headed for the door, carrying the sack in one hand and holding up the baggy pants, which were way too large for me, with the other. I tripped on one leg of the pants in an unintentional imitation of Buster Keaton.

No one laughed.

Chapter 20

At the laundry and dry cleaner's in Saint Symphorien, the Vietnamese girl promptly demanded payment in advance. She did a double take when I said I had fallen into a wine vat but she didn't ask what color wine.

Crossing the lobby of Le Relais du Moulin had been tricky but I managed it by close observation and fast footwork. One shower was insufficient and I had to take a second. A heavy dosage of cologne bestowed on me more "presence" than I would have wished and I realized that I would not be able to embark on any undercover missions until it had worn off. I got into the car and on to the highway.

A Porsche scorched past me and then a BMW with Swiss plates. The traffic thinned out as I got farther into the countryside and I was cruising placidly when I saw a terrifying sight.

Across the top of the windshield came drifting what looked like an enormous dragonfly. I had a chilly feeling that came from the memory of the horrifying creature that had flown over me in Colcroze—and dropped a murderous beehive. This one was very similar, then I was able to make out a framework of slim girders, a set of wheels, and a human figure seated in their midst.

It was an ultralight aircraft—"a flying bicycle" as some called it. The large wings were diagonally striped in red, white, and yellow, and I found some satisfaction in the fact that they were not green and brown as the other creature—well, aircraft—had been.

This one was low and dropping quickly. My first scare was that it was about to make some lethal attack on me, but that evaporated as it crossed my path and veered away. Nevertheless, I didn't take my eyes from it, being fortunate that there was no high-speed Teutonic traffic on this stretch.

The aircraft drifted lower and lower until it fell out of sight beyond a wooded hill. It was so low that it had to be landing. I slowed and turned into a well-used dirt road that wound into a pine forest.

So I hadn't been dreaming after all. I had seen a real aircraft in Colcroze—at least, a real ultralight aircraft. Moreover, the man flying it had dropped a crowded beehive on me, and as Colcroze was deserted and apparently had been that way for centuries, it was no accident.

This strongly suggested that being pushed into the wine vat had been no accident either. The inescapable conclusion was that someone here didn't like me. Perhaps there was more than one person who didn't like me—difficult as I found that to accept.

The pine forest opened up into a large field with some wooden buildings in one corner. A windsock flew over them and the air hummed with the sound of small engines. A large compressed-air tank with crumbling blue paint stood to one side, and sunk into the ground, a fuel container with a BP crest poked up nozzles and valves.

Six of the ultralight aircraft were dotted around the field. Men and women were near them. I stopped the car and watched. One man came out of one of the buildings, carrying a fuel can in his hand. He took it to one of the aircraft and emptied the can into it. Another man came out of the same building and I stared at him. He had his hands in the pockets of a leather jacket and he sauntered toward the same aircraft. I shaded my eyes against the sun to get a better look at him. I wasn't mistaken—it was Alex Suvarov, the golden-haired Russian I had met on Masterson's yacht.

I hadn't looked at his card when he had given it to me but I looked through my wallet, found the card and read the name.

Escadrille Demoiselle it said, and underneath it had the English translation—Dragonfly Squadron.

I had thought it near impossible when he had told me that one of the couriers in his service had brought a film script from Orange to Nice in an hour and a half. I had been thinking of a fast car, but with an ultralight aircraft it would be easy.

I examined the aircraft one by one. A machine was taxiing slowly and had red, white, and yellow bands in a diagonal pattern across the wings. That was the aircraft I had seen making its landing approach. One of the stationary machines had its propeller turning and accounted for another engine noise. Its wing was two shades of blue. Of the other four machines, two were different combinations of red and white and the third was silvery gray with black markings. It was the remaining machine that had already caught my eye, though. It had green and brown wings in an unmistakable and unforgettable pattern—it was the aircraft I had seen over the ghost village of Colcroze.

I drove to the buildings across the field and parked. I followed Alex Suvarov out to the ultralight that had just been fueled. It was one of the two with red and white markings. I passed the silvery gray machine where a man and a woman were engrossed in a discussion that involved downdrafts and wing loading factors. When I reached Suvarov, he was giving compass readings to the other man, who was apparently preparing to take off.

The man climbed into the bucket seat and fastened his seat belt. His hands moved on the controls and the engine growled louder. The ungainly aircraft moved forward, bumping a little over the grassy surface. Its pilot guided it past the other aircraft and I expected him to taxi to a runway to take off. Instead, he just accelerated the engine and the craft rolled forward, rising into the air like a released balloon.

It was a breathtaking sight to a neophyte like me because it was not far short of a vertical takeoff. As the ultralight disappeared over the pine trees, Suvarov turned and saw me. His face lit up with recognition.

"My friend!" he cried. "I am so glad you have come to see us!"

He sounded genuinely pleased and his words rang with sincerity. His smile faded, though, as he saw my expression.

"Is something wrong?" he asked.

I pointed to the ultralight with the green and brown wings. "Does that aircraft operate from this field?"

"Yes," he said, still puzzled. "All the aircraft here belong to members of the Dragonfly Squadron."

"Who does that one belong to?"

His eyes moved over my face. "That one? Why, that's mine."

Chapter 21

"Were you flying it two days ago?"

"Two days ago . . . that was Tuesday . . . no, I didn't fly that day. I was at Sophia Antipolis, the science park. A company there is interested in a contract for the rapid exchange of engineering designs between their drawing office and the Aerospatiale plant at the Marseille airport."

"You were there all day?"

The welcoming look had died by now and he was becoming increasingly cool. "Why are you asking these questions?" he demanded.

"Because an ultralight with those precise markings on the wings dropped a beehive on me. I was nearly killed."

A smile twitched his lips. "A beehive . . . ? Was dropped on you? Where?"

"It was in Colcroze," I said.

He said slowly, "Colcroze—the ghost village. You must have been the only one there. No wonder you thought the beehive was dropped on you."

"It *was* dropped on me," I said angrily. "I *was* the only one there—that's how I know it was aimed at me. And the ultralight that dropped it was that one."

I pointed an accusing finger at the innocent-looking bundle of slim girders supporting a wide-span wing. He followed my finger. "Come with me," he snapped, and we walked to one of the wooden buildings.

Inside, it had a few desks, some file cabinets, a couple of phones, and a wall cabinet holding maps and books. A huge relief map of the South of France covered most of one wall and on another were photographs and certificates.

Suvarov led the way to one of the tables where a large ledger lay open. He flipped the pages. "Tuesday . . . here it is . . . you can see for yourself: No one flew on Tuesday." I scanned the scribbled entries. He motioned to a slight, wispy Frenchman with an old-fashioned flying helmet in one hand. "Guillaume, were you here on Tuesday?"

The man shook his head.

"Do you know who was here?"

Guillaume reflected. "I don't think anyone came on Tuesday, not that I know anyway."

Suvarov stood, irresolute for a moment. Then he looked over the table, picking up another ledger. He turned to one of the pages that had a colored tag. "This is the flight record of my aircraft," he said. He pointed to a column. "This shows the kilometers flown—you can see, it shows 42,017. I entered that on Monday when I came back from a flight." He snapped the ledger closed. "Let's look at the aircraft."

We went outside and as we neared the ultralight, I was struck by its flimsy appearance. The bucket seat had a panel with only three instruments. Suvarov indicated one of them. "The French Aviation Authority insists that we keep close record of kilometers flown. Ultralights are relatively new and the authorities haven't yet decided how to rate them, so a lot of data is kept. This aircraft has flown 42,171 kilometers. . . ."

He regarded me with a very different expression. "That means it's been flown 154 kilometers since I took it out on Monday."

"How many air kilometers is Colcroze from here?" I asked.

"About 70," he said quietly. "Hmm . . . maybe you are right."

We walked slowly back to the wooden hut. "We fly each other's aircraft occasionally," he said, talking as much to himself as to me. "Someone was here on Tuesday and flew this aircraft." He clapped a hand on my shoulder and his voice was hard. "I'll find out who it was."

I believed him, not entirely because of his golden hair and bright blue eyes and general appearance of an honest man. I felt that he was angry at a person who would take his aircraft without his knowledge and use it for such a purpose.

"And now, let me show you what a wonderful machine this is," he said.

He was a devoted enthusiast of the ultralight, a passionate and articulate flag-waver in support of what he believed to be the forerunner of a major method of transport in the future.

"Flying is man's oldest dream," he told me. "Two-thirds of all living creatures can fly—is it any wonder that people want to do so too? For centuries, the most ingenious brains in history wrestled with the problem. Sadly, most of them sought to imitate the birds and flap wings. It wasn't until 1903 that two brothers who owned a bicycle shop made the first flight."

"The Wright brothers?"

We were standing by his aircraft. I had overcome my aversion to those terrifying brown and green markings. The Dacron sheeting and the aluminum tubing and girders seemed a harmless structure as well as a pitifully weak way to challenge nature.

"Yes. From then on, aircraft developed in two ways: military applications and big airliners. You see, it's an interesting contrast to the car. American industry set out to make a car available to everybody, led by Ford's Model T. Soon, everybody had a car . . . life could have been different. If World War I hadn't broken out at that time, it's quite probable that everybody would have had a plane."

I listened to him, fascinated.

"So how has the ultralight developed now?" I asked.

"Private flying was strangled by safety measures. Small private planes were safe and reliable, but these gains were achieved only at high cost. The average person couldn't afford to buy a private plane and the upkeep and operating costs were prohibitive.

"The hang glider was the answer: simple, cheap, nothing mechanical, no power, and no operating costs. It became a popular sport, then, inevitably, the people doing it wanted more—more control, more power than just the wind. So they put a chain-saw engine on a hang glider. Then came a bigger wing, then a few simple controls, then more power . . ."

"It must have been hard to know when to stop," I said.

"Exactly. More progress along those lines and we would have been back to the light aircraft that we had set out to avoid!"

"But you've managed to arrest that progress and the ultralight is the result."

Suvarov patted the aircraft beside him as affectionately as if it were a favorite horse.

"Two hundred pounds empty weight, can climb to ten thousand feet, can stay in the air three hours, can take off and land on a tennis court. In the air, I can turn off the engine and just float. I can hear dogs barking, hear music from convertibles."

He turned to face me. "I know what you are thinking. The pilot of this machine could spot a person in a deserted village, could drop a missile of some kind on him—a hand grenade, a bomb, or even a beehive."

I nodded. "Someone did. The ultralight is an ideal craft for the job, too, isn't it? The engine's very quiet, so you wouldn't hear it until it's almost over you. It flies low, so in terrain like Provence's, it's out of sight most of the time."

"That's true," said Suvarov. "Tell me, why would someone want to drop a beehive on you?"

"I'm here on a very simple job—I'm writing an article on vineyards in the south of France that are owned by English. The Willesford vineyard is the first one. The day I arrived, a man was found gored to death by a wild boar. That seems to have frightened a lot of people. I went to the winery to get some information for the article and somebody pushed me into a wine vat."

His eyes widened, but to his credit he managed not to smile.

"Provençal folklore contains several characters like you—who attract danger and disaster."

"That's not me at all," I protested. "All I want to do is write an article."

"Somebody doesn't like you. Could there be a reason for that?"

"Lewis Arundel at the Willesford vineyard says that people think I'm here to scout out land for retirement homes."

He turned away to test the rigidity of a strut. Was he contemplating the veracity of my statement, I wondered. Did he know something, anything?

"Is that why you were in Colcroze?" he asked, fingering a support wire. "To write an article?"

"When I was on a tour through the south of France some years ago, I was taken to a few ghost villages. They made an impression on me that I never forgot. So I thought that while I was here, I might write an article on them, starting with Colcroze."

"Except for being pushed into a wine vat, you might have thought that the beehive fell on you by mistake from a passing aircraft." He turned to look at me again. "Is that right?"

"Highly unlikely. Anyway, it wasn't just a passing aircraft—it was an ultralight."

He nodded reluctantly. "Mine in fact."

"Well," I said, brightening my tone of voice, "we've been through all that. You're going to find out who was flying the aircraft that day."

"I am," he said seriously, then his tone lightened too. "Now, how about a flight in an ultralight?"

"What! Er, no, thanks . . ." I was trying hard to think of a good reason to refuse. The craft looked fragile enough in the air—standing alongside one on the ground was all I needed to know that I wouldn't trust one with a bottle of Haut Brion 1990 let alone my life.

"It's kind of you to offer but I really can't."

My refusal didn't insult him, in fact it amused him. He grinned at my discomfort. "It's all right. Lots of people feel nervous about ultralights when they're first introduced to them."

"I'm glad you understand. In London, where I live, I don't even have a car. I hate mechanical things and loathe flying—I even hate underground trains, though unfortunately I have to use them a lot."

"Don't worry about it. Maybe I'll get you to change your mind."

"Where would you put me anyway?" I asked. "This one hardly has space for the pilot."

"We have a couple of two-seaters in the other hangar. We just completed modifying them so we can use them for training and also as aerial taxis."

"Taxis?" I said, appalled at the thought.

He grinned even wider. "Sure. We can whisk a person from A to B in a fraction of the time a ground taxi takes and we can land and take off almost anywhere, including many places a helicopter couldn't get near—and, of course, at a fraction of the price."

"They are considered safe enough to carry passengers?"

"Certainly. The safety record of ultralights is far better than that of conventional aircraft. They're impossible to crash and burn, for instance."

"Crash and burn!" I said, horrified.

"They're one-quarter the weight of a light plane and are usually traveling at half the speed. That means that if a ground impact were to occur—"

"A ground impact? Is that a crash?"

"Yes. Then the ultralight hits with only one-sixteenth the energy of the light plane. The pilot invariably walks away from an ultralight crash. Little damage is done, and anyway, the fuel tank only holds five gallons. Moreover, I can shut off the engine at five thousand feet and land anywhere within a five-mile radius. The glide ratio of ten to one makes landing without power easy." He grinned his Dawn Patrol grin and we walked back to my car.

"It sounds very—er, safe," I told him. "Perhaps some other time . . ."

Chapter 22

I was earlier than usual returning to the Relais but I told myself that I would do a lot of cogitating in the pool. It was notably warmer today. A platoon of cicadas in the plane trees buzzed with self-importance while high in the clear blue sky a few birds floated as serenely as if they had never heard of gravity.

I must have dozed off—it was becoming a habit I must avoid acquiring, although this time I did not encounter any monstrous insects upon awakening. Instead, I had a well-honed appetite and by the time I had changed, drunk a Kir, and gone down to the dining room, the honing had reached razorlike proportions.

I was waiting for Madame to arrive with her listing of the day's catch when she came bustling up to say, "M'sieu, there is a lady who wishes to speak with you." She batted her eyes in the classic matchmaking manner.

"Did she give a name?" I asked.

"No, m'sieu."

"Is she—?"

"She is young, m'sieu, and attractive."

"Ask her to join me," I said.

Madame Ribereau smiled understandingly.

"Very well, m'sieu."

It was Veronique Morel. She was wearing a dark blue suit with matching shoes. She looked very smart and trim but she put a hand to her mouth in embarrassment.

"I am sorry. I did not mean to interrupt your meal."

To the French, nothing is more reprehensible than delaying, or interrupting the all-important process of eating. The French do not simply eat—they dine. It is crass behavior to disrupt that ceremony.

"You're not interrupting," I assured her. "I haven't started yet."

"But . . . I should not have—I will wait in the lobby."

"Nonsense," I said firmly. "Sit down and join me."

I signaled Madame Ribereau, a close enough observer to have a waiter appear immediately with another chair.

"I really must not . . ." Veronique said, still spilling out apologies.

"You don't have to eat if you don't want," I told her. "But please sit."

Still she hesitated until I said, "It will spoil my meal if you don't."

That did it. The waiter brought a chair and she sat.

"A Kir? A glass of wine?"

"No, no, really, I just wanted to tell you something."

"Two Kirs Royales," I told Madame, who ducked her head and left. She would have preferred to hear what it was that Veronique wanted to tell me, so I was sure she would be back very quickly with the drinks.

"This is a very good auberge," I told Veronique. "Do you know it?"

"Yes," she murmured. "I have eaten here a few times."

She had a lovely face. I hadn't noticed at our original encounter just how attractive she was—after all, with a shiny revolver aimed at my middle, I was distracted from such perceptions. She had firm, regular features that were far above ordinary, but it was the eyes that were most striking: large and luminous, full of tenderness and understanding but strong and unwavering.

Madame arrived with the drinks. She handed me a menu and gave me the briefest of inquiring glances as she still clasped a second menu. I nodded and she handed it to Veronique.

She was still a protester. "No, really, I—"

"Madame, do you still have some of that superb Pâté de Grives?" I asked.

"Indeed, m'sieu."

"You must taste it," I told Veronique. "It really is excellent."

I gave Madame a quick nod. She was gone before Veronique could protest further.

"First, we'll drink to health, happiness, and good fortune," I said, "then you can tell me your news."

We drank. "This is very kind of you," she said, recovering her composure. She took another sip of the Kir. "What I want to tell you is this—a postcard came to the house for Edouard. It was from the public library in Saint Symphorien, notifying him that a book he had borrowed was overdue."

Madame arrived with the pâté and triangles of

toast. We were going to get priority service, I could tell. Veronique daintily spread some pâté on a piece of toast and agreed enthusiastically that it was, as I had said, excellent.

"What was the book?" I asked.

"The *Almanac de Reszke*."

I had another sip of Kir. The name meant nothing. "What is it?"

"It deals with the aristocratic families of France. It tells of their origins, shows family trees, indicates who they are related to . . ."

"When we had our first meeting—in the cave—you mentioned that your husband was researching the aristocratic families of Provence. How did you know that?"

"The last time I was in his office, he had on his desk a list of books dealing with that subject. Edouard had put a big red star next to the *Almanac de Reszke*."

I urged her to have some more pâté and she did, leaving just enough for me to have a couple more toast triangles. "Go on," I urged. "Do you have any idea what it means?"

"Until the revolution, the aristocracy ran France. There were over ten thousand of them—princes, barons, dukes, earls, counts, viscounts. Half of them died on the guillotine or at the hands of the mobs. Today's survivors keep a low profile, but they have a lot of influence."

"I'm surprised to hear that," I told her.

"Ah, but it is not because they are aristocrats but because they are in positions of wealth and influence. Their education and background give them all the qualifications needed to be successful in banking, insurance, industry, the armed services, government, farming . . ."

Madame returned, eager to know if we had decided on a main course.

"I couldn't," Veronique said. "No, really, I—"

"Let's just find out what Madame has for us today."

Merou, a Mediterranean fish belonging to the same family as grouper, was the catch of the day. Daube, a rich dark beef stew and a Provençal favorite, was also on offer but I decided on the third choice—paella. Madame assured me that it was extra good today with freshly caught shrimp and squid as well as chicken.

"Have just a small portion," I urged Veronique. "You can't let me eat alone."

"*Très bien,*" said Madame, giving Veronique no opportunity to decline. "And to drink?"

"Do you think Sancerre goes well with paella?" I asked Veronique.

"Well, yes, but—"

"*Parfait,*" said Madame.

"So," said Veronique when Madame had gone, "I went to Edouard's office." She leaned forward and her face was animated. "The mail had been picked up from the floor. It had been sorted. Judging from the postmarked dates, he had been there a couple of days earlier. Anyway, the files on the Willesford case were gone."

"Gone! Did you look around?"

"Yes, they were not in his office. I went through the books on his shelves—he has a lot of them—and I found the *Almanac,*" she said, her eyes brighter than ever. "A marker was in one page and an arrow was drawn to one name. It was the viscomte de Rougefoucault-Labourget."

"Did the *Almanac* tell anything about him?"

"The Rougefoucault branch of the family is very old. They were prominent during the Cathar rebellion and Robert, the head of the family at that time, led a column to relieve Simon de Montfort at the Siege of Valence. King Philip Augustus gave him a château and a huge tract of land in Provence as a reward. A marriage with the Labourget family made them even more powerful a century later."

"Doesn't tell us much, does it?"

"Maybe that's why Edouard was at the newspaper office. They have records of old Provence families."

She looked down at the tablecloth and brushed away a couple of crumbs that weren't there. "There's something else . . . I want to tell you that I have not been completely honest with you," she said in a small voice. I wasn't completely surprised—in my business, honesty is as rare as a good German red wine.

Madame chose that moment to arrive with the Sancerre and when it had been poured, tasted and approved, and the bottle settled into its ice bucket, Veronique continued.

"We have had . . . difficulties in our marriage. I suspected another woman but maybe he just spent more time working."

As we drank the Sancerre, she told me of their earlier days of marriage when she had been part of her husband's business. She had known the details of all the cases and had often helped him to put his reports together. It was only after he had become involved in the Willesford case that he became more secretive and began to shut her out.

"What do the police say about his disappearance?" I asked.

"The police?" She looked alarmed, surely the normal reaction of a law-abiding person when the police are mentioned.

"Yes. You told them he was missing, didn't you?"

"I told them. They know nothing."

The paella came. The French sausage in it was not as spicy as the chorizo sausage in the traditional Valenciana version, but otherwise it compared well. It contained peas and beans but not artichoke hearts as in the original. Similarly, it had clams but no mussels. Madame served Veronique the same size portion that she gave to me and the girl turned out to have a very healthy appetite. Her plate was so clean it would not justify a dishwasher and the basket that had contained half a dozen rolls was empty. I had only had two of them, but nobody was counting.

She smiled apologetically. "I didn't know I was hungry," she said.

Madame beamed with approval though she tut-tutted when we declined a liqueur. I walked with Veronique out to her car, an elderly but serviceable Diane.

"We need to visit the newspaper office," I told her.

"We?" she asked hesitantly.

The contrast struck me—the contrast between this uncertain girl and the tough broad who had held a gun on me in a cave. I was reminded of a line from *My Fair Lady*, something to the effect that "women are irrational, exasperating, irritating, vacillating." This one certainly vacillated—between scared girl and pistol-packin' mama. Still, I was convinced that this part of my investigation could be carried more effectually with her than without her—she was French.

"I'll do it by myself if you really—"

"No, I'll come with you," she said.

"Tomorrow? After lunch?" I suggested. "Let's meet in Saint Symphorien, about two o'clock. By the fountain in front of the *mairie*."

She nodded. Those luminous eyes glowed briefly, then she was gone.

Chapter 23

The cream-colored Rolls Royce Phantom that pulled up at the entrance to Le Relais du Moulin caused most of the heads breakfasting in the garden to turn. I drained my coffee cup and went out to the vehicle as though this were just part of an everyday scenario.

Grant Masterson greeted me as I joined him in the capacious and luxurious backseat that was large enough to hold board meetings. He was scanning a computer readout of what looked like stock market reports.

"Beautiful morning for a truffle market."

"No wonder the Greeks, the Romans, and the Moors all liked Provence," I said.

The Rolls moved onto the driveway so smoothly and silently that there was no sound except the slight crunch of gravel.

"That's Helmut up there at the wheel," Masterson said. "Master chauffeur."

In the driving mirror, Helmut met my eyes and inclined his head slightly. He wore a peaked cap and under it looked to have a very close-cropped haircut. He looked tough and capable and I wondered if he doubled as bodyguard too. A man as wealthy as Grant Masterson must need one.

"Three terms in the Legion," Masterson said, "so when he wanted to quit and take a quieter job, I snapped him up."

"The French Foreign Legion?"

"Of course. Helmut's from Bremen but he likes the soft life down here on the Côte d'Azur, don't you, Helmut?"

The chauffeur's eyes moved fractionally and his cap dipped a quarter inch in recognition. Masterson leaned forward and touched a button. "Coffee?" he asked. Mounted in the back of the seat before us was an electronic coffee maker. It was quiet but still made more noise than the Rolls's engine. I was tempted to ask for a cappuccino but I just said, "Thanks, I will."

The liquid in my cup stayed as calm as if we were stationary even though we were cruising at least sixty miles an hour around the curves. Masterson pushed the computer sheets away. "I enjoyed your party," I told him. "I talked to some very interesting people."

"Bertrand—from the casino—for instance?"

"No, I missed him. The professor held several of us enthralled, though."

"Ah, yes, planetary influences . . . unfortunately a lot of people associate his ideas with astrology whereas his theories are quite sound and based on scientific evidence."

"So I gathered. I was particularly interested in his ideas on improvements in wine."

"He does sound very convincing," Masterson agreed.

"Do you have any financial interest in the wine business?"

"Not really. My delicatessen chain will sell wine, but only because the two go together—when people buy delicatessen goods, they often like to buy their wine at the same time. That means, of course, that we can only sell the better vintages."

We rolled almost silently through the countryside, climbing steadily.

"How's the article coming along?" he asked casually.

"I'm behind schedule due to finding the body," I said, assuming that he knew about Emil.

"Body?" he asked in alarm.

I told him about it. "I hadn't heard," he said, and I reflected that a multimillionaire is probably concerned about events on a higher plane.

"Sanglier, they think?"

"Yes."

"Vicious creatures, or so I've heard. I'll probably think twice before ordering it in a restaurant again."

It was still early as we drove into Aupres but already cars were lined up on the grass verges coming into the village—an indication that the parking areas were full. Such a problem, however, meant nothing to Grant Masterson. Helmut simply drove to the center of the village, dropped us, and nodded when Masterson told him to come back in a couple of hours.

Aupres was a typical market village and its square was the venue for the twice-weekly market that saw produce coming in from the farms. The Hôtel de Provence sat behind iron gates on one side and the town hall, with three steps leading up to it to emphasize its importance, fluttered a large tricolor flag from a long white pole. Vehicles were parked everywhere including a number of places they shouldn't occupy, but on such occasions the law turned a blind eye. Vans, trucks, and pickups dominated and the area set aside for motorcycles was just as crowded.

"You probably know more about this," Grant Masterson said, "but I asked around and it seems that the whole village is the venue for truffle sales. Any farmers or hunters who find truffles can bring them here and sell them, and the buyers may be commercial or entrepreneurs or just anybody who wants to buy a truffle."

"So I believe. I've heard that this village has hardly changed since Roman days when it comes to truffle marketing."

"Look over there," Masterson said.

At one of the tables in front of a tiny bar, two men were arguing and we edged closer, trying to appear uninterested. An empty coffee cup was near each of them but their mutual attention was on a plate on which sat an ugly, dirty, misshapen, knobbly lump of fungus the size of a walnut.

"Looks like a turd," said Masterson inelegantly, "but it's really a black diamond."

It was a truffle, the most sublime food known to man and by far the most expensive on earth.

"It's been brushed," I pointed out to Masterson. "They used to sell them just as they were pulled from the ground—the idea being that they were in their natural state. On today's market, the price is so high that the weight of even a few particles of soil clinging to them makes them more expensive, so now they usually brush them."

He shook his head. "Can't understand it," he said.

"They don't taste that great to me, yet some people are willing to pay a thousand dollars a pound for them."

"The Italian white truffle is getting to be popular because it's less than half the price," I pointed out.

"The customers who will come to my delicatessens won't want those," he said firmly. "They'll want the best and that means the black truffle."

"You probably know that there's steady trade in white truffles that have been turned black."

"That's what I've heard. Now there's a 'black' market if ever there was one. Just how do they do that?"

"They soak the truffle in tannin solution, then set it in a bowl containing an iron salt."

"Isn't there any way of spotting truffles that have been counterfeited that way?"

"There is," I said. "Take a cut with a knife and the veining is different. The false one—the white truffle—doesn't show the characteristic light-colored veining of the black truffle."

"I'll have to remember that."

The two men were becoming more heated. We moved a little closer to hear their dialogue. The seller was scoffing at the amount offered by the prospective buyer.

"This isn't a turnip I'm selling you, it's a truffle," he said acidly.

The other snorted. "It should be a blue truffle at the price you're asking."

"I'll tell you what I'll do. I'll let you have it for eighteen hundred francs—and that's only because you're married to my cousin. If it was anybody else, believe me, the price would be double."

The haggling continued. Masterson turned to me.

"We've seen black truffles, you mentioned Italian white truffles, now this guy's talking about blue truffles. What's the story on them?"

"They don't exist. It's a hoary old Provence legend. It's like King Solomon's mines, the Holy Grail, or a fragment of the True Cross."

Masterson nodded toward the two men.

"They've broken the price barrier. I think they're about to finalize."

He had evidently been in enough price negotiations to be able to recognize the signs. Sure enough, one nodded, then they shook hands. The buyer wrapped the truffle in a paper napkin and stuffed it into the pocket of his jacket. Notes changed hands. They ordered another cup of coffee and all evidence of a business transaction was gone.

Masterson was shaking his head in a mixture of admiration and amazement. "Extraordinary way to do business. No one has ever been able to cultivate the truffle, did you know that?"

"So I understand. Lots have tried, though."

"That alone makes it unique among the foods we eat." Masterson was obviously intrigued by this dirty-looking, unappetizing tuber that he wanted to sell in his delicatessen chain.

We passed an ancient pickup truck, open at the back so that the tailgate provided a convenient negotiating platform. A whole family had apparently struck it lucky, for truffle hunting is not unlike gold mining in that chance plays a major role. A bottle of red wine, unlabeled, stood there, its contents lubricating a deal involving a few ounces of the ultimate delicacy.

"The Romans loved truffles, didn't they?" Masterson asked.

"Yes. Caligula was especially fond of them and

ate great quantities. Then in the Middle Ages, they were so revered that it was believed they grew only where a bolt of lightning had struck the earth."

Masterson motioned toward a bench on the edge of the parking area where a small park had forced its way into existence under the plane trees despite the sandy ground. A man who looked like a farmer held a small balance in his hand, a simple affair of aging bronze. We moved a little closer. The balance pan with weights on it crept higher as the man poured chopped truffles into a bag on the other pan.

"I just mentioned the Romans," Masterson said, awestruck. "That's exactly how they sold truffles in those times. Two thousand years might not have gone by for all these people care!"

"Going to make any purchases?" I asked him. "Or do you only want to soak up the atmosphere?"

"Main thing I want to do is get knowledgeable enough that I can make sure my buyers are getting a good deal. Most food commodities are straightforward, but truffles and truffle dealing are all mysticism and tradition." He shook his head in bewilderment and I smiled involuntarily.

He gave a wry grin. "I know—I shouldn't let it frustrate me, but this is a whole new world for me. It's hard to accept that the rarest foodstuff we have is bought and sold off the backs of trucks and using weighing scales the way the Romans did."

"I can understand that. Of course, in Paris, you could buy truffles in a more sophisticated environment. . . ."

"And at higher prices—no, no, I wouldn't have missed this for anything. How do people know about it, though?"

"Word of mouth mostly. There's an occasional handwritten notice nailed to a tree in neighboring villages."

"Well," he said, "let's go back to the square for a while and then I'll buy a truffle or two just for the experience. Will they take a platinum card?"

"They probably won't take a French bank note over two hundred francs. I understand that forged five-hundred-franc notes are coming in from Holland again."

We watched a few more transactions being negotiated. An unshaven young man came into the square on a noisy motorcycle and set up shop with some small and grubby specimens spread out on the saddle of his bike. One enterprising character in a bulky hunting jacket had a moving van that was empty except for three or four dozen bottles of juice in which fresh truffles had been marinated. A large woman in a plaid shawl had a picnic table with small packets of truffle shavings for sale, but she wasn't doing much business.

"They are too easy to adulterate," I told Masterson.

Eventually, he bought a fine-looking truffle, firm and fleshy, very dark in color. He paid a thousand francs for it, which pleased him immensely. He was probably getting more satisfaction out of this than some of his million-dollar deals and it was no doubt a rare occasion when he conducted a transaction personally and walked away with the merchandise in his hand.

The seller was a wizened old man with a face nearly as dark as the truffle. The price Masterson paid was maybe higher than longer haggling might have secured but he was impatient and the amount was presumably trivial to him.

"What are you going to have your chef do with it?" I asked as we walked away.

"I have three chefs," Masterson said. "One French, one Italian, and one Japanese."

"Don't they disagree all the time?" I asked, determined not to approve such extravagance.

"I try to keep them segregated. Each has his own responsibilities."

"Which one will get the truffle?"

"I'll probably have them share it and see who can make the most imaginative use of it. They're all pretty inventive. What do you suggest?"

"The choice is unlimited. Truffles go into soups, salads, sausages, and soufflés. You can put them with lobster, oysters, veal, fish, poultry, pasta. They improve everything eatable."

We returned to the spot where Helmut had left us and stood talking until the cream Rolls cruised up to us out of nowhere and we climbed into the luxurious air-conditioned interior. Helmut made a neat turn despite the narrow crowded street and we flowed out of Aupres in quiet comfort.

I was appreciating some of the advantages of being a multimillionaire.

Chapter 24

The Vietnamese girl in the cleaner's brought me my clothes accompanied by a cheeky grin. "Boss say, next time, drink white wine not red."

I walked round the square to La Colombe. It was close to lunchtime and I wondered if the enigmatic dowser from Wales, Elwyn Fox, would be here. He had given me the impression that it was a favorite hangout of his. Sure enough, he was sitting in the same place at the end of the bar. I took the stool next to him.

He finished draining his stein and turned casually, then greeted me cordially when he recognized me. "Ah, the journalist! How are ye? What'll ye have?"

"I'll join you in a beer," I said, and the barmaid manipulated the pump handle with a deftness born of long practice.

"Heard anything new about Emil?"

"No," I said, "but I don't really expect we will, do you? He was gored by a wild boar and it is hardly likely to confess."

The barmaid set the two beers in front of us and Fox took a long swig of his as if he were dying of thirst. In addition to being weather-beaten, I noticed that his skin was bad and that he had several small warts. His eyes were alert though, brown and lively as a squirrel's.

"What about the dowsing? How's that going? Having any luck?"

"It's a slow business. Frustrating at times."

"Must be," I commiserated. "Go weeks at a time without any success, I suppose?"

"Aye, sometimes."

"But you're always successful eventually, I believe you told me."

He nodded and drank more beer. The Welsh nation has a reputation for being loquacious but Fox wasn't living up to it. He emptied his beer glass and I watched as the barmaid refilled it. Maybe that was the answer . . . I waited until he had taken several swallows and tried again.

"I'm always looking for spinoffs," I said. He gave me an inquiring look.

"I came here to do an article on wine and vineyards. Poor Emil's death gave me the idea of another article on wild boar in Provence—it would go well in a hunting magazine. Now you've given me another idea."

He looked dubious. "I have?"

"Dowsing. Anything along those lines is popular today—New Age, they call it. People are interested in flying saucers, crop circles, spoon bending, angels, Bermuda Triangle, Atlantis . . . Dowsing fits right in, could be fascinating."

He didn't display any great enthusiasm for the idea. "I suppose so," he said grudgingly.

"I'll bet you've had all kinds of exciting experiences."

He drank beer while he thought. I hoped he wouldn't think as deeply as he was drinking.

"Costa Rica was what you would call exciting."

"In what way?" This was like pulling teeth. I hoped the beer was strong enough to be effective.

"The Nicaraguan rebels were particularly active at that time. The area I had to work in was under dispute by both countries and in those jungles, nobody really knows where the frontier is."

"Bad time to be looking for water," I said, and his muttered "Aye" struck me as being hesitant. I followed it up.

"Costa Rica had a water shortage? With all those rain forests?"

The barmaid came, anxious that Fox's well wouldn't run dry for lack of beer. I mentally applauded her timing, wanting to keep the Welshman well lubricated. When he had lowered the level in the new glassful, his reservations about talking to me were evaporating and we were getting to the congenial man inside.

"It wasn't water I was dowsing that time. It was oil."

"You dowse for that too? Find any?"

He grinned with satisfaction. "I found it. Trouble was, due to the war, the Costa Ricans couldn't get equipment in to drill for it—and without oil exports, they couldn't finance the war."

"And you were in the middle of the shooting?"

"I was bombed and shot at by both sides," he smiled proudly.

"I should have realized you dowsed for other things than water," I said, keeping the conversation moving. "I remember reading about Uri Geller— when he became famous with his spoon bending, people said, 'If you're so clever, why can't you make yourself a millionaire?' So he did—he located

mineral deposits for the mining companies and
made a million dollars in less than a year."

Fox nodded. He seemed relieved at the change of
topic.

"I met Geller. Very impressive, he was. Some
called him a phony but he wasn't that. They called
him a showman too, and that he certainly was.
Funny how people think that if a person is a showman, he can't be genuine."

"A legacy of the great Barnum," I said.

"He had an explanation of his own powers, did
Uri," Fox went on. "He told me he had a very severe
electric shock from his mother's sewing machine
when he was a boy. It was only after that his powers
were first noticed."

He was still talking about Geller. I wanted to get
back to Fox.

"But you're primarily a water diviner, aren't you?
You mentioned some work looking for oil as well
but with you, isn't it mainly water?"

My question made him nervous and he fidgeted
with his beer glass.

"Water's more of a challenge, y'see. It's part of
nature, that's what makes it so difficult. Divining is
finding the location of a material that is different
from its surroundings. Water is not that different—
it's one of the basics . . . earth, air, fire, and water,
that's what our ancestors believed our world was
made up of and that's what makes water harder to
find."

He drank the last mouthful of beer and looked
wistfully at the glass. "I suppose I should be going."

"I should too," I said.

"Back to the vineyard?"

"I can't wait to have another delightful session

with the charming Simone. Is she running for Miss Cordiality again this year?"

Fox chuckled. "She is a bit of a grim girl, isn't she? O'course, you can get just as much information from Lewis. He's a smart lad, knows all about the place."

"Lewis Arundel? Does he? I might try him."

I put a couple of notes on the bar. We said farewells and I left. A backward glance as I went out the door saw him ordering another beer. His mention of leaving had evidently been a ploy to terminate our conversation. I tried to work out what it was in our conversation that made him edgy. What did he have to hide?

In referring to Geller Fox had said that some people called him a phony. Was that Fox's sore spot? Did people call *him* a phony? Was he a phony?

I had said I would meet Veronique at two o'clock because I hadn't been sure what time I would be back from the truffle market, and it was now one-thirty. I walked to the *mairie* and near it was the French equivalent of a tea shop—a bakery that sold bread and pastries for takeout as its primary business but also had three or four tables. I decided on a complete change of pace and ordered a glass of tea and a *pan bagna*. The long bread roll filled with anchovy fillets, onions, and olives mixed with olive oil is one of the staples of vineyard workers during the harvest and is satisfying—but only just. I found myself counting the hours to dinner but I manfully declined anything further despite the wonderful baking smells. I had another glass of tea and watched for Veronique's arrival.

Chapter 25

La Voix it was called—The Voice. It was in a street so narrow that with a stretch, I could touch the buildings on both sides.

"What are we looking for?" Veronique asked me before we went inside.

"I wish I knew," I told her, and she flashed me a look that clearly suggested an unfavorable comparison with her husband when it came to investigating. She wore a pink shirt with a bolero-type red jacket and a white skirt and looked charming.

The newspaper office might be old on the exterior but the equipment in it was surprisingly modern. The proprietor, Monsieur LeQueux, was out soliciting advertisements but his daughter was in charge in his absence. She was a healthy, plump, farm girl in appearance but she knew the business from A to Z. She was about the same age as Veronique and the two of them had an immediate rapport.

Elise was sympathetic when she heard of Morel's disappearance—which was mostly due to Veronique's use of a trowel in laying on the tragic aspects of being a woman alone. Elise glanced at me, intrigued, when Veronique introduced me as "a family friend," and pronounced herself anxious to do whatever she could to help.

She remembered Edouard Morel's visits very well. He had been here three times, she said. On the first two occasions, he had wanted to see "these files"—she indicated rows of microfiche. They were records of births, marriages, and deaths, but Elise said it had been only the latter that Morel had wanted to see. She quickly had us set up and scanning them.

No, it wasn't any specific names, Elise said. Morel seemed to be noting the ages and cause of death of everyone whose decease was reported. We went through them, starting from the present. As I jotted down these items, one fact rapidly became apparent—the locals lived to a ripe old age. The majority were eighty or over, several ninety, and there were even four centenarians.

During the last three years, only one death was violent—an eighty-eight-year-old man had fallen under his own farm tractor. All the others were of natural causes, the ailments causing death predominantly pneumonia, heart failure, and cancer. We went further back—and then further. No change in the pattern was evident and Veronique snapped off the viewer with an exasperated sigh.

Elise said, "It's Doctor Selvier's article that brings most people here." She noted our blank look. "His article on wine?" She reached for a plastic folder. "I had to put it in here," she said. "It has been so popular. We have been asked for reprints by so many people—not just Monsieur Morel."

It was an article that had appeared in *La Voix* three months ago. The author, Doctor Selvier, wrote of the generally beneficial effects of wine drinking

and quoted several authorities in support of his recommendation. He went on to laud the Saint Symphorien wines as being especially valuable for their
ability to retard oxidation in the body and thereby
bestow antiaging characteristics. Willesford wines
were used as examples and I noted that there was no
mention of the Peregrine wines. The doctor's conclusion was that drinking wine prolongs life.

"This Doctor Selvier," I asked Elise. "Where
does he practice?"

"Why, right here," she answered in surprise.
"He's our village doctor, here in Saint Symphorien."
She gave us directions.

"Before we go, there's just one other thing we'd
like to check—" I looked meaningfully at
Veronique.

"Oh, yes," she asked Elise, "the last time my husband was here, did he ask to see your records of
Provence aristocracy, the history of family names
and so on?"

Yes, he did, said Elise, and she took us over to
some shelves holding a number of huge, bulky tomes
that had not yet been reduced to slips of plastic. She
was called away by the phone and Veronique and I
quickly located the appropriate volume and turned to
a page not quite turning yellow. Veronique's finger
moved down it and I heard her gasp.

"What is it?"

"Look!" she said in a whisper. "The last viscomte
de Rougefoucault-Labourget was a colonel in the
army. He died at Dien Bien Phu in 1954 leaving no
heirs. The line is extinct!"

French villages are heterogenous in their makeup
and it was not unusual to find that the doctor's office

was in one of the older, restored parts of the village where money and effort had been lavished on several streets to turn them into expensive residences.

Doctor Selvier's was as expensive as any, a stone building on three floors and comprising his offices and his home. A svelte dark-haired woman in an impossibly white nurse's uniform sat in the front office. She looked as if she would have been more at home in Paris than a village in Provence. She gave us a delightful smile and told us that visiting hours had ended fifteen minutes ago. Veronique explained that we merely wanted to ask the doctor a couple of questions about his article on wine. She continued, saying that I was a journalist from England and had to catch a plane in the morning, so if there was any way the doctor could spare us five minutes . . .

When we were ushered into his office, he gave his watch a meaningful glance. Veronique kept her story brief, stressing the angle of an English journalist writing about French vineyards. She added that she was here as my interpreter.

Doctor Selvier was a handsome man, graying at the temples, vigorous and with a deep resonant voice. He must have had a fanatical following among the female populace and I noticed Veronique responding to him.

"Oh, yes, that article," he said. "It brought a lot of comment even though I didn't say anything that other doctors and researchers haven't said already. Drinking wine has many beneficial effects."

"One of them being longevity?" I was glad to hear Veronique leap in with that question early.

He turned his gaze on her. "Certainly. Wine lowers the blood pressure; relaxes the nervous system, thereby reducing the strain on the arteries; facilitates gastric secretion, so helping digestion; and is diuretic, thus encouraging the elimination of organic wastes. With all those improvements in the body's operating condition, it is bound to perform for a longer duration."

"Do you believe, Doctor, that the wine from some vineyards is more beneficial than others? The wine from Willesford, for instance," asked Veronique.

"I have found it higher in iron and tannin, richer in mineral salts than the wines from several other vineyards," he said. His delivery was a little more paced now, not as free-flowing as his earlier stock statements. He studied me as if wondering how much I understood.

"So people live longer?" I said.

"There are other factors, of course. The so-called Mediterranean diet of fruit, bread, and olive oil is extremely healthy. Most people here eat that way." He went on smoothly. "We don't know enough yet to be able to analyze many of the characteristics of wine. Nor do we know enough to be able to measure their effects on the human body."

"I have one more question, Doctor. Why isn't the wine from Peregrine the same as the wine from Willesford? The vineyards are adjacent, the climate is the same, the soil must be the same. . . . What is the difference?"

His pause was a fraction longer this time.

"I don't know. I haven't studied the wine from Peregrine." He didn't sound as if he had any interest in doing so. He wriggled his left wrist, the one with the watch. Perhaps he hoped it would buzz. Instead, the brunette nurse came in to remind him that he was requested at the hospital. They must have had a prearranged code for that interruption. We thanked him and left.

"He likes publicity," Veronique said. "He liked the publicity he got when that article appeared, but he doesn't seem so anxious to talk about it now."

"Strange," I said. "An English journalist might have gotten him more coverage. I wonder why he was so cool?"

"We came in off the street," Veronique said. "Perhaps he would have been different if we had called for an appointment. These provincials like formality."

"You may be right," I agreed. "Didn't you think, though, that the doctor was strangely dismissive of Peregrine? It's not in the true scientific spirit of investigation to praise the Willesford wines and ignore Peregrine's."

"Perhaps Willesford paid him and Peregrine didn't."

She wasn't just being cynical. She might well have hit the nail on the head.

Chapter 26

Veronique dropped me off at Le Relais and as it was still only four-thirty, I decided on a visit to the Willesford vineyard. The place was at the heart of this puzzle that grew more perplexing the more I discovered. I suspected I was learning the wrong things, but how was I to know which were the right ones?

I parked as far away from the farm cart as I could. It still stood there, just as it had with Emil leaning against it. I went inside to find Simone's office empty. Wandering in search of someone, anyone, I ran into Lewis Arundel.

"Ah, the pride of Fleet Street," he said with his usual tinge of sarcasm. "Know any more than when you started?" he asked.

"Quite a lot," I said. It was equally untrue whether applied to writing an article or investigating a mystery, but it might shake him up a bit.

"Just had a few drinks with the Welsh wizard," I said breezily, trying to jar loose some information from him. He invited me into his office, which was a smaller version of Simone's with glass on three sides.

"Is he still trying to get the twig to twitch?" he asked.

"I think he's being very successful." The lie got even more of his attention.

"Really? Hot on the treasure trail, is he?"

I wasn't sure what he meant by that but I wanted to keep the ball rolling.

"I was surprised to find a dowser here," I continued, still being chatty. "I didn't realize water was a problem."

He leaned back in his chair and put one long leg up on the corner of the small crowded desk.

"No problem here," he said flatly.

"Then how can it be a problem over at Peregrine? The terrain is the same. How could they have a problem with water and you not?"

He pulled open his desk drawer and rummaged around until his hand emerged with a packet of cigarettes. When he was puffing contentedly, he asked, "Told you he was dowsing for water, did he?" He sounded amused.

"Well, maybe he didn't. He told me he was a dowser and I assumed he was talking about water. He did mention previously dowsing for oil in South America."

"He was quite a hot shot at that, I believe." Arundel puffed a poor imitation of a smoke ring, frowned, and tried again. It was no better. "Dowsed lots of other things too."

"We talked about Uri Geller—he made a million dollars in less than a year finding metal deposits." I paused, thinking. "Is that what you meant when you said 'treasure' a minute ago?"

"Never did get the hang of these," Arundel said.

He blew another plume of smoke that no geometrician would ever have recognized as a ring. He took his leg off the desk, leaned even farther back, and regarded me with the faintest of smiles that was really more of a smirk.

"You can't blame poor old Elwyn," he said solicitously. "These hills have been alive for centuries—not with the sound of music but with the tread of seekers after the Treasure of the Templars."

"I suppose I've heard legends. . . . I didn't know people were still looking for it though."

"More than ever. People still enter the lottery, don't they? Odds are about the same and you don't even have to buy a ticket."

"I didn't realize that it was supposed to be around here, either."

"Several regions claim it in campaigns that are no doubt spearheaded by the local chamber of commerce."

His phlegmatic manner made it hard to tell how much he was merely trying to stir things up. As an occasional drinking companion of Elwyn Fox's though, he might know a lot about him.

"So there's no water problem," I said.

"We don't have one at Willesford. Can't speak for the Peregrine crowd."

"Do you know any of them besides Gerard?"

"You've met him, I suppose? Yes, nice chap, knows wine. But any others? No, I've never seen a soul." He gave me a searching look. "Interested in Peregrine, are you?"

"It's a close neighbor of Willesford so I have to be. But you're right—it's Willesford I'm writing about. What about these rumors that Peregrine wants to buy you out?"

"It wants to expand—where else can it go?"

"It must think you're a valuable property."

He shrugged carelessly. "We are."

"But surely you're not *that* valuable a property?"

"How valuable?" His eyes opened a fraction wider. "I don't know how much Peregrine has been offering. Do you?" The last question came as a swift jab.

"No," I said, "but it must be on public record."

He laughed. "Peregrine? It's incorporated in Monte Carlo. You know what that means."

"I suppose that means it's about as accessible as the Mafia's account books," I conceded.

"So if you know what the latest offer is, you have some red-hot information."

"Just rumors . . . ," I assured him, adding quickly, "Don't your wines have something of a reputation for their medical value?"

"All wines are medically valuable, aren't they? Since the National Institutes of Health stated that wine can cut the risk of heart attacks by seventy-five percent, the public has been putting wine on a par with penicillin. 'The Mediterranean Diet,' they called it."

"Yes," I agreed, "and when CBS put on a TV special in the US calling it that and linking wine drinking with a low mortality rate from heart disease, it was said that wine sales there went up thirty percent. But what about the locals? Don't they believe that drinking wine helps them live longer?"

"I doubt it. They just like to drink it." He puffed away the last millimeters of the cigarette. "What makes you ask that?"

"Doctor Selvier's article in *La Voix*," I said airily.

"Oh, you saw that, did you?" He grinned. "Didn't hurt our sales any."

"So you don't make wine in any special way?"

"Special! Of course not."

"Maybe the grapes . . . or the soil . . . or even planetary influences?"

Surprisingly, he didn't laugh. "Ah, you've been talking to the professor. Yes, there are accounts of extraordinary results from applying knowledge of the movements of the planets."

"You believe them?" Such a belief didn't fit with his otherwise skeptical demeanor.

"I don't disbelieve them. I understand that Rahmani has reached some extraordinary conclusions from his work."

His phone buzzed and he answered it. His French was fluent and the call was from a buyer who wanted a prompt shipment. Arundel took down the order and, hanging up, said, "Another satisfied customer. Didn't say if he wants the wine for medicinal purposes." He got to his feet. "Have to get this moving. He wants delivery tomorrow."

I walked out of the office with him.

"If there are any more questions, don't bring them around tomorrow. There'll be only a skeleton staff on duty."

"Not a national holiday, is it?"

"A local one—the Feast of Saint Symphorien, the patron saint of the village. We'll all be there."

"Maybe I'll come too."

"You should. There's something for everybody and lots of good wine."

"Willesford wine?"

"Naturally." He gave me a lazy grin and stalked off across the yard.

Chapter 27

Saint Symphorien's day of the year was bright and clear. It was only midmorning and already the crowds were gathering. Tape barriers had been erected around the square to prevent parking and this time the police meant it. Shop windows were gaily decorated and buildings had red and white flower arrangements hanging from windowsills. Music blared out from speakers on every corner. Delicious aromas of baking bread, biscuits, and cakes declared that the bakers were making sure no one went hungry.

A light breeze ruffled the banners that stretched across street corners and a buzz of excited anticipation filled the men, women, and children thronging the square.

Provence is famous for its festivals. Even the smallest village has at least one a year and even the poorest puts on a brave show. It looked as if Saint Symphorien was really going to celebrate today.

A couple of sweating soldiers hurried past me, still adjusting their blue tunics, white trousers, and red trimmings. A sergeant would have been apoplectic at the sight of their headgear—one wore a blue and white pillbox shako and the other a sheepskin busby. A photographic flash temporarily dazzled me—it was Monika Geisler taking pictures of the crowds and the decorated square.

I pushed my way over to her. She looked like a stylish guerrilla, but then I saw that her light green battle-dress outfit was more likely supplied by St. Laurent than a quartermaster. She snapped off another shot of a tiny girl in lace and crinolines, then saw me.

"Staying away from beehives?" she asked with a sparkling smile.

"And deserted villages. I see you're working today."

"Never miss an opportunity."

"You'd better have lots of film."

"It's wonderful, isn't it?" she said, looking around. "Are you staying for the parades?"

"I'll probably be here most of the day."

"Good. See you later then." She laughed as a clown smoking a big cigar approached and quickly raised her camera.

A Von Suppe overture coming from the speakers was drowned out by a marching band representing the local high school, their jaunty enthusiasm overcoming their occasional failure to keep in step or stay in tune. Trombones blared, cymbals crashed, and drums thundered across the square. Proud parents pointed out their talented offspring and applause rippled through the crowd.

I scanned the sea of faces and saw Gerard Girardet, but he was too far away to hear me call. The thump of percussion persisted, but when it was finally lost in the distance, lines of small children filed through, dressed in Provençal costume, the girls looking particularly proud in their lace bonnets.

Another band came, dressed in crimson and green minstrel costumes with embroidered hats, tiny bells at ankles and wrists, and playing ancient Provençal instruments. Some carried the galoubet, a three-holed flute, others the tambourin, a hand-held drum, as they danced and weaved the farandole, one of the oldest dances in southern Europe. The effect was a tinny sound, limited in range and repetitive, but peculiarly hypnotic.

"I see ye're a music lover," said a voice behind me in English.

Elwyn Fox wore his habitual leather windbreaker that he evidently found appropriate to all climates, temperatures, and occasions. He looked flushed and even more bleary than usual. His complexion was grainy but his eyes were bright as if they suppressed an inner excitement.

"I'm getting into the spirit of the festivities," I admitted. "No place quite like Provence for the traditional songs and dances."

"True, true. I'm into the jollifications myself—a great day it is."

He squeezed alongside me. At closer range, I could see that the light in his eyes hinted at something more than the pleasure of enjoying a country fete.

"You look as if you just won the lottery," I told him.

He was almost rubbing his hands with glee. He wanted to tell me all about it but something was holding him back.

"You finally found water," I said. "Millions of gallons of it—pure and sweet."

He shook his head. "It was a wonderful day yesterday," he said joyfully. "Wonderful."

"If you didn't find water, what did you find?"

Abruptly, his mood changed and the eyes under the heavy brows regarded me with an unfocused stare.

"What is it?" I asked. "What's wrong?"

He didn't reply. I don't think he could hear me—he was in another dimension. He shivered as if caught in an icy blast.

"You—I see you—" His voice was weak and he was looking through me as if I were glass. Whatever he could see terrified him. He tottered and was about to fall. I grabbed his arm.

"What's wrong? Are you ill?"

He struggled unsuccessfully to find words, then he pulled loose, stumbled away, and was lost in the crowd. I tried to spot him but it was impossible.

Local veterans were next on the parade list: World War II, Indochina, and French Foreign Legionnaires. The loudspeakers bellowed a stirring military march and the throngs cheered and waved.

Fox's strange attitude bothered me and I was still pondering when squeals arose from the children in the crowd and there was a surge backward. The cause was a bizarre creature like a giant green crocodile with scaly skin and bulging eyes. It raised its head, opening mighty jaws and now showing resemblance to a dragon as ribbons of red paper streamed out of its mouth, propelled by a blower inside and suggesting fiery breath.

"What is it?" I asked an old man standing nearby.

He smiled. "A 'Barasque'—it is said to guard the sacred treasure."

"What treasure is that?"

"Why, the Treasure of the Templars, of course."

The monster came slithering over the paving stones while children clung tighter to parents' hands and even a few women screamed. Fearsome growls came forth and sudden forays at the edge of the crowd made it sway like a field of corn in a strong wind.

As the creature left the square, doubtless seeking more pulses to accelerate, the music from the speakers ended and a voice advised us that the ride of Gabriel Bonnard was now to be recalled. A mad clatter of horses' hooves on the cobblestones heralded the entry of a big black stallion, galloping fiercely and urged on by a rider in a pale blue uniform who was carrying a large satchel. As near as I could determine, he was bringing a French version of the Message to Garcia, and a motley crew following him had little chance of catching him.

I turned to look for Elwyn Fox. His condition troubled me. I wanted to help but I could see no sign of him. Instead, I saw a head of golden hair that could belong only to Alexis Suvarov. He saw me at about the same time, pushed his way in my direction, and pumped my hand.

"Glad you could come," he said jovially. "Everybody's here . . ." He squeezed sideways to allow his companion to come forward. It was Simone Ballard. She wore light blue stretch pants and a blue and white sweater with white sandals. She looked quite attractive and her nod of greeting was accompanied by what was, for her, very nearly a smile.

"So you two have abandoned ultralights and wine for the day, have you?"

It was Simone who answered. "This is Saint Symphorien's biggest day of the year. Everyone comes. Besides, we have a stand selling Willesford wine and we're taking turns at it."

"Good. I'll come and have a glass or two," I said.

Suvarov's face became stern as he addressed me. "I'll know in a day or two who flew my Demoiselle on that occasion we talked about."

Simone looked at him puzzled but he made no attempt to enlighten her.

"Staying for the aioli?" he asked.

"Yes."

"Good, we'll see you then." They were hailed from a nearby window and wormed their way through the masses of people, presumably to get a location with a better view.

I thought about the aioli. It is the traditional lunch in Provence on festive occasions and takes place in an outdoor space, usually a park. The name derives from the word for garlic, *ail,* and the dish is made by pounding garlic cloves into a paste with egg yolks. It is seasoned and olive oil is added until it becomes like a thick mayonnaise. It is served in huge mounds, accompanied by boiled cod, snails, fennel, green beans, hard-boiled eggs, potatoes boiled in their skins, carrots, onions stuck with cloves, and sometimes squid cooked in its ink.

Some of the dishes that accompany the festive aioli I find a little bland, particularly the boiled cod, boiled potatoes, and boiled carrots. Still, when the dish originated, boiling was one of the few ways of cooking food. It was easy, and in those days healthy cooking was considered to be an oxymoron. I decided to go and contribute one more garlic exhalation to the cloud that would envelop the village in the afternoon.

It was eleven-thirty and the people showed no signs of moving so I presumed that more parades would come by before lunch. I had time to find out what had happened to Fox and I decided to start looking in the one place where he was most likely to be. Every establishment dispensing food and drink of any kind was open today and La Colombe was no exception, though it was empty but for a sole drinker. I joined him at the bar.

"I was worried about you. Are you feeling all right?"

A stein of Fox's favorite medicine was on the bar top before him and held only another two inches. He finished that in one gigantic swallow and the bored barmaid, with nothing to do, promptly refilled it.

"I'm all right," he said. His voice, though quiet, was steady, but he didn't look at me.

"Do you have these attacks often?"

"From time to time."

"Do you know what causes them?"

"It's nothing physical. It's this—this sense that I have. Sometimes it comes over me like a cloud. I feel chilled, drained." He shivered and reached eagerly for his beer glass. When he had drunk half of it, he finally looked at me. His eyes were somber. When he spoke, his voice was grim. "Be careful. I don't know what else to tell you. Just be careful." His voice throbbed with urgency.

"You were elated when I saw you earlier. You must have found whatever it was you were dowsing for."

"Elated?" He thought about the word. "Aye, ye could say I was elated."

The cries and shouts from the crowd in the square were growing louder and I decided to ease up on my interrogation for the moment and then tackle him hard when he had relaxed.

"Let's go out and see what the excitement is all about," I suggested.

He hesitated. The bar was a safe haven to him

and he didn't want to leave it, but he finished his drink and nodded agreement. We went outside.

The crowd was thin here in front of the bar and we were able to move to the rope barrier. The increase in noise had been caused by a medley of entertainers. There was a stilt walker, a little out of practice, whose immensely long blue pantaloons flapped as he swayed uncertainly over the cobbles. After him came a fire-eater whose blasts of flame caused the children to gasp loudly. There was a distinct smell of brandy and I gathered he was enjoying his job.

The clown I had seen earlier now had a string of small dogs on separate leashes and all of them were intent on tripping him up. His falls and near falls brought shrieks of laughter. A juggler was next. He wore a moth-eaten tuxedo and he kept green bottles moving through the air while the crowd held its breath. When he dropped one bottle, it bounced and he swept it up neatly with a practiced swing.

The applause was drowned in a rumbling roar as a huge wooden wagon drawn by four powerful farm horses rolled slowly into the square. It was packed with monks in brown robes, cowled and hooded. I turned to Fox.

"This has some local significance, does it?"

"Aye. Gerard was telling me about it. During the Cathar wars, Saint Symphorien changed hands several times. The Cathars had this plan to recapture it from the Papal forces." He darted me an uncertain look. "Ye know who the Cathars were?"

"Medieval heretics, weren't they?"

"That's right. Their beliefs were opposite to those of Rome, and the fighting was bitter—armies on both sides were big and powerful, mostly experienced soldiers returned from the Crusades."

I motioned to the colossal wagon. "So these monks were prisoners of the Cathars? Being taken to be executed?"

Fox tapped the side of his nose. "Ah, you'll see in a minute . . ."

The big wooden wheels creaked and the sweating horses snorted, their manes waving and their eyes gleaming. Behind the rough staved sides of the wagon, the monks stood silent and still, features hidden behind their brown robes. The monstrous vehicle moved slowly past us and clattered on around the square. The crowd was quiet now, adults and children watching, waiting. The wagon swayed under its heavy load of dozens of men.

It was only about twenty yards away when a shot was heard. It was the signal for the "monks" to strip off their robes and be revealed in sinister black military uniforms.

"Cathar storm troopers!" said Fox excitedly.

Crossbows, pikes, swords, lances, and long-handled axes appeared menacingly and the crowd gasped. The wagon was a frightening sight, packed with men intent on dealing death and mayhem. Then the sides dropped down and the troops spilled out in all directions, yelling and howling.

"So that's how the Cathars regained control of the village," I said, turning to Fox.

He didn't hear me. Beads of perspiration trickled down his face and his eyes were filled with horror. Surely he wasn't that affected by a pageant, no matter how well done, I thought. He was staring petrified at the would-be warriors and I tried to see what had such an effect on him.

A row of crossbowmen were advancing toward us. Fox seemed to find something specially menacing about them. Their weapons were aimed over the heads of the crowd—all except one. Fox's arm shot out, pointing. That soldier's crossbow loomed in my vision as, from his crouched position, the bolt was released.

The people were shouting in excitement but if anyone else saw the discharge, the warning was lost in the noise and confusion.

I had a momentary glimpse of a black pointed shape hurtling at me, growing larger and larger . . .

Chapter 28

The bolt from the crossbow passed so close that I could feel its hot breath singe my cheek. As thoughts tumbled through my brain, the first of them postulated that I had been hit. Hadn't I read that you didn't feel the pain at first? That idea was immediately dispelled by a horrible gasping sound from behind me and I turned amid cries and shouts of terror to find Elwyn Fox falling to the ground, his hands desperately grasping the long, black metal bolt protruding from his throat.

The next minutes were a chaotic jumble of events with one emerging as dominant—the gendarme, Aristide Pertois, was there, bending over Fox even as the Welshman gurgled his last precious seconds of air and died with a flow of blood spreading across his chest.

It wasn't until I was in one of the offices in the *mairie* that my mind came back to normal. Pertois had somehow found an official to open up the building and Fox was carried inside. The gendarme told me to follow him and I was too stunned to do otherwise. Fox's body was taken into one room while Pertois led me into another. He murmured a few words to one of the men and a minute later a small glass of brandy was pressed into my hand. Pertois disappeared for a while. I lost track of time, then he came back to sit on the edge of a table facing me as I sprawled in a chair, physically and mentally devastated.

"A horrible thing," he said quietly. I nodded.

"Tell me exactly how it happened."

I did so, glad of the opportunity to do something, whatever it was, even if it meant reliving those ghastly moments.

"What did you talk about in La Colombe?" he asked.

"He told me that yesterday was a wonderful day."

Pertois leaned forward. "Did he say why?"

"I said he must have found millions of gallons of water in his dowsing efforts. He shook his head but he was still so pleased with himself that I assumed he had found something else. It seemed unlikely to me that he was looking for water but I had no idea what else he could be dowsing."

"What did you think he was dowsing for?"

"I've heard stories about treasure. The Treasure of the Templars in particular."

He sat back onto the table, not taking his gaze off me. "Provence is full of such stories. They probably told you the Templar treasure is guarded by dragons too, didn't they?"

"Yes, and I saw one of them today."

"In the parade—yes." His agreeable tone suddenly developed a razor edge. "Out of your line anyway, isn't it? You're writing about vineyards. Why are you investigating dowsers and treasure?"

"It seemed like a good subject for another article. Vineyards are still the subject I'm mainly interested in. Besides," I went on, not wanting to be too docile,

"I'm not investigating, I'm just gathering information."

His steady gaze didn't waver. If skepticism could be expressed in silence, he was a master at it. I told him the rest. "When I was talking to Fox, he seemed to be having some strange seizures. It was if he were having extrasensory experiences. He warned me of danger. Then when the Cathars came flooding out of that wagon, he pointed and looked terrified—as if he were seeing a vision. Seconds later, the crossbow went off."

"Eh bien," he said, the French equivalent of "Ah, well" and just as meaningless. "I must go. We will continue tomorrow at nine in my office. You know where the Poste Provisoire de la Gendarmerie is?"

He described its location. I went out into the sunshine where people were still moving around, determined to enjoy the rest of their ruined day. I was still undecided on where I would go as I drove out of the village. The two vineyards seemed to be the obvious places. Whatever was going on revolved round them. . . .

The Peregrine vineyard was first. I parked near the shining stainless steel barrels and went to the door of the only building. It was locked, as I might have expected. I circled the building, looking for another door. There was one in the back but it was locked too.

It was a small facility for wine production. I guessed the output of the vineyard to be about a thousand liters an acre as it was fairly good-quality wine. There were about four acres, so that was four thousand liters—just over five thousand bottles. It was small. Barely enough to support Gerard let alone show a profit for a Monte Carlo–based conglomerate.

I strolled down to the rows of low bushes that held the grapes—the heart and soul of the vineyard. They looked healthy, and in the time between now and the harvest would grow appreciably. Professor Rahmani came to mind. How much larger and juicier could he make these grapes if he applied his ideas to them? Another thought occurred—*was* he applying his methods?

From this position, the chalky cliffs and their yawning black holes looked innocent, yet held a touch of hidden menace. I could see them from the same angle as when I was with Gerard and had seen a figure appear, then hastily duck back out of sight. Surely . . . I shaded my eyes to see more clearly . . . There was no mistake. There was movement on the ledge in front of one of the cave mouths.

Chapter 29

The last time I had climbed up here, it had been to find a shiny revolver pointed at me. I would be more careful this time. I studied the geography in more detail before I made a move. The ledge ran across the cliff edge and three-quarters of the way up. The only way up to it from where I stood was the same that I had used on the previous occasion, at the west end. I could see cave mouths along the ledge. At the east end of the ledge, a trail snaked up and onto the ridge at the top where eucalyptus trees grew in what looked like dense woods, though the ground sloped back and out of sight.

I made the climb keeping a careful eye on the ledge whenever it was in sight. I saw no further movement and reached the ledge hardly out of breath. At the mouth of the first cave, I paused and listened. It was quiet but for the soft buzz of cicadas. I walked carefully along and into the third cave— the one where I had seen movement from below.

The antechamber was large and could have housed dozens of people. The walls looked ancient and caves ran in three directions. I froze—I thought I had heard a sound and I held my breath. There was only silence. I took a step then stopped . . . there was something, a sort of scuffling sound, a scraping. I listened, then gave it longer. My heartbeat had settled down to a dull thump by that time and I decided to look briefly into each cave, going as far as the penetration of the outside daylight permitted.

I had taken no more than a dozen steps when I was hit by a fast-moving body that seemed to weigh a ton. I crashed to the ground, the wind knocked out of me, trying to see in the semidarkness who my assailant was and how I could protect myself. I could make out only a long dark shape, then to my horror, there was another—and another.

Before I could roll away, I was engulfed in massive fleshy bodies and the porcine stench confirmed my worst fear—sangliers, wild boars. Slobbering jaws brushed my face and I tried to jerk myself clear, but wherever I turned there was another of the creatures. I fought to get to my feet but their hairy, bristly carcasses were everywhere, grunting and snorting. I expected to feel the excruciating stab of a tusk at any second and kept rolling this way and that to avoid their aim. Their prickly hide was disgusting as it rasped my skin and I could feel spines rip my clothes. Boar saliva trickled down my face and revolted me but the fear of a daggerlike tooth ripping into me was worse.

I continued to roll and twist to escape the inevitable thrust of one of those spearlike tusks while the memory of Emil Laplace's body with its myriad bleeding wounds rose vivid in my mind. I was so exhausted from the buffeting and beating that I was taking that I seemed to be floating in a world of smelly, snorting, massive shapes. I was battered and aching and losing consciousness when a shock wave reverberated through the cave, a hollow boom that sent echoes bouncing off the walls and made my eardrums tingle.

The sangliers growled in what I hoped was apprehension. They backed away. One of them ran, snuffling and snorting, into the safety and darkness of the cave interior and the others followed. I lay there in the stillness, hardly able to believe that I was still alive. I gulped a lungful of the stinking air and staggered out into daylight.

At the far end of the ledge, I took the path that went up to the top of the ridge. Scrubby undergrowth covered the ground and the trees looked invitingly safe. When I was close to them, I took stock of myself. I could hardly believe it but I couldn't find any blood. Why had a sanglier killed Emil and not me? Not even a flesh wound!

My clothes were a mess, my shoes were badly scuffed, and I had splintered a fingernail but it was a negligible price to pay. My spirits rose as I began to fully appreciate that I had no splintered bones and no lacerations. I wondered what the noise had been that had frightened off the sangliers . . . then it came again.

In the confines of the cave it hadn't been an identifiable sound, but out here there was no mistake. It was a gunshot, and the leaves in the eucalyptus trees crackled. I dropped to the ground—had I escaped the frying pan to enter the fire, in this case gunfire? The explosion came again and this time it was much closer. Where could I hide? Back in the caves? Not likely! Before I could make a decision, a man came into sight. He was carrying a large gun and it was pointed right at me.

This was clearly not my day. Almost killed by a crossbow bolt, nearly mauled to death by wild boars, and now shot at with a very loud gun. . . .

The man came closer. It was a shotgun he carried, and as he approached me he snapped it open at the breach. Was I reprieved? Why? He was wearing hunting clothes—denim pants, a jacket with large pockets, big boots, and a floppy hat. He looked familiar.

"Hello!" he greeted me jovially. "How are you?"

There were several answers but I wasn't ready with any of them. I recognized him now—it was Marcel Delorme, the elderly wine master at the Willesford vineyard.

"I hope I didn't frighten you," he said. "I thought it was a good day to do some hunting with everyone at the festival."

He was staring at my clothes. No wonder. I looked like a tramp down on his luck. "Did you have an accident?" he inquired solicitously.

"I was attacked by sangliers. I'm lucky to be alive. Your gunshot scared them away."

His eyes were big. "Sangliers?" He started to laugh. I didn't join him. "Sangliers?" he spluttered. "You were in one of the caves?"

"Yes and several of them attacked me. What's so funny?"

He wiped away a tear. "There are no sangliers here in the caves. Those are just pigs."

"Nonsense. They were huge, they mauled me—nearly killed me."

"They were being friendly, they were kissing you. This breed of pig is very affectionate." He was still chuckling at this city slicker who didn't know the difference between belligerent boars and passionate pigs. I wondered if there was a possibility that he was right and that was why I had no injuries.

There was no chance that I was going to admit it, though.

"Well, it's a good thing you came along anyway. You saved my life."

He was starting to laugh again and argue that statement, but he caught my eye and thought better of it.

"Do you want to come and get cleaned up?" he asked instead.

"Thanks, but I'd better go back to the auberge and clean up properly."

He nodded. "I'll try my luck a little longer, then. I saw some fat quail up here but haven't been able to get any yet."

"Those pigs . . ."

"Yes?"

"They live in the caves?"

"They were Emil's. He bought them some time ago. They were extremely attached to him—they are very friendly animals."

"What did you think about his death?"

He got a faraway look in his eye and avoided my gaze.

"That couldn't have been his own pigs. They are all female, they don't have tusks. He must have run into a real sanglier—a wild one." He brought his attention back to me. "Were you looking for something in the caves?"

"Just curious," I said. "Did the Romans really use them for storage?"

"So they say." Like many rural French, history in his own backyard didn't interest him much.

"The Templars too?"

"People come looking for their treasure." He sounded dismissive.

"Do they ever find any?"

He shrugged. "Who knows? If you found any, would you tell?"

He had a point there. He pulled out a couple of shotgun shells and snapped them home.

"I must get on with my hunting now. Good day to you."

Once again, I had to run the gauntlet to get to my room without raising an alarm. I had a warm, relaxing bath, firmly resisted the idea of a glass of champagne, and phoned Sir Charles.

"It's not two weeks already, is it?" were his first words. His next were a short time later after I had described Fox's death.

"An accident," he said anxiously. "Nothing to do with our business."

"It's not clear yet."

"What's all this dowsing?" he wanted to know. "Never heard of a vineyard hiring a dowser," he muttered after I had told him what I knew of Fox's activities.

"Nor did I. Could be unconnected."

"Hmm," he said. "Anything else?"

I thought it better not to worry him with tales of beehives falling from the sky and near drowning in a vat of red wine. As for being attacked by a herd of killer sangliers and nearly having my head blown off by a shotgun—well, there are just some things an investigator doesn't report.

I went down for a swim, changed, and went into the lounge, where I ordered an atypical scotch and soda. I settled down with it in a comfortable armchair and looked through a pile of magazines on the table. My browsing came to an abrupt stop as I came upon an article headlined "Seeking the Treasure of the Templars." It was in a *National Geographic*–style publication and the whole issue was devoted to the myth and legend of Provence. I recalled only fragments about the Templars and this was an excellent summary of their history.

They were monks who were also warriors. They protected pilgrims on their way to the Holy Land during the first Crusades. They took their name from the Temple in Jerusalem, swearing to win it back for Christianity. By the time of the later Crusades, they were the most powerful organization in Europe. They paid no taxes and were richer than most countries.

Inevitably, as their power and wealth increased, envious eyes were cast upon them, and King Philip of France, his own finances in disastrous shape, denounced the Templars as devil worshippers and seized their possessions. Many Templars were killed and others tortured to death. Frequent and determined efforts to find the treasure had been unsuccessful, though there was a lot of truth in Marcel's statement that anyone finding any of it would hardly be likely to let out the news. Metal detectors, ultrasonic beams, X-rays, and other technical equipment had been employed in the search as well as . . . I reread the phrase twice . . . "as well as dowsers."

Had Elwyn Fox been one of those dowsers? Who could have hired him? Had he been killed because of what he had found? I remembered him telling me what a wonderful day he had had the day before. Had he actually found treasure?

Henri, the headwaiter, came to bring the menu and tell me that one of the specials of the day was crayfish, so his recommendation was to start with the *gratin de queues d'ecrevisses*. I told him that he evidently went along with the French proverb that "the best cooking is that which takes into consideration the products of the season." He beamed and agreed, going on to say that for the next course, the kitchen had just received some *daurades,* a popular Mediterranean fish that is at its best when eaten straight from the sea. Henri proposed it poached in champagne and I concurred, After three attempts on my life, I deserved a good meal.

The main course required a lot of deliberation. Sweetbreads in nantua sauce was a contender, and chicken described as being "in the style of Sacha Guitry" was another. I knew that the great writer and director was a lover of good food, but I didn't know which dish it was that he enjoyed so much that it was named after him.

"And what else can you offer?" I asked blithely.

Henri sighed and proposed beef stroganoff as a subtle rebuke for daring to decline such a sublime presentation. I finally settled on another of the "products of the season"—Partridge à la Valentinoise, which Henri said was roasted until just pink and served with a sauce of meat glaze, wine, Armagnac, fresh cream, and black pepper.

The gratin was a little bland but the *daurades* were perfect. The partridge was excellent, too, though I had pangs of regret for not ordering Sacha Guitry's favorite chicken. A white Châteauneuf-du-Pape went very well with it and I even had a dessert—a soufflé with Grand Marnier. I watched some terrible French television for a while—a soap opera episode in which revelations of incest, blackmail, and betrayal were followed by recrimination, revenge, remorse, and reconciliation. I think the episode ended with a suspicion that the family jewels had been replaced by replicas, but that started me in more speculation about Templar treasure. . . .

Chapter 30

"Not red wine this time! What happened? You get into street fight?" The Vietnamese girl in the cleaner's in Saint Symphorien grinned as she wrote up a slip. "This may take two days—you very hard on clothes."

The "Poste Provisoire" of the gendarmerie was not easy to find. Pertois had told me that it was in the primary school, but classes were in session and I had no wish to interrupt the flow of wisdom that was being imparted to French youth.

Finally, I spotted a—well, shack was the only description—a wooden construction with a tricolor flag flying above the door and a shiny new telephone line running into it.

I knocked and went in to find Pertois sitting at a school desk that might have fitted him once but didn't now. His long legs stuck way out in front of it and he had a pile of papers in front of him on the tiny top; other piles were on more desks. Around the walls were shelves, mostly empty, and Pertois waved a hand at them.

"This used to be the book depository for the school. They no longer use it and have kindly loaned it to me as a *poste provisoire*."

He carefully withdrew his legs from the small cramped desk, completing the motion with a flourish like pulling a cork from a bottle. He stretched to his maximum height, which was a full six feet. Behind the round lenses, his eyes were like disks of black coal.

"We haven't been able to find the man who fired the crossbow yet," he said. "We don't even have a physical description. Can you help? You are the only one who recalls seeing him."

"I had only a fleeting impression. I couldn't point him out in a lineup."

"Height? Build?"

"I'm afraid not. In those robes, I don't remember any distinguishing characteristics. He was not exceptionally tall, or short. He wasn't noticeably heavy . . ."

He nodded, resigned.

"There was one thing though . . ."

"Yes?" He leaned forward eagerly.

"The way he fired the crossbow—he must have been familiar with it. There was no hesitation or fumbling. He swung it up and fired as if he were well practiced in using it."

Pertois grunted. "That might be some help. It's not a common accomplishment." He paused. "You still think he was shooting at you?"

"Fox believed I was threatened and after two attempts on my life, I naturally suspected it was a third when a crossbow bolt seemed to be fired at me."

"*Two* attempts on you?" He fixed me with a piercing stare through his round lenses that plainly said I had been holding out on him. "I fished you out of a wine vat—that was presumably one. You didn't tell me about the other."

I told him now. He rubbed the top of his short, scrubby black hair in a ruminative gesture as he listened. "I was groggy from sleep when I half-woke and saw this huge thing above me. It looked like a giant insect—like a dragonfly. Naturally, I wasn't going to tell anybody—it would have sounded too absurd."

"Demoiselle . . ." He used the same word that I had used, the French for dragonfly. "That's what they call those aircraft—those flimsy little things that look as if Louis Blériot might have flown them."

I went on to tell him the rest and about Suvarov. "It was his aircraft," I concluded, "but he says he wasn't flying it. Says he was in Sophia Antipolis—I suppose that could be checked. I saw him at the festival and he said he was close to finding out who flew it that day."

Pertois grunted. Abruptly—most of his movements were abrupt and jerky like a marionette—he swept a pile of papers off a desk and waved a hand at it. I sat on the top, not wanting to get trapped in it whereupon school memories might come flooding back. Pertois sat on another. "Two attempts on your life! And now I find you standing next to Elwyn Fox who is shot dead!"

Was this the time to bring up the charge of the sangliers? I thought not.

Pertois shifted his position on the uncomfortable desk top.

"You say you have never heard of Andre Chantier?"

"Not until you asked me about him when we talked in the bar. You said he worked at the Willesford vineyard but left."

He nodded. "He left, yes, and was found dead a week later." After a pause he said, "So you can see why I was perturbed to find you standing over a dead body at that same vineyard."

"I suppose so," I admitted.

He squinted at me. "And why is someone so determined to kill you? Because you are writing an article in a magazine?"

He had boxed me into a corner very neatly. "Fox warned me," I said, trying to extricate myself. "How was Chantier killed?" I asked.

"I didn't say he was killed. I said he was found dead. He was drowned."

"You mean he drowned or he *was* drowned?"

He looked away, pondering how much to tell me. "We had a little luck. As part of a national program, the medical examiner's office was trying out some new methods. These concerned the analysis of stomach contents and went as far as analyzing water in the stomach and lungs. You see, water varies in different locations. The differences are small but we were able to determine that although Chantier's body was found in Marseille harbor, the water in his lungs was the water of Ajaccio in Corsica."

"A triumph for French science," I commented.

"In addition, the forensic people were able to establish the time of death fairly accurately and you didn't have anything to do with it."

I eased my position on the desk. "I'm glad to hear you . . . You say you *know I had nothing to do with it?* How?"

"Because you were in Scotland at the time."

It would have been forgivable if he had looked smug. All I could do was goggle at him.

"How do you know that?"

"Our Sûreté office in Paris talked to Scotland Yard. An inspector there called Hemingway vouched for you. He mentioned your unfortunate habit of having your food investigations become mixed up with criminal activities."

I probably showed my relief. Better to have my cover blown than be a murder suspect. Pertois continued.

"Chantier's death seemed merely strange at the time, but then the private detective, Morel, began poking into Willesford vineyard affairs. When you found Laplace dead, the vineyard was obviously at the center of the case. I called Willesford in London and asked what you were really doing here. Sir Charles didn't give me much detail but he authorized you to tell me whatever I need to know. You can call him and verify this, of course."

"Of course," I said weakly.

"With two—or perhaps three—attempts on your life and now three deaths, you're becoming a one-man crime wave, aren't you?"

"Not me!" I said fervently. "It's this vineyard—"

"My first reaction was to have Sir Charles recall you. This is a murder investigation and it might be better for both us if you were out of it. However, he didn't agree. He reminded me that I am a French policeman and he is a British lord. He pointed out that he would not accept such a—well, such a request."

"So you're stuck with me," I said brightly. "We have to cooperate."

He sniffed. It wasn't the vote of confidence I would have liked but it would have to do. He slid off the desk and stood before me. He said reluctantly, "It also means that I have to confide in you. I am not a gendarme."

Chapter 31

I instinctively glanced at the door. Was it locked? Was I trapped in here with an impostor?

"I'm Huitième Bureau," he said as if that were an explanation.

"I've heard of the 'Deuxième Bureau,' the famous French Secret Service, but I didn't know you'd got as far as eight."

"You haven't heard of it," Pertois said, understandably self-satisfied. "Good, well, our attempts to be . . . shall we say, discreet, have been successful, then. Wine, as you know, is one of France's most important products. We are still, after many centuries, the world leader in wine production." It was a point I would enjoy debating with him—but this wasn't the time to do it. "The Huitième Bureau was set up to handle all crimes involved in any way with wine and the business of wine."

"Subsidized by the Association des Vins de France, no doubt," I suggested.

"Funding has never been one of the Huitième Bureau's problems," he said smoothly, as aware as I was that financial support of law enforcement agencies by private organizations is forbidden under the French constitution.

"Sounds very sensible," I said. "The Inspector Hemingway you mentioned is with the Food Squad at Scotland Yard—a roughly similar concept."

He gave this a dismissive nod. "So when this mysterious drowning of a Willesford employee occurred, I was sent down here to investigate. It is one of our procedures to have an Huitième Bureau operator pose as a gendarme."

"You know about wine?"

"My father was a wine merchant. I learned a lot from him."

"So you operate sort of like the Deuxième Bureau?"

"Ah, they are an espionage organization. We are not permitted to engage in such activities."

"Of course not," I murmured, carefully keeping my tongue out of my cheek.

"We have not been able to find the man who fired the crossbow. No one noticed this man more than any other and as the volunteers came from several villages, he wasn't obvious. An examination of the bolt hasn't revealed any useful information yet, either, but that is continuing."

"What do you know about Fox's activities as a dowser?"

"There seems to be adequate water for both vineyards. I have wondered what he was dowsing for but my superiors would be critical if I spent any time pursuing that question. They are not so tolerant of so-called New Age inquiries."

"You were suspicious about the death of Emil Laplace, weren't you?" I asked. "I can see that Chantier's death started your investigation but what did you find out about Emil's death? Was it really wild boars?"

"The wounds were certainly made by boar tusks but the more we examined the wounds, the more it seemed that those tusks were not on a boar at the time."

I shuddered. The conclusion was unpleasant. "Any idea who?"

"Nothing firm."

He might be confiding in me because he wanted my help but it was obvious that despite all that he had imparted, there was still a lot I hadn't been told. Nevertheless, I felt a relief that I didn't have to keep up my journalist cover with Pertois. Still, there might be a few other points I could clear up.

"Did you know about Morel?"

"I guessed that he had been hired by Willesford."

"What about his disappearance?"

"Is that what it is?"

"His wife thinks so."

"Did she tell you she has a million-franc insurance policy on his life?"

I shook my head and he was casual as he went on. "You've been seeing quite a lot of her, haven't you?"

"I was looking through the caves above the vineyard when I first met her. She was looking for her husband." His eyebrows went up a couple of millimeters at that and I hurried on. "We agreed to cooperate in trying to find her husband." I outlined our efforts since then and Pertois looked skeptical.

"The conclusion is that drinking Willesford wine helps people live longer? And this is why Peregrine wants to buy it?"

"Sounds absurd, I know, but, yes, that is one explanation. You know about wine—you think it's possible?"

"Hmph," he said, "wine is good for the health—many doctors recommend it."

"Doctor Selvier, for instance?"

He stood up and walked to and fro in front of the desk a couple of times. Finally, he said, "I think that will be all for now. We will be in close touch from now on—very close."

We shook hands. His grip was firm and strong. "Be careful," he said, and I didn't like the tone of his voice. "Call me if you learn anything—anything at all."

"You think I'm still in danger?" I asked him nervously.

"If there is another attempt on your life, I don't want to hear about it from someone else."

On that bleak note, he led me to the door and let me out. It had been locked, I noticed.

Chapter 32

❧

The road from Saint Symphorien to the ultralight airfield was not the place to be today. France's most popular sport—bicycling—had commandeered the route and an endless stream of crouching, sweating men and women with yellow and blue number tags on their backs struggled to overtake their rivals. Feet flashed in dizzying circles and the metal tubular frames reached scorching speeds.

I was more tired than the cyclists when I finally turned into the airfield. I braked abruptly and pulled in under a clump of trees as a movement in the sky caught my attention. I turned off the car engine and then I could hear the buzz of the ultralight. It had the green and brown wings that I recalled with a shiver—it was Suvarov's aircraft, the one that had dropped the beehive on me in the ghost village of Colcroze.

The nose dipped as I watched, then one wing tilted and the frail craft swung into a landing approach. It grew larger as it floated down, the wheels touched, and within seconds it had rolled to a stop. A car drove slowly from the wooden buildings to the aircraft. I had recognized the plane and I also recognized the car—it was a red convertible and its racy outline told me that it was Monika's Maserati.

Glad that I had waited and watched, I sat there as Suvarov released his belt and climbed out of the aircraft. Monika got out of the car and went over to him. He lifted a box from a strap and shelf assembly by the pilot's seat. It was the shape and size of a shoe box and he handed it to her. She took it reverently as if it were fragile or precious and they talked for a couple of minutes. She walked back to her car and the engine revved up noisily as she stamped on the accelerator. The convertible snarled into a U-turn and headed in my direction.

The encounter was conducted in a clandestine manner that made me curious. I wondered what was in the box and where Monika was going with it. I hastily started the engine and pulled deeper into the trees and out of sight.

She raced by and I gave her time to reach the main road, then I followed. When I turned out, the red dot of the Maserati was heading north into the foothills and I went in pursuit. The cyclists had spread out now as the climb up into the hills slowed them down. They were less of a hazard and had coagulated into small groups.

I managed to keep the red car in sight most of the time, losing it on the twisting, turning road but finding it again. North we went, the cyclists thinning out still more, but I had the thought that it was just as well they were on the road. The way Monika drove, they would keep her from noticing that she was being followed. I wasn't concerned that she would recognize my black Citroen, which looked like thousands of others all off the same assembly line.

We were heading toward the eastern part of the

Var, the upper section of Provence. A ruined castle was perched on a hilltop, looking precarious, but it had probably been there for a thousand years. We entered a tiny village and I stayed a cautious distance behind the convertible as it slowed through the narrow street, but as we left the village, the red Maserati was pulling away.

We had driven for nearly an hour when I saw Monika make a turn onto a side road. As I reached it, Monika was no longer in sight, but the imposing sign indicated where the side road led.

Le Petit Manoir it said, and I recognized the name immediately as one of the homes of gastronomy and highly recommended by Michelin, Kleber, and Gault-Millau.

All this and the road only led to a restaurant! Well, it was well past noon, and at the worst I could have lunch. I drove down the road. It came out on the edge of a spectacular, beautifully manicured green lawn; on the surface of a miniature lake rimmed with stone, water lilies lay placidly.

The restaurant had a large patio at the lakeside that made a delightful outdoor dining area. The building itself was timbered with mullioned windows and had an imposing entrance of heavy beams and huge paving stones. A semicircular gravel drive ran from where I was to the restaurant entrance and a parking lot lay off the left. Only a few cars were there—it was evidently early for serious diners.

Monika's red Maserati stood right in front of the entrance and I was just in time to see her going in to the restaurant, the box under her arm. I thought a valet might come out and park her car but nothing happened for several minutes. Then she came striding out of the restaurant, an eye-catching picture in tight-fitting light brown slacks, a russet brown belted jacket, and dark brown boots. Her blond hair fluttered back as she walked purposefully to the car, empty-handed. She jumped in and started the engine. With a clatter of gravel, she was completing the semicircle and heading back toward me.

I had to think fast. She had driven an hour to get here, so her journey must have had some important purpose—to deliver the box that Suvarov had given her. She was rounding the end of the drive, gravel still spurting up behind her. There was a wide space just ahead and I pulled into it, shielded from view.

I didn't have to worry about her seeing me. She picked up speed as she left the gravel and came scorching along the dirt road. I had a momentary glimpse of her looking straight ahead as she raced past. I listened until the sound of her motor had died, then drove slowly to the parking lot.

The restaurant foyer was elegantly spacious. Massive beams supported a timbered ceiling, and a suit of armor stood at the door to the dining room. Weapons hung on the paneled walls and a massive basket of flowers gave a softening touch. Tapestries in soft golden tones lightened by faded yellows and reds added to the medieval atmosphere, and a huge black iron chandelier hung overhead. Black iron sconces on the walls held electrified candles.

A young man in a tuxedo welcomed me in friendly fashion.

"Good morning, m'sieu. You have a reservation? The table is for how many?" My response of "one" didn't impress him but he looked through an old ledger thicker than a New York phone book. He was frowning when I heard voices behind me. A tall, distinguished man with silvery hair and another man in a tuxedo came walking to the exit.

."When will the next shipment come in?" asked the silver-haired man.

"Three or four days," said the other. "They are getting more frequent now."

"Good. Monsieur le Viscompte tells me that the quantities are increasing too."

"Yes. I am managing to move more and more . . ."

Their voices died as they went out of the lobby and I could no longer distinguish the words.

Outside, tires crunched on gravel and a long black Mercedes pulled to a stop, the engine running. A chauffeur in a light gray uniform, peaked cap, and gloves stepped out and opened the rear door for the silver-haired man. He got in and the car drove off.

The young man who had greeted me was conferring with the tuxedo-clad man who had come across the foyer. The latter turned to me. "Good morning, m'sieu. I am the maître d'hôtel. You wish a table for one?"

I confirmed it and he smiled with pleasure as he said, "We are pleased to accommodate you, m'sieu. Please come this way."

"The man who just left—I thought I recognized him. Who was he?" I asked.

He hesitated for a long second.

"You mean Monsieur Blanc?" he asked lightly.

"That is his name? Perhaps I am mistaken."

"Yes, Jean Blanc. He is a wholesale butcher in Castellane."

Jean Blanc is the French equivalent of John Smith or John Doe. I couldn't think of the man's real name but it certainly was not Jean Blanc. As I followed the maître d' into the dining room, I was racking my memory, but the identity of the man escaped me. His name was as well known to me as his face. But who was he? It was not idle curiosity. He carried under his arm the box that Monika had brought.

Chapter 33

I was glad this meal was a legitimate business expense after I had looked through the menu. It was going to run close to a thousand francs, I calculated. Well, if it was going to cost that much, it seemed that an aperitif wouldn't add a lot to the bill so I ordered a vodka martini. While waiting for it to arrive, I returned to the vexing question of the silver-haired man to whom Monika had given the box. I knew the face . . . but from where? A politician perhaps. Nothing connected. A fashion designer maybe? A theatrical impresario? Still nothing.

The incident was more suspicious for another reason . . . why had the maître d' told me that the man was a wholesale butcher from Castellane? Did butchers travel incognito? Of course, many celebrities choose not to have adulating crowds identify them—but a butcher!

The martini arrived. I scanned the menu again, setting aside mere monetary considerations and concentrating on the food. A waiter came with a ramekin of tapenade, that appetite-sharpening mixture of anchovies, black olives, and olive oil, mashed into a thick black paste. With it was a basket of crunchy bread, hot from the oven. Some like to add capers to tapenade and others get even more innovative, but this was a good basic example of back to the original.

For the first course, the choices included a mussel salad, a lobster gazpacho, quail eggs with pureed asparagus and a puff pastry topping, but I decided on the tagliatelles with a coulis of truffles. It was an excellent choice; the truffles were extraordinarily tasty and I had never had a better example of how they can influence the flavor of a dish without having a dominating flavor of their own. Even the pasta scintillated under the influence of the truffles.

The headwaiter came, suggesting the day's specialty—baked sturgeon served on a bed of sorrel. The popular Mediterranean fish known as Saint Pierre sounded enticing, being served with leeks and truffles. I decided on the sole Colbert, the simplest of sole dishes in which the fish is dipped in egg white, rolled in bread crumbs, then lightly fried. It would be a test of the quality of the fish, with nothing to obstruct its taste.

I had not had a beef dish since I had been in Provence, but I decided that it was time I did. Doctor Salisbury, the famous dietician of an earlier era and originator of the Salisbury steak, maintained that a person needed at least three pounds of beef a day, but modern thinking slashes that to one beef meal a week. So this would be mine. The Pieces de Boeuf à la Royale with truffles caught my eye—this place certainly went in heavily for truffles, but I discarded that in favor of the next item on the menu.

The rib steak Beaujolais came from Charolais beef, the best in France, and in preparing it this way a large quantity of Beaujolais wine is used and simmered down to less than a quarter of its volume along with shallots, garlic, thyme, bay leaf, and brandy. It was expertly done and served with tiny pureed potatoes, the minuscule French peas known as Petits Pois, and a ragout of morels, a mushroom cultivated in Provence. There was no escape from the truffle, for the morel ragout had slivers of truffle to accentuate the woody flavor.

Congratulations to the chef were fully deserved. After some discussion with the sommelier, it was a bottle of Volnay that had accompanied the meal. The Clos Ducs was tempting but I restrained myself and chose the Pommard-Epenots at one-fifth the price. It was smooth, full-bodied, firmly tannic, and exotic with wild berry aromas.

Back in the car, I studied the map. The journey out here had been a tense drive with the sole objective of keeping Monika's red Maserati in sight and I wasn't sure exactly what part of the Var I was in. The menu gave the address of Le Petit Manoir as the village of Palliac and I finally located it. As I did so, another name, very close on the map, leapt out at me—Pontveran. Why did that name strike a chord? I remembered a card . . . the one Professor Rahmani had handed me on Masterson's yacht. The Institute for the Study of Planetary Influences the card had said, and the address was in the Var—in Pontveran. I checked the road numbers and direction and headed that way.

A few palatial homes studded the hillsides, perched on narrow ledges of land that gave them magnificent views. I passed a clinic for respiratory diseases, the pure, clean air at this altitude no doubt accounting for its location. The bicyclists were gone, having continued straining muscles and sinews all the time

I had been indulging myself with food and drink. I felt no remorse.

A signpost to the institute appeared before I reached the village of Pontveran. I followed it along a paved road and came to a pair of large metal gates. There was a speaker and a button on one of the brick posts. I gave my name and said I wanted to see the professor. He came on the line himself, asking me to repeat who I was. I reminded him that we had met on Masterson's yacht and said I was accepting his invitation to see his facilities. I was prepared for him to be testy and speak of appointments but he sounded affable and invited me to come in. The gates swung open.

It was a long stone block building that looked like a museum. It had two stories and plenty of windows. Several wooden outbuildings were scattered off one side and the grounds were so extensive, I couldn't see where they ended. The entrance had double glass doors, and a young Arab girl stood there, smiling. She led me through the building and up a flight of stairs. The corridors were wide and offices and laboratories seemed to alternate. I had little chance to see anything, for at the top of the stairs the girl tapped at a door, opened it, and motioned me to enter.

French decorators are fond of Oriental carpets and a large, expensive-looking one almost filled the room. Professor Rahmani came walking across it, his hand outstretched. The craggy face was more suited to a construction worker than a scientist. His unruly hair still stood up from his scalp and he had an ungainly way of moving his body, but his reception was friendly.

"Ah, my friend! How kind of you to favor us with a visit! Please come in and sit down."

His antique desk was surprisingly small but magnificently carved. The walls were white plaster in the Provençal style with photographs and copies of letters all over them. A table was piled with books, many of them appearing to be very old. A long wooden cabinet was against one wall, its carving matching the professor's desk. The one unusual feature of the room was a large freestanding model of the solar system with the sun as a bright golden orb and the planets around it, each painted to represent its main characteristics, Earth blue, Mars red, Neptune black, Jupiter brown, and so on.

"When we met on Grant Masterson's yacht, your views sounded fascinating," I told him, "and as I'm writing about vineyards, naturally I'm interested in any influences on grapes. You said you can grow grapes that are larger and juicier by making use of your theories?"

"I have done so. Without any loss in quality, either. In fact, the taste was fuller and richer."

"You did this in collaboration with a vineyard, I suppose?"

"No, it was done here."

"There must be many of the local vineyards that would like to take advantage of your ideas," I suggested.

He growled a negative. "None of them are receptive to new ideas. They want to keep on making wine the same way it's been made for the last five thousand years."

"They've all turned you down?"

"Yes, all of them."

"Did you make any wine from the bigger, juicier, tastier grapes that you grew?"

"We don't have wine making facilities here." He

went on to contrast the wine industry unfavorably with the Citrus Guild. "Now, with oranges and lemons, we get considerable support . . ." He went on at length on that topic and I had to steer him back onto the grape track.

"Let me take you on a tour of the premises," he offered.

Much intriguing work was being done. Some of it seemed worthwhile research but I wondered if the rest had any real hope of success. Many projects were focused on yeasts and molds.

"These are the plants that contain no chlorophyll," Professor Rahmani explained. "They are unable to photosynthesize sugars and have to live on the decaying remains of other organisms."

"What's the purpose of such research?" I asked. "Or is it just research with no immediate likelihood of any application?"

"Oh, it has a strong likelihood of bringing tangible rewards. One of the plant groups includes the tubers."

"You mean potatoes?"

"Yes, potatoes, and also yams and water chestnuts. All are valuable foodstuffs and ways of growing them larger and more quickly have very real attractions, especially in poor areas. You will have heard of the terrible potato famine in Ireland in 1845 when a million people died of starvation due to their dependence on the crop and another million and a half emigrated?"

"A national disaster that has never been forgotten."

"Precisely. We are hoping that our work will make the potato immune to the blight that caused that famine."

"Presumably you have no difficulty in raising money for this research?"

Rahmani smiled, making his irregular features yet more uneven.

"Raising money is always difficult, but for these projects it is easier than most."

"Your . . . can I say, unorthodox, views on the influence of planetary movements must limit your sponsorship," I said, being as delicate as I could.

"Oh, not all of our work involves the planets," the professor said, not at all perturbed. "We have excellent facilities and staff so we accept contracts for more, as you say, orthodox research. Come, I'll show you some of these."

Outside, fields and small plantations were growing various crops. Boards and charts at each one recorded figures in great detail. It all seemed extremely efficient and I told the professor so.

"We are aware of the importance of keeping careful and extensive information on every aspect," he said. "Sometimes, unexpected sources yield data that contribute in ways we hadn't anticipated."

I left, thinking that I had a few more pieces of the puzzle in my hands. The problem was—I wasn't sure where they fitted.

Chapter 34

"Another death!" snapped Sir Charles. "What's going on there? Who is it this time?"

It was the last thing I wanted to do but I had to make it the first. I had two champagne cocktails, then called Sir Charles, and he was not patient. Our conversation began with him telling me of Pertois's call. Sir Charles said he knew that the Association des Vins had an investigative branch and that he told them little other than that I was investigating on his behalf. "I didn't even want to do that," he grumbled.

Mention of a dowser threw him into further perplexity and I foolishly let slip a word about treasure, which stretched the conversation still longer. We concluded with him agreeing that I should continue for a few days more after I had recklessly promised results in that time.

The dining room was only partly full and Madame was excited over her purchase of a small quantity of *bar,* a sought-after but uncommon Mediterranean fish that is usually called striped bass in English. I promptly ordered it. For the first course, I had grilled eggplant with strips of red pepper flavored with basil, garlic, pine nuts, and lemon juice. The bar was "Duglere" style—covered with tomatoes, onions, thyme, garlic, and bay, then poached in white wine. It was excellent, served with green beans only. I was debating between dessert or just coffee when Madame said there was a lady on the phone for me, so I took it in my room.

It was Veronique. Her voice was shaky. "Edouard just phoned me."

"What did he say?"

"He said he wanted me to come to his office, then he hung up."

"Are you sure it was your husband?"

She hesitated. "It—it sounded like his voice but I'm not absolutely sure."

"What are you going to do?"

"I'm going—now. That is—" she hesitated again, "if you'll come with me."

Before I could ask myself if this was a good idea, I was already saying, "All right. I'll come."

"The office is at 24 rue de Brabant. It's just near the Opera House. Do you know where that is?" I told her that I did. "There's a little café called Marie's—let's meet there. In about an hour."

"Veronique—" I said quickly before she could hang up.

"Yes?"

"Remember that revolver you pointed at me? Bring it."

There was a pause then she said, "I will."

Even with Nice's parking problems, it was still a few minutes short of an hour when I left the car and walked to the café. She was inside, drinking a cup of coffee and smoking a cigarette. I noticed that there were several butts in the ashtray. She had already put a banknote under her saucer. She stubbed out the cigarette, gave me a half smile, and we went out.

"It's very near," she said. "Edouard used to come in here quite often." She sounded quiet but firm. I didn't ask her if she had the gun.

We turned down the first narrow street, which was one block from the Opera House. At one end, the Mediterranean shimmered, a vertical slit of blue with sea and sky merging. We went the other way. The street had cars parked illegally on both sides, half on the sidewalk. Somewhere a horn was blaring, leaned on by a trapped driver. Veronique led me down a tiny alley, which garbage cans made an obstacle course and hadn't been cleaned since the Nazis left.

Veronique stopped at a rusting steel door, opened it with a key, and turned a big handle. She led the way up steep narrow stairs and I followed, my eyes on a level with her slim ankles. At the first floor, we stopped, although the stairs went on up. A door had a wood panel saying Edouard Morel; Investigations. Veronique knocked and the sound was loud and hollow, but it brought no response. She turned the knob but the door was locked. She brought out the same keyring and used the smaller key on it.

It was a small compact office with the usual furniture of a tight-budget operation—that is to say, no gadgetry beyond a telephone. She picked up a handful of letters from the floor and looked through them. She put them on the desk and shook her head. "Nothing of importance."

I pointed to the corner of the office. "What about that?"

At first she was bewildered, then she saw the wastebasket.

"It's full! Yes, that is different." She lifted it and upended it on the desk. We went through the items together. An invitation to a luncheon at the Hôtel Mercure, an offer of a credit card with unbelievably low interest rates from the Banque Commerciale de Nice, a reminder to renew a subscription to a news magazine, an electricity bill, a request from the Socialist Party for a donation, a lot of advertising leaflets and a restaurant receipt were all it contained.

Veronique was looking at the restaurant receipt.

"Where is it from?"

"La Toque Imperiale in Ajaccio, Corsica, dated four days ago."

I recalled that the unfortunate Andre Chantier, the worker at the Willesford vineyard, had been found drowned in Marseille—his lungs full of the water of Ajaccio.

She said suddenly, "Look!" Morel had a large spike on his desk with several notes speared on it. We should have noticed it sooner as the note on top had "Veronique" in large printed letters on it. She carefully detached it and smoothed it out. We both read it.

URGENT. SORRY——COULDN'T WAIT. COME AT ONCE TO FORUM IN HERCULANUM. KEY IN TOP DRAWER.

"He must have been here. Do you recognize his writing?"

"This printing—I'm not sure. It has to be Edouard though, doesn't it?"

"I suppose so." I wasn't convinced—everything connected with Edouard Morel was shadowy and uncertain, but I wanted to reassure her.

She opened the top drawer of the desk. A large bronze key was there with a cardboard tag tied to its ring. The tag was labeled only with the letter *H*. With it was a printed brochure describing the site.

"Herculanum? That's the old Roman town, isn't it? The one that's still being excavated?"

"Yes. But what can it have to do with Edouard?"

"I don't know. Are you going out there?" I asked Veronique.

She gave me a stern look. "Of course. Aren't you coming?"

If it was going to be a reunion with her husband, I didn't particularly want to be present, but I doubted it was that straightforward. "You did bring that gun, didn't you?"

She nodded.

"Right," I said. "Let's go."

Chapter 35

An hour and a half drive northwest of Nice, the ancient city of Herculanum spread over a large hillside, houses and villas crouching behind walls denuded of their roofs, temples and halls awaiting the crowds of two thousand years ago, public baths dry and silent, soaring arches untouched by time and massive columns rearing into the sky seeking a purpose.

A large sign explained that a Neolithic settlement had been here originally and was then rebuilt in about the year 150 A.D. by the Greeks. They did not establish a colony but moved on, leaving the site to be developed by the Romans a hundred years later. The location was perfect for the Romans' purpose as it lay close to both of the routes between Spain and Italy, one over the Alps and the other along the coast. Work to restore it was continuing, a sign said. We sat for a moment, awed by the thought of a city dead for so many centuries, destroyed by the barbarian hordes from the East, though its stones remained.

Veronique had said little on the drive here. I presumed she was having mixed thoughts about a reunion with a husband who had so mysteriously disappeared. I had presumed that Morel would be at his office when we arrived. The finding of the note and the key made it appear that the change of venue had been planned and that he had no intention of being at the office. The choice of the Roman city of Herculanum was peculiar, but perhaps a public place suited Morel's plans better.

"There should be cars and people here," Veronique said.

She was right. Where were all the tourists and visitors? It was evening and perhaps the place was closed. Ahead of us was the triumphal arch of Augustus Caesar and near it, the mausoleum with a ninety-foot tower. All was quiet.

A freshly painted sign outside the main entrance gate caught my eye and I drove over to it. The site was closed for a week while important work was being done to strengthen the safety precautions, it said.

Veronique thumped one small fist on her knee in frustration.

"It can't be closed!" she said angrily.

"That key . . . ," I said. "He must expect you to go in."

Her anger at her husband for playing these games with her showed on her face but she calmed down quickly and gave me a brief, apologetic smile.

"You're right." We looked in all directions.

"Down there," I pointed. A smaller gate suitable for individuals to pass through led to a building that was probably offices. A large board displayed a map and identified the various ruins and their functions. The forum was clearly identified.

I parked, Veronique produced the key and gave me a triumphant smile as it turned in the lock. I glanced around nervously. Not a soul was in sight nor was there any sign of humanity.

"This is very strange," I told her. "This is not a normal place to meet."

"We are here," she said, and with simple French logic added, "so now we go in."

We were moving into the shadow of the hill and the sun was behind it, dipping as it ended its day's work. The light was dimmer now and the shapes of the buildings raised by Roman hands centuries ago were stark and grim.

Veronique shivered. "Where do we go?" she asked.

"According to that map, we go this way. Be careful, the ground is very uneven and it's getting darker by the minute."

It couldn't have been my words—but lights came on. Some were mounted on poles, others were on the ground. They made the sky instantly darker.

"The lights are on a timer," I said with a ring of confidence. "Security."

Veronique threw me a nervous glance. Security could also mean guards or large and vicious dogs— I could read that thought in her eyes.

We walked past gaping doorways and shattered stone walls. The soil was densely packed from the thousands of feet belonging to curious folk of the twentieth century who wanted to see how their forebears had lived. They saw a surprisingly sophisticated city with swimming pools and thermal baths, temples and ball courts, three-story homes with fountains and courtyards, shops belonging to bakers, butchers, carpenters, and wine merchants, a theater, and a town hall with fluted columns and shaded patio. The site was getting rapidly more eerie, with fantastic shadows interlacing into strange patterns.

The forum consisted of two low, crumbling walls and a third and fourth largely restored. Mosaic tiles covered the floor and some vestiges of the original colors miraculously still remained in them. I had thought a forum was always an open square, but apparently it could also be a hall where indoor meetings could take place.

There were two wide steps leading in, splintered and broken, with weeds forcing their way through the cracks. We went forward cautiously, a light on a pylon outside casting beams ahead of us.

Veronique uttered a faint cry. . . . A figure was huddled in the far corner. Our footsteps clattered loudly on the tiles and then we knelt beside him— for it was a man, and one glance at Veronique's face told me that it was unnecessary to ask . . .

"Is he . . ." she was asking, and it was another unnecessary question. Part of his head was crushed in and blood ran down his face. By his feet was a chunk of marble the size of a brick with blood on it too.

Veronique rose to her feet, shivering, her face pale. She swayed and looked about to fall. I put my arms about her and she clung to me tightly.

A voice said, "You will both step away from the body. I have several questions that you must answer."

I recognized that voice as its owner stepped into view over one of the low crumbling walls. It was the "gendarme" from the Huitième Bureau, Aristide Pertois.

Chapter 36

This Aristide Pertois was a very unusual detective. How did he come to be on the scene so promptly? was my first thought. I wasn't sure how long Edouard Morel had been dead but the blood was only just beginning to congeal, so it wasn't very long.

Pertois was also a very stern detective. The affable front he had presented to me after the murder of Elwyn Fox had disappeared and I didn't like the hard glint in his eyes. His small black mustache was menacing and even his short, bristly black hair looked threatening. It was evident that my association with corpses was getting too frequent for him.

Veronique sat with a woman detective at a hard, cold steel table in the gendarmerie at Saint Remy, the post nearest to Herculanum. I sat on the other side of the woman detective and Pertois was opposite. The woman had taken our fingerprints and footprints. Veronique had been invited to empty her handbag on the table and Pertois had examined her revolver after giving her a look of reproof.

"You have a permit for this weapon, of course?" he demanded.

"My husband does." She was tight-lipped and pale but otherwise quite composed.

"Madame, I asked if *you* have a permit."

"No, I don't."

"It is a serious offense to carry a gun without a permit."

"My husband was killed with a piece of marble—he wasn't shot," she replied spiritedly.

"You say he was killed. Why would you not suppose that it was an accident?"

"He is a private detective. He has been on a case where others have died. He has been missing for some time. It is far more likely that he was killed."

Pertois regarded her. "You say you found this note in his office."

"That's right." Veronique's voice was firm.

"And this key was in his desk drawer?"

"Yes."

"What else did you find there?"

Veronique shot a glance at me. "There was a receipt from a restaurant."

"Which restaurant?"

"La Toque Imperiale in Ajaccio."

"Had your husband been in Ajaccio?"

"I don't know. I haven't seen him for some time."

"Have either of you been in Ajaccio?" he said, looking from Veronique to me. We both shook our heads.

"So neither of you knows anything of this death? You arrived here to find the body?"

"That's correct," Veronique said. Pertois looked at me and I nodded.

Pertois switched his questions to the subject of Veronique's knowledge of her husband's movements during the recent weeks. She answered him carefully but without adding any embellishments.

"And you were at his office today? Because of this phone call?"

"Yes."

"Even though you were not sure it came from your husband?"

This went on for some time and many women would have lost their temper, but Veronique hung on, face drawn and occasionally slightly acid-tongued at being asked the same question three or four times.

I expected the same treatment, but when Pertois had finished his verbal battering of Veronique, he simply said:

"I shall require statements from both of you. Please be in the Poste Provisoire at eight-thirty in the morning." He turned to Veronique. "How did you get here?"

"We came in my car," I cut in.

Pertois looked over at the woman detective. She was middle-aged and austere. She nodded. "We can find a car to take her back." She glanced at me but Pertois said, "M'sieu will be staying."

As Veronique rose to go, I went over to her. "Are you all right?" I asked.

"Yes. I think I'll go and stay with my sister in Cap d'Ail for a few days." She turned to Pertois and said calmly, "May I have my handbag?"

He hesitated, then nodded to the woman detective.

"You may have your bag and its contents except for the gun. We will give you a receipt for that. Leave us your address and phone number in Cap d'Ail."

The woman said, "We have also kept the key. It will be returned to the site office at Herculanum."

When the two women had gone, the Huitième Bureau man turned to me.

"Once again, m'sieu, you are there when a death occurs."

"Veronique—Madame Morel—received the phone calls and the note. I went along with her because she asked me."

"Tell me exactly what happened from the time she phoned you."

I went through it step by step. He didn't interrupt and his coal black eyes never left my face.

"And you say he was dead when you arrived at Herculanum?"

"You know he was!" I said heatedly. "You came in seconds later."

He grunted. "Actually, I was there before you."

"What!"

"I was in my car near Saint Remy when a call was relayed from my office. An anonymous caller said a man was being attacked at Herculanum by a man and a woman. I came here and found the body. I saw you two arriving and watched to see what you would do.

I stared at him in exasperation.

"Then you know we didn't have anything to do with it!"

"It looks that way," he said nonchalantly. "Unless one of you killed Morel, left Herculanum, and then returned there to *find* the body."

"But you don't believe that!" I pressed.

"This soft earth will show how many sets of your footprints are present," he said confidently.

"And you let us think that we were under suspicion?" I said angrily.

He gave me a pleasant nod. "Yes."

"So we were being framed?"

"It would appear so. Had I been in my office, it would have taken much longer to get here. I would have arrived to find you standing over the body."

"It's beginning to make sense," I told him. "I thought it was strange to be called to Morel's office only to find that he wasn't there, and then to be redirected to Herculanum. It's obvious now."

"Under less fortunate circumstances, the two of you would have been in a very dubious position," said Pertois. "An estranged wife, her paramour, a quarrel resulting in a dead husband, and a million-franc insurance policy—a most suspicious combination."

"You have concluded that it was murder, haven't you?"

"Officially, I have to wait for the medical examiner's report but it looks like it. I could find nowhere for that piece of marble to have become detached and fallen on Morel's head."

"You haven't had any reports on his movements in the past weeks?"

"No."

"Any news on the crossbow bolt?"

"The bow and three bolts were stolen from a museum about two months ago."

"Here? In Provence?"

"No, a museum in Porticcio."

"Where's that, Italy?"

"No, it's in Corsica. It's just around the other side of the bay—from Ajaccio."

"Ajaccio! That place keeps turning up, doesn't it?"

"It does," Pertois agreed.

"Not just from the water in Chantier's lungs," I added.

"Hmm . . ."—he rubbed his chin thoughtfully— "and also the restaurant receipt you found in Morel's office. I must remind you once again to be careful," he went on. "We have enough corpses in this case already. Another would complicate it even further."

I presumed this to be an example of French black humor but in case it wasn't, I said nothing. He pushed his chair back in a dismissive gesture. I stood too as I said: "You referred to me as Veronique's paramour—I presume that has the same meaning in French as it does in English. I'm not her paramour."

"I will keep that in mind." He walked me to the door. "I had your car brought here. You will find it in the visitors' parking lot at the back of the building."

"How did you do that? I still have the keys."

"Poof!" he said dismissively. "We do not stand on formalities here in France."

Chapter 37

I drove back to Le Relais musing on what an unusual detective he was. It was fortunate that the
Huitième Bureau had established a role in this business before I had arrived, otherwise I might have
been stuck with some starchy official without imag-
ination or ability.

I went up to my room as slowly as possible. That
way, I was able to delay doing something I *really*
didn't want to do. When I dialed Sir Charles Willesford's home number, I did that slowly too.

He sounded quite jovial. It was a mood I knew
wouldn't last long.

"You're reporting progress already?" he sounded
astonished. "It's only been a few hours and—"

I seized on that. "Well, I *have* found Edouard
Morel . . ."

"Excellent! What have you learned from him?"

It was going to be all downhill from now on, I
could see that. I told him the whole story and he interrupted me with only a few bewildered questions:

"Hit on the head with a piece of *marble?*"

"In a *Roman ruin,* you say?"

"You were with Morel's *wife?*"

"She has a *million-franc policy* on his life?"

There was a lengthy silence and I could hear him calling for a strong whisky and soda. His wife was obviously very efficient and his voice was stronger as he resumed. "I was going to tell you to drop this investigation. Too many people are dying. But—well, maybe . . . you say you're close to the answer . . ."

He didn't add, "so we might as well risk your life a little longer." Still, I didn't like being a target and a natural stubbornness was asserting itself.

"I think we can get to the bottom of this business if I hang in there just a little longer," I said heroically.

He grunted. He didn't want to see the money he had invested so far completely wasted was what the grunt meant. "Good man," he added.

"I'll keep you informed," I told him and hung up before he could get maudlin or I could change my mind.

Chapter 38

I was in the middle of breakfast the next morning when the call from Suvarov came. He sounded serious as he said, "Can you come to the airfield this morning? I have some information for you."

"I'll be there in half an hour," I told him.

The ultralight field was crawling with activity despite the early hour. I parked and surveyed the busy scene. A wheel was being refitted onto one machine and a man was casually lifting the aircraft with one hand to accommodate a jack.

A thin buzz came from an engine running at low speed and it sounded like someone pruning a hedge. I recalled that Suvarov had told me how some of the earlier ultralights had used chain-saw engines. Overhead, a blue and white ultralight was making random circles at a lazy speed.

Suvarov was easy to find. His shock of golden hair made him stand out and I walked over to where he was tightening some wing struts with a wrench. He and another man were disagreeing over how tight they should be and I waited until they reached a decision. Suvarov nodded, handed the wrench to the other, and straightened up. He saw me and came with his hand outstretched.

"I am glad to see you. How is the article going?"

"It's coming along," I said. "So who flew your aircraft that day?"

"His name is Johann Ditter."

"What do you know about him?" I asked.

"He came here a month or so ago. He was German but spoke French well. He'd had flying experience in light aircraft and a few dozen hours in ultralights."

"What was he doing here?"

"He didn't say—and he hasn't been seen since your beehive incident. One of the pilots did some checking for me and found he'd moved out of the address he'd originally given us and no one knew where he'd gone."

"None of your pilots got to know him?"

"No. He was something of a loner, it seems. No friends, no acquaintances, didn't attempt to get friendly. Maybe something to do with his years in the Legion."

"He was an ex-Legionnaire?"

"Yes."

"Do people often drift in and out of here that way?"

"Ultralight pilots are like an unofficial clue. When one goes to another region, he heads for the nearest field, maybe flies, maybe just hangs around and chats."

"But this Ditter didn't chat?"

"No. Seems he didn't try to get to know anyone and when anyone talked to him, he wasn't communicative."

"What did he look like?"

"Medium height and build, military bearing, close-cropped hair."

I thanked him and moved on quickly. "Terrible news about Fox," I said. He agreed.

"Did you know him well?"

"Not well. We had drinks together . . . oh, three or four times. I tried to sell him on the idea of using an ultralight to do his dowsing but he never took me up on it."

"Would that have been an efficient way of doing it?" I asked.

"That might have depended on whether he was dowsing for water or if it was something else."

"That question bothered me too," I said. "I don't know what else it could have been, though. Do you?"

The blue and white ultralight overhead came in, touched down, and stopped as abruptly as if caught in an invisible net. Its engine roared. Well, in a normal aircraft it would have been a roar. In the case of the ultralight it was a whine like a petulant eggbeater. The craft rolled forward until it was going little faster than a running man, then it lurched up into the air, floating away like a leaf in a strong wind.

"Thomas is practicing landings," Suvarov said. "He broke an axle support the other day and wants to develop a lighter touch." He watched the plane climb and bank. I said nothing, waiting for him to answer my question.

"I was up in my Dragonfly one day and I saw Fox. He was on Willesford land, up above the caves. He seemed to be looking for something."

"He was dowsing, was he? Not just out for a stroll?"

"He had something in one hand. I'm sure he was dowsing."

"And on Willesford land . . . ," I said, trying for some reaction, "when he was hired by Peregrine."

"Puzzled me too," Suvarov said and gave me his dazzling grin. "But then it puzzles me every time I fly over those vineyards. Poor little Peregrine hemmed in on all sides by mighty Willesford. Don't know how it survives. But you're the wine expert, you tell me—how does it?"

"Another puzzle," I agreed.

Thomas was coming in again, his craft sinking to the ground. Suvarov winced as the wheels hit, bounced, hit again.

"He hasn't got it right yet," he said, shaking his head. He watched the ultralight come to a stop, pivot, and surge forward into another takeoff run.

Chances of finding the German, Ditter, were slim. He had evidently been hired to do the job and, his mission fulfilled, had been moved on. Had his mission been fulfilled? I wondered. If the intention had been to frighten me, it had worked, though it hadn't persuaded me to drop my investigation. If the aim had been to sting me to death—well, that might have worked but for Monika's timely arrival.

I drove to the schoolyard headquarters of the gendarmerie and arrived right on the dot of eight-thirty as instructed. Veronique was already there and said a demure "Good morning." Pertois was on the phone and apparently fending off a superior who was pressing for more rapid results. Pertois seemed to be doing very well and even promised an early resolution. He caught my eye as he hung up and gave me a "what else can I say" shrug. Gallic shrugs can cover a wide range of meanings and situations and someone should write a book on them.

He had put in a lot of hours since I had last seen him. He had typed statements ready and went through Veronique's first. She made a few comments and he crossed out the disputed passages in the statement and substituted her words. She seemed ready for a confrontation but Pertois gave her no opportunity to find one. He obligingly made all the changes she requested, and in no time at all she had signed the statement.

The two of us saw her to the door.

"Everything all right?" I asked her. She managed a small smile.

"Yes. I slept fairly well. I'm taking care of my sister's two children today while she does some shopping. She doesn't have many chances to get away—they're just under school age. They're both very active, so they'll keep me occupied."

"Good. Call me if there's anything I can do. Give me your phone number in Cap d'Ail too."

She nodded, gave me the number, and left. Pertois and I went back and sat down. He pulled forward my statement and went through it with me. I signed it and he put it into a neat pile on one side of his desk.

"I have news," I said and told him about Johann Ditter, the beehive bombing pilot. He scribbled a few notes. "I'll see what I can do," he said, "but it doesn't sound very promising."

He put the note on a spike. A plastic envelope was near it. He opened it, took something out, and flicked his thumb. A golden spiral fluttered upward, then collapsed into his hand. He paused a moment, then slapped down a coin on the desk top. He leaned back.

I stared at the coin. It looked like gold. I looked up to meet his level gaze. Through the round spectacles, the black eyes showed no expression.

I reached out and took the coin, examining it. It was old and worn, no longer shiny but showing no corrosion. The crude letters around the edge were just distinguishable: They read "Louis IX—Roy et Empereur." The other side depicted the sun over a building and showed the date 1269 in Roman numerals.

"Gold," I said. That didn't require any vast leap of intelligence but it was all I had. I slapped the coin onto the table even harder than he had.

"Yes, it's gold," he said.

"Did you dig it up?"

He didn't smile, but there was a slight twitch that sufficed.

"I received it by special messenger this morning." He leaned back and shuffled until he was somewhat comfortable in his metal chair. "Among routine bulletins came one from a gendarme post in Cotignac. They had raided a pawn shop after being informed of numerous stolen items that had been disposed of there. They found this in addition to the goods they were looking for and I asked to see it."

"What does it tell you?" I asked.

"The pawnbroker was anxious to lighten the sentence for fencing stolen goods and he said a man came in with this coin and asked for a valuation. A ten-franc gold piece of this date is naturally very valuable. The pawnbroker said he was concerned that it might have been stolen from a museum"— Pertois gave an indignant snort—"a likely story!" He continued, "Anyway, the man said he had a lot of them and wanted to know what they were worth."

"A lot of them? They'd be worth a fortune, wouldn't they?"

"Certainly. I phoned Professor Duplessis at the

University of Bordeaux. He's an expert in rare coins. He confirmed my suspicion—namely, that if such a thing as a Treasure of the Templars existed, it might be expected to contain a number of coins like this."

"I recall that when we talked about the Templar treasure right after Fox was killed, you were disinterested."

"I still am. If the treasure ever existed in the first place, treasure hunters would have found it by now."

"Marcel Delorme at the vineyard pointed out to me that anyone finding the treasure would keep it quiet—fear of thieves, the publicity . . ."

"Mainly the taxes," added Pertois, practical as all Frenchmen where taxation was concerned.

He squirmed in the uncomfortable chair, then he picked up the coin and put it back carefully into its plastic envelope. "I am under a lot of pressure in this investigation," he said. "I need some results and I need them soon."

"Me too," I said. "If I don't make some progress within the next few days, I may well be recalled to London."

Pertois flicked one finger through his mustache in a reflective gesture.

"We need to move quickly and decisively," he said at length.

"Good," I agreed, and waited. "Doing what?" I asked finally.

"I will contact you . . ." That meant he didn't know what to do. ". . . very soon." And that meant he didn't know when.

Chapter 39

I parked in the main square of Saint Symphorien and made my way to the cleaner's to pick up the clothes that had barely survived the encounter with what I firmly considered to be sangliers. There was no way I was going to admit being almost killed by amorous pigs.

"Had to mend lot of rips and tears," said the girl, explaining the amount of the bill. They had done a good job and the pants and jacket were serviceable, though not qualified for banquet occasions.

On my way back to the car, I was edging past a newsstand that took up half the sidewalk, as do many in France. It had the usual array of gaudy-cover magazines and I was several paces beyond the stand when I realized that something had stirred my memory. I turned back to the stand and studied the display.

Then I saw it, the red and black cover of the popular magazine *Paris Eclat*. It was one of those periodicals that relentlessly pursue the famous and the wealthy. Many such publications would expire from lack of circulation if it were not for the shenanigans of the British Royal Family, but on this occasion it was a French face that had caught my eye. The caption read, "Joseph Tourcoing," and no wonder my subconscious had been jogged—he was the silver-haired man I had seen taking the box that Monika had brought to the Petit Manoir.

I bought the magazine and hurried back to the car. Tourcoing was almost as famous a name in French cuisine as Bocuse, Robuchon, or Guerard. I read through the article on him.

Tourcoing was born in Pau and grew up in the shadow of the Pyrenees. He went to a small, local cooking school because nothing else interested him. He found himself becoming more and more fascinated by cooking and went to work in a restaurant in Saint Jean Pied-de-Port. From there he progressed to Biarritz and rose to popularity at the famed Miramar Hôtel. Seeking wider experience, he worked with the renowned Gerard Boyer at Les Crayeres in Reims and with Alain Senderens in Paris. In 1986, when Senderens sold his restaurant, l'Archestrate, Tourcoing put his life savings into opening his own place, Le Reveillon.

He was a purist, the article said. His oysters came from Quiberon, his prawns from Roscoff in Brittany, and even his salt was special—he bought only the special gray Guerande salt that has been collected since the seventeenth century by workers called *paludiers* using long wooden rakes and working only by hand. Tourcoing's own favorite specialty dish was roasted duck served on a bed of its own crushed giblets with vegetables.

One of the luminaries on the Paris scene, he was innovative and always eager to experiment despite retaining a love of the traditional, the article continued. He had just gained a third star from Michelin.

So why his visit to Le Petit Manoir and why was

he masquerading as a butcher from Castellane? What was in the box and why had Monika pushed the Maserati to its limit in order to bring it to him? I now had a lot more questions to add to the long list that already baffled me.

Perhaps the box contained gold coins like the one I had held in my hand. Maybe Tourcoing was planning a chain of restaurants and he needed financing for them . . . I put a stop to this speculation. It could go on and on.

I recalled seeing a bookshop on the next corner. I locked the car and went to it. I found the section on travel guides and located a shelf of the excellent French *Entrée* series, each book dealing with a different part of France. I selected the book on Provence and turned to the pages on Palliac.

Le Petit Manoir was the first restaurant to be listed, as befitted its status. The service and decor were given high marks and the food was highly recommended. The reader was warned that the prices were elevated even though the quality justified them. Some of the dishes were described and reference was made to the extensive offerings of foods containing truffles. Le Petit Manoir was "a truffle lover's heaven," said the author. It was the concluding paragraph that leaped out from the page, though:

"Alfred Rostaing, the owner and head-chef of Le Petit Manoir, continues to improve on his own high standards," the entry stated, "and if he maintains this rise, he may soon eclipse even his cousin, Joseph Tourcoing of Le Reveillon fame in Paris."

So . . . the two of them were cousins. What did that mean? It meant nothing right now but I filed the fact in my mind and was returning the book to its place when my stomach reminded me that it was lunchtime. I opened *Entreé to Provence* again and saw that it showed three places recommended for lunch. One of them was Le Chaudron, not far from here.

It was a delightful place with vaulted ceilings that dated back to when it was a wine cellar and shop, a plaque informed me. Now it had a reputation for seafood and the menu included bourride, the thick, creamy fish stew; baudroie, a Mediterranean fish that is no longer too common; grilled sardines; and another unusual dish, poutargue, a pâté made from red mullet roes, blended with salt and baked in the sun. It is then formed into small balls and cooked quickly in hot oil.

There aren't many opportunities to enjoy poutargue for it is a specialty of the Bouches du Rhône area, and is rarely found elsewhere. I ordered it to start and as a main course, a tuna steak Provençale style. For many people, tuna means opening a can, but there is no resemblance between that product and a fresh steak of tuna. The fish grows to three feet in length and its flesh is firm and savory. Being a little oily, it is ideally suited to the Provençal style of cooking which calls for studding it with anchovy fillets, marinating in olive oil and lemon juice, sautéing with onion, garlic, and white wine, then baking in the oven, basting frequently.

It was a very good meal and I drank a half bottle of a Willesford white wine with it, the one carrying the name Pont Vieux on the label. It was surprisingly good, the reason for my surprise being the unbelievably low price of eleven francs. I had avoided it until now because I had assumed that at such a price, it would be barely drinkable. Instead it was a fine Chardonnay, well balanced and as the wine buffs would describe it in their hyperbole, ". . . with flavors of oak and vanilla, finishing with ripe pear and a vibrant acidity."

Why was it selling at such a low price? The question bothered me all through the meal even though it did not spoil my enjoyment of it. I don't let anything do that. The waitress brought a fine-looking Tarte Tatin to the next table and I was sorely tempted but resisted manfully. Some describe it as an "upside-down apple pie," but when well prepared, it is considerably better than that.

At La Relais du Moulin, Madame Ribereau had a message for me. It was from Monika and I called the number given. There came a series of clicks, then some musical notes. A buzz followed, then one of those silences that only telephones can provide—a silence that is not a silence. On this occasions, no heavy breathing followed and I supposed it was a satellite relay telephone link. Perhaps Monika was in some impenetrable jungle either driving an all-terrain vehicle at an outrageous speed or modeling for Christian Dior. She came on the line promptly, though, and wasted no time getting to the point.

"I'm doing a photographic assignment at a Provençal fair," she said crisply. "Traditional dances, displays, exhibits . . . there's a wine tasting, too, and some good food. Thought you might like to come along—it's your kind of thing."

"Where is it?"

"An old château, only a hundred kilometers or so from the Relais. It's a big event. I think you'll enjoy it."

"Sounds great," I said.

"Good. Pick you up about ten o'clock tomorrow morning."

"Okay, I'll be ready."

"Pack an overnight bag," she said breezily. "I have an invitation—the accommodation there is said to be excellent."

The connection broke with a few more clicks and tones.

Chapter 40

The next morning, I had plenty of time for an invigorating swim and a change into undamaged clothes, of which my supply was running down. I packed an airline carry-on bag and was sitting outside in the morning sunshine when the grating of tires on gravel announced Monika's arrival.

I climbed into the Maserati alongside her and made sure the seat belt was tight. She looked entrancing in a dove gray pants suit with vermilion piping.

"I don't know how you keep your hair looking that way with all your activities," I told her.

She tossed her head and her hair swirled in a glittering fountain of yellow gold.

"I'm lucky. It stays this way, I don't have to do much to it."

She let in the clutch and the engine snarled as we raced out to the main road. There, she accelerated to the speed limit and well beyond it, though her control was expert. She didn't allow even a tire to cross the white center line—in contrast to most French drivers. She shifted gear on the tightest of bends with a sure, deft touch.

I was reluctant to say anything that might disturb

her concentration, but it seemed that driving fast and conversing were two things she could mix as smoothly as if she were mixing a martini, so I asked about her racing record. She told me of successes in Australia, Italy, and Japan, near successes in Mexico and Argentina, and a crash in South Africa.

"The car was completely demolished," she said casually.

"Weren't you hurt?"

"I walked away from it. Not a scratch."

"You must love race driving," I told her.

"I love anything that has excitement."

We were going north but the road was not familiar. Signposts flashed by but on the rare occasions when Monika was driving at a speed at which I could read them, the names meant nothing. Eventually I caught a fleeting glimpse of a sign pointing to Digne so I knew we were in the northern part of the Var, one of the two regions of Provence.

On a craggy ridge, a shattered ruin of a castle thrust up fingers of black stone. Fields of lavender blanketed hillsides, and when I saw herds of sheep, I knew we were reaching a fair altitude.

Despite Monika's ability to drive and talk at the same time, I preferred to avoid any distraction. An occasional sideways glance at her proud profile and steady hands reassured me that she was in full control. She drove on and slopes covered with olive groves spread a dark gray-green blanket over the terrain. We passed a sheep farm and an old mill, but vast expanses of empty land lay between the few signs of civilization.

At length I noticed that she was slowing, and she gave me a quick look.

"There's a little restaurant along this stretch.

Watch out for it—it's easy to miss." I looked at the dashboard digital clock. It was nearly one o'clock.

We found it—the Belle Aurore. It had a pleasant shaded garden and we both had braised salmon, the specialty of the house. The proprietress was delighted to explain how her husband, the chef, prepared it. He put fresh-caught salmon in a pan with white wine, tomato puree, butter, and some crushed garlic cloves, then braised it in the oven. He removed the fish, boiled down the liquid, added a spoonful of cream, cooked a little, then added hollandaise sauce, mixed, and poured it over the fish. It was superb and we had an unexpected treat with it—the white wine from Cassis. This comes from vineyards that are crowded between the Mediterranean and the hills of the Esterel, making expansion impossible, so it is hard to find. The cellar of the Belle Aurore had several bottles left.

"This is a section of road familiar to rally drivers," Monika explained. "The tight turns and the narrow road are exhausting, so the Belle Aurore is a popular place to stop."

I must have dozed off after we resumed our journey for eventually, through a somnolent haze, her voice penetrated. "We're almost there."

Within a couple of minutes, she slowed and turned into a wide entrance at the side of the road. A drive weaved through a dense pine forest along a rough road that looked as if it had been recently cleared. Then the forest thinned and we came to a pair of massive iron gates, set in a towering stone arch. A stone wall, weathered and cracking but still intact and about eight feet high, went in each direction as far as the eye could see.

Two men on tall ladders were mounting an elaborate metal shield on top of the arch. I could make out a dragon with wings and the armored helmet of a knight but I couldn't identify the rest of the heraldic emblems, nor could I decipher what appeared to be Latin lettering at the bottom.

One of the men on the ladders gave us a wave. He hammered a couple more securing spikes and the other man gave it a shake to make sure it was firm. They came down the ladders and set them against one side of the arch. I saw that they wore black uniforms with red trim.

"I suppose that's the symbol of the fair?" I said to Monika.

"No," she said. "It's the family crest of the owner."

"Our host?"

She nodded. "Yes, the viscomte de Rougefoucault-Labourget."

Chapter 41

Monika drove in slowly through the huge gates. The two men both had close-cropped hair and one called something to Monika in German.

I was having second thoughts about this visit. It was the spider and the fly syndrome. It was clear that I was the fly and I was now suspecting the name of the spider.

"Do you know this viscomte well?" I asked her point-blank.

"Fairly well. He's sponsored me in a few races."

"There's a rumor that he's dead."

It was fortunate that we were creeping along slowly. She turned to stare.

"What?" She recovered and laughed, seemingly with relief. "What nonsense! He's very much alive. He's trying to revive interest in the fair. He wants to make it once again into the major event it used to be."

So I had tracked down the viscomte, Dien Bien Phu notwithstanding. Or he had tracked me down. Anyway, there was surely safety in numbers, and the activity in the grounds suggested large crowds, judging from the tents and marquees.

People swarmed everywhere and the air was

thick with cries and chatter. The sun was near its zenith and it was warm despite the altitude. The smells of herbs and flowers mingled with the tang of freshly cut grass. It was all very bucolic. Through all the noise came a thin buzzing sound. Monika slowed even more and pointed. "Look!"

A speck was visible in the sky. In the sparkling air, it could be seen clearly as it dropped lower. It grew in size and became a craft with large rectangular wings and a flimsy frame.

"It's Alexis!" Monika said excitedly. "That's his new two-seater—look, there's someone with him!"

It drifted nearer. There were two figures inside the cube of girders. The craft came lower, banking slightly, and sank out of sight on the other side of the château.

"Who's his passenger, I wonder?"

"I can't see from here," she said, shading her eyes.

I saw the château clearly now for the first time. It was built in the style of the fortified manor house—a very large and substantial dwelling but with battlements, towers, and arrow slits dating from the days when the home would have to be defended against Moors, Saracens, pirates, freebooters, bandits, and quite often one's envious neighbors.

Monika parked and a servant in the black uniform with red trim came out of the house, took our luggage, and led us inside. We went along a hallway and emerged into the main hall. It was impressively cavernous, with wood-paneled walls, armor and weapons, banners and tapestries. Voices echoed from the high ceiling where a massive chandelier hung.

An elderly gray-haired man appeared and introduced himself as Gilbert. He was the head of the household staff and told us that the viscomte was not here yet but was expected during the afternoon. He had the servant who had carried in our bags show us to our rooms. We were both on the third floor, Monika's room a few doors down the corridor from mine.

The carpets here looked new and the hunting prints on the walls were in new frames and under sparkling clean glass. The room had mullioned windows with a seat all round the window alcove. The bed looked new, too, and the wallpaper had a subdued flower print; clean, fresh rugs were spread on the polished wood floor. The whole château had obviously had a thorough rejuvenation very recently. I took a shower, put on a shirt and slacks, and went out, locking the door with the big, old-fashioned key.

I considered knocking on Monika's door but decided to do some reconnoitering on my own first. There were no other rooms on this floor but bedrooms, so I went down the wide staircase to the floor below. It appeared to be the same and I had hardly stepped onto the staircase to go down to the ground floor when a uniformed servant materialized at my elbow.

"Can I help you, sir?" he asked politely in German-accented French.

It was not the same man as the one who had carried in our bags, but he was the same type. Medium height and build, military bearing, and close-cropped hair—the description had a very familiar ring. The uniform was impeccable, black with red trim at the collar and cuffs of the jacket and a red stripe down the pant legs. He looked tough and efficient.

"Just looking around," I said affably.

"Very good, sir. The bar is, of course, always open. The fair will be on until six o'clock and dinner will be at eight."

I gave him a nod. He stood, motionless. I went on down the stairs and into the hall. It was empty and I examined the rooms running from it. There was a billiard room, a recreation room with Ping-Pong, darts, and two computers set on game programs, a meeting room, and another room that was set up as a cinema.

The bar, which was comfortably furnished to the standard of a good club, was empty. A quick glance indicated that it was very thoroughly supplied with every kind of drink. I went back into the hall and out through the main entrance. There were two massive, carved wood doors that were undoubtedly old but had been carefully refinished and restored. One swung open slowly and silently, despite its mass, a tribute to newly oiled hinges.

I wandered among the stands and stalls. One was giving a presentation on the Felibrige. This was a group of poets and romantics who deplored the way the old Provençal language, customs, and traditions were dying out. Organized by Frédéric Mistral, a familiar name throughout Provence, they made a great number of people aware of their heritage, and when Mistral won the Nobel Prize for literature, the Felibrige received even greater support.

A reading in the Provençal language from Mistral's own work, *Mireio*, was billed for every hour on the hour. Copies of his books and plays were on sale and troubadours in costume stood nearby, eagerly awaiting the call to sing and play.

A large number of people were clustered around

the Willesford stand, sampling the wines. I watched from a distance. Two white wines were being offered for tasting—the Pont Vieux and the Bellecoste. The rosé that they sold as Val Rosé was being offered too. I didn't see any of their better wines being poured. I strolled on to see what other festival delights were on display.

Music caught my attention and I headed in that direction. A team of tumblers and jugglers were putting on an act of great dexterity and I watched them for a while. I was expecting to encounter Monika, snapping away at her shutter, but there was no sign of her.

An enterprising farm had an aromatic and visually attractive show of their products, including sausages of various kinds, pigs' feet, and other pork products. It seemed just the place to ask some questions about pigs and sangliers, and the heavy-set, red-faced man on the stand knew all the answers. Cheese appeared to be the main product, though. The most pungent French cheeses are made from *lait cru,* raw milk that has not been pasteurized. This prevents cheese makers from selling outside of France and obliges them to make strong efforts to sell in their own neighborhood where their loyal consumers are used to the cheese artist's moldy masterpieces, complete with ashen rind, blue bacterial tracks, and a pungency that could pierce armor plate.

A familiar figure approached—it appeared to be an English country gentleman having an at-home day in his gray slacks and white long-sleeved shirt. His aristocratic nose wrinkled at the assault of the cheese fumes.

"Hope the stuff tastes better than it smells," said

Lewis Arundel in that languid tone. "But then it would have to."

"You a friend of the viscomte's?"

"Known him a while."

I was well enough acquainted with Arundel's laid-back style to know that this was his normal reaction to such questions.

"Is he here yet?"

"Haven't seen him," Arundel drawled.

"He's alive and well then?" I asked casually.

"Of course," he said quickly. "Why wouldn't he be?"

We strolled along past a stall that was at the opposite end of the spectrum from the last one. This had herbs and spices of Provence in bottles, jars, cans, bouquets, air-fresheners, sacks, and a dozen other ways. The fresh clean scents of marjoram, rosemary, and basil were strong in the air.

I was determined to press hard on Arundel.

"The reason I'm particularly interested in talking to him today is that I believe him to be responsible for four murders."

He stopped in midstride. His eyes widened in what looked like genuine surprise. "You're not serious."

"Not only that but he's also involved in two—perhaps three—attempts on my life."

A smile was starting to play around his mouth. "A serial killer, for sure. A bit of a bungler though, isn't he? I mean, you're still alive."

"This isn't funny," I said, getting angry.

Arundel resumed walking, very slowly. "In fact, it's funnier than you think," he said. He seemed to be deciding whether to go on. He made up his mind. "When you were pushed into the vat of Mourve-

dre—that's one of the murder attempts you're referring to, isn't it?"

"Yes."

"Well," he said with a lopsided grin, "that was
me. I pushed you in." He went on quickly, "You
were nosing into matters that didn't concern you. If
I hadn't pushed you in, someone else would have—
Simone probably."

"What matters didn't concern me?"

"You might as well know," he shrugged. "You
probably know already. According to law, we're
only permitted to add twenty percent Mourvedre to
a wine. We've had excellent results increasing that
to about twenty-five percent—doesn't sound like
much, I know, but it's one of the secrets of the high
quality of our red. The record book that you were
sneaking a look at gives the actual percentages. Oh,
it's not that much of a secret—not worth killing
somebody for, anyway—but I thought pushing you
in might warn you off."

"I might have drowned," I said furiously.

He laughed out loud.

"Nonsense. I was prepared to pull you out before
that happened. We didn't know that gendarme was
on the premises. He got to you first."

"And the beehive?"

He looked puzzled. "Beehive? What beehive?"
He either didn't know or wasn't going to admit to
that one. "When you talk about murders, you surely
don't mean Chantier and Laplace?"

"And Fox and Morel."

"It seems like a long string of unfortunate events,
I know, but accidents happen. It's been years since
we've had anybody hurt in our vineyard until now."

"Is that the way the viscomte tells it? A string of unfortunate accidents?"

"Yes." His eyes searched my face. "Well, you know him. Does he seem like a mass murderer to you?"

"I don't know him."

His expression changed. "You don't? Well, you'll meet him then you'll see. The whole idea is preposterous."

"Andre Chantier's drowning—was that preposterous?"

"The currents in Marseille harbor are treacherous," he said.

"He wasn't drowned in Marseille but in Ajaccio."

He stopped again in midstride. "Ajaccio?" he said hoarsely.

We resumed walking, past a stall adorned with objects carved from olive wood. The wood is very hard and durable and is made into walking sticks, ashtrays, letter openers, pipes, candlesticks, and even small animals.

Arundel was less talkative now. His face was strained. A man in the uniform of the staff walked past us as if on patrol. Again I noted that they all had a similar bearing and competency. They all looked like tough customers.

We stopped at the next stand. It had the Peregrine name above it in large letters and the small wooden counter had glasses and a stack of brochures. Arundel hailed Gerard.

"We'll drink anything—even your awful stuff, Gerard. And make sure the glasses are clean, please."

Girardet smiled a polite smile, evidently used to

Arundel's mocking manner. He poured wine for us, a pleasant white though not as good as the one he had given me on my first visit to the vineyard. Arundel noticed it too.

"This is the cheap stuff, Gerard. Where's the good wine—if you make one?"

Gerard reached under the counter and produced an unlabeled bottle.

"I didn't know you could tell the difference. Try this one."

Arundel poured his wine out onto the grass and said, "Fresh glasses again too."

Gerard smiled his polite smile once more. This time the wine was good and had the same superior taste as the one I remembered. Arundel just grunted and said, "Better, Gerard, but not much. Come on over some time and I'll show you how to make real wine." He emptied the glass, then said abruptly, "I'm going to get ready for dinner. See you later."

My mind was buzzing—it began when I saw that honey was on the next stand. In Provence, bees are catholic in their choice of flowers to pollinate, so their product may be flavored with thyme, sage, lavender, lemon, lime, or eucalyptus, and all of them were represented here in every size of jar and bottle. I approached the large, capable-looking woman in charge. "Can you tell me something about bees?" I asked her, and she not only could but did. She answered my questions thoroughly and I went up to my room, very satisfied.

Chapter 42

The dining room resembled a restaurant in Paris of the last century. Stained-glass windows had medieval scenes of bucolic frolicking and on the walls between them hung Manet oils depicting famous restaurants of La Belle Epoque. The elaborate ceiling of dark wood and gilt gave a baroque splendor to the room; lighting was provided by white-shaded bronze lamps mounted on tall narrow mirrors. At the head of the long table was a chair so magnificent, it was almost a throne. The back and arms were framed in hand-carved mahogany and the back had a padded coat of arms in crimson and gold.

The bar had been sparsely attended and now we were all seated for dinner, though it was barely eight o'clock. The chairs on either side of the impressive throne at the head of the table were taken by Simone and Monika. Monsieur le Viscomte was evidently exercising a certain "droit du seigneur." Next to Monika, Gerard Girardet gave me a friendly smile from his place opposite Doctor Selvier. Lewis Arundel and I were next. Then came Professor Rahmani and Alexis Suvarov, obviously already acquainted, Suvarov sounding as if he were close to selling the services of his new two-seat ultralight. The two cousins completed the assembly: Alfred Rostaing of Le Petit Manoir at Palliac where I had eaten so recently and the silver-haired visitor there whose face had baffled me, Joseph Tourcoing of Le Reveillon fame in Paris.

The cousins were discussing Menton near the Italian border, the only gap in the culinary eminence of the Riviera. Rostaing was asserting that it was so bleak that the Casino was the only place to eat. The two were contemplating remedying that situation by buying a restaurant there and remodeling it, both architecturally and gastronomically.

Waiters entered and began setting a hot hors d'oeuvre in front of each guest. I tried to catch Monika's eye but she picked up a fork and began on the hors d'oeuvre. Instead, I complimented Simone. "You look terrific," I told her. She wore a light blue dress, gathered across the shoulders, and her hair glowed—not as strongly as Monika's brighter blond, but for her, soft and warm. She acknowledged with a slight smile.

The aroma of the hors d'oeuvre was enticing but I couldn't identify it from its appearance. It was a soufflé and had been prepared by a master. The top was a delicious brown but not crusty. As I broke into it with my fork, I recognized it as a variant of a Normandy-style crayfish soufflé, but the flavor was so superb that for a moment, all thoughts of plots and crimes went out of my head.

The crayfish were so fresh they must have been flown in within the last hour or two. A salpicon of shrimp, oysters, and mushrooms had been added, and the chef must have put in the eggs the way that is authentic but rarely followed because it is time-consuming and tedious—the egg yolks added first, then the beaten egg whites. This makes a vast difference to the texture, but it was the taste that was stilling conversation all over the room.

I glanced down the table to where Joseph Tourcoing, the great chef from Paris, was nodding in appreciation. Alfred Rostaing was scooping up the soufflé, oblivious to everything. The incredibly wonderful taste was clearly augmented by the thin slices of truffle. I expected to hear a comment from some quarter on the absence of our host, but this superb hors d'oeuvre was occupying everyone's attention to the exclusion of all else.

The conversational level was still at this low ebb when the door opened.

The person entering walked to the elaborate chair at the head of the table and sat.

Chapter 43

"I hope you are all enjoying yourselves."

The words brought an immediate response from Joseph Tourcoing.

"Monsieur le Viscomte, this soufflé is magnificent! Never have I tasted better!"

Murmurs of agreement ran from seat to seat.

"Really superb, monsieur, really superb!" confirmed Alfred Rostaing, the other restaurateur in the room. He said it quickly so as to return at once to finishing the soufflé.

A waiter had placed this outstanding hors d'oeuvre before the viscomte as he sat down and he lost no time in dispatching it, nodding with satisfaction as he did so. Waiters flowed in, removing the soufflé dishes and replacing them with another dish. A wine was being poured and I contrived to get a glance at a label. It was a Musigny Blanc, a white burgundy that is lighter than most and fresh enough that it remained aloof from intruding on the meal.

The next dish was a mousse, just a tiny mound, and I heard Rostaing comment quietly that it was prepared from river trout. Flecked with minute chips of truffle, it was excitingly different and the small portion made it all the more tantalizing.

The excellence of the food had almost distracted me from the surprise of seeing our host. I was beginning to put the pieces of the puzzle together but that which concerned the identity of Monsieur la Viscomte had caught me completely unawares. I looked at him again. He gave me a smile and a nod and resumed his conversation with Monika. She was resplendent in an iridescent silvery gown that was a startling contrast to her usual sporty style.

Following the mousse came Goujonettes of Lotte, Mediterranean fish that had been cooked in *nage*. This is a recent development in French cuisine and comes with the trend toward lighter, lower-fat cooking. A *nage* is an infusion of herbs and vegetables used strictly for poaching fish. Previously thickened with cream, the modern way is to use vegetable puree. Scallions had been blanched in the *nage* and I guessed that the seasoning came from ginger, coriander, and lemon-grass. Slivers of truffle adorned the fish, and again murmurs of admiration rippled through the room.

There was a switch of wine at this point. This one was a Premier Cru from the Peregrine vineyard, more assertive than the Musigny but balanced and charmingly flavorsome. The viscomte must have acknowledged the quality of the best wines from Peregrine, I thought—then I realized that until now I had missed the point of this completely.

I looked again at our genial host, the Viscomte de Rougefoucault-Labourget, now discussing a fine point of vine growing with Gerard Girardet. Most of the aspects of the mystery were falling into place and I wondered just how many of those in the room had already known the identity of Monsieur le Viscomte . . .

He was Grant Masterson—millionaire business-man, owner of the spectacular yacht *Windsong*, and the man who had invited me to accompany him to the truffle market.

The table service continued to be ultra-smooth. The lotte was followed by Becasseau Truffée. Becasse is woodcock, one of the tastiest and tenderest of game birds. The becasseau is a bird under seven months old and the trick is to get birds right on that border-line of age so that they are large enough to be meaty but young enough for the flesh to be delicate. These were perfect, and although my mind was really on the viscomte . . . Masterson, I could not help being interested in the discussion between Tourcoing and Rostaing that concerned the cooking of the dish. They were concluding that it was sautéed in very hot butter, chicken livers and truffles were added, then it was finished with lemon juice and brandy. It was served with straw potatoes, the very fine crisp sticks, and accompanied by cardoons, popular in Provençal country cooking but seldom used by known chefs. This was clearly a shame because the large edible thistle is a close relative of the artichoke and, if attentively prepared, even more delicious.

The wine waiters poured a Pomerol with it—the Trotanoy that is made from several grape varieties, principally Merlot and Cabernet Franc. It was fruity but only enough to accent the game, and the steely tannin gave it character.

A lemon sabayon in a very tall fluted glass had champagne poured over it upon serving and cleaned the palate perfectly. Then came the dessert, Brandied Truffle Fritters. The batter was light as a feather and a comment from Doctor Selvier that this was a very rare dish was quite true. It requires thick slices of truffle and these make it too expensive to calculate.

Conversations flowed on a dozen subjects but my participation was limited to nods and simple answers. Finally, Monsieur le Viscomte—as I had now come to think of him—announced that coffee and liqueurs would be served in the library. Cigars for the men, he stated, adding with a laugh that they were for the women too if they so wished.

In twos and threes, the assembly rose and proceeded in the direction of the library. As I passed the thronelike chair at the head of the table, the viscomte put a hand on my arm.

"Let's go into my study. You and I have a few things to talk about. . . ."

Chapter 44

It was a dream of a study, most of the books leather-bound and mellow with age and gilt lettering. Subdued orange lamps cast a restful glow and two large globes on floor stands showed the ancient and modern worlds. Masterson indicated a couple of deep leather armchairs and we sat. A waiter appeared and took our orders for coffee and I went along with Masterson's suggestion of the Ethiopian brand.

I found I was thinking of him as Masterson again, now that we were alone. He leaned back and eyed me with an amused grin.

"It took a long time for you to figure it out, didn't it?"

"Yes. The meal tonight clinched it, of course. It was not just a meal—it was also a statement."

He considered that. "I think that sums it up—yes, a statement."

"Every course contained the truffle," I said. "But they weren't just truffles—they were a sublime improvement on the original, they were truffles raised to the nth degree."

He nodded, pleased. "So what's your summary?"

"The blue truffle is still a legend, of course and

always will be, but we can call this one the blue truffle. Chantier found it—a hybrid, some natural offspring of the finest black truffle with a very much higher percentage of glutamic acid, the component that enables the truffle to accentuate the taste of any food it accompanies. Chantier cooked it for his friend, Emil Laplace.

"Chantier probably knew only that it was a supertruffle but Laplace recognized its potential value and bought some truffle pigs to look for more. It was convenient to spread a rumor about sangliers—that would keep others away and would explain the presence of the pigs. Finding that the truffle grew only on Willesford land, Laplace struck a deal with Arundel to sell it. As he didn't have the money, Arundel approached you, and he's been working for you ever since. You probably told him he could take over control of the vineyard when you bought it. At the same time, you were telling Girardet he'd be in charge."

He regarded me, unperturbed.

"What you have been doing is testing out all these truffle dishes by using Le Petit Manoir. I don't know how much you told Rostaing, but he knew he was onto something good and sent samples to his cousin Tourcoing to try out on the Paris market."

I paused to let the waiter bring and pour the coffee. Masterson sipped.

"Don't you find this Ethiopian brand really excellent?" asked Masterson.

I marveled at his complacency but was not going to let him know it.

"Yes. The pity of it all is that you found it necessary to kill several people to develop this blue truffle, sensational as it is."

Masterson shook his head, slowly and sadly.

"I'm disappointed that you think that of me. I was rather hoping you might join me in this great crusade to bring the food world a breathtaking discovery." He sipped his coffee approvingly. "I didn't kill any of those people, you know."

His barefaced denial took me unawares. "Chantier?" I asked.

"Drowned accidentally."

"Laplace?"

"Gored by a sanglier."

"Fox?"

"An accident. A crossbowman stumbled and his weapon discharged. He shouldn't have had a bolt—"

"Morel?"

"Signs warn against unauthorized prowlers in Herculanum. Those two-thousand-year-old buildings are just not safe."

I gazed into his face. Somehow, he looked different from my companion at the truffle market. . . . "You don't really believe all that."

"Certainly I do." He gave me an injured look. "I'm Grant Masterson—I haven't killed anybody."

I had the creepy feeling that his acquisition of the title of viscomte was segregating his two personalities—and establishing a convenient way of dismissing responsibility. It was probably the same approach he had used with Arundel, others, too, perhaps including Monika.

"You brought in Fox to dowse for truffles . . ."

Masterson nodded. "The pigs weren't doing the job. We turned them loose."

"But then Fox's dowsing found a large bed of truffles. He was so pleased, he was drinking and talking about it. You had the crossbowman kill him before he could say too much."

"Professor Rahmani has the task of cultivating the truffle," said Masterson. "And, d'you know, he may succeed! If he does, I'll be sorry I let my enthusiasm soar and made those offers for Willesford. Suvarov and his ultralights took care of local transport, of course—with the help of an experienced rally driver."

He went on in chatty fashion. "The first blue truffles we found had a very short life—we had to rush them to the table. We handle them better now."

"Your two red herrings worked very well," I said. "The story of the Treasure of the Templars, the planting of that coin at the pawn shop—that was good. Even better was the tale of the wonderful wine that helped people live to a ripe old age."

"Everyone wants to believe that's true," purred Masterson.

"You had stories spread around about how many old people were in the region. Doctor Selvier was a willing helper too."

"The doctor likes seeing his name in print."

"So all the villagers were convinced that Willesford wine helped them live a long time."

Masterson pulled a wry face. "That was the original intention, but they're a stubborn lot. Too many of them were not convinced."

"But they all drink Willesford wine," I protested, puzzled.

"Of course they do," grinned Masterson, "but to get them to do it, I had to subsidize the bars, cafés, restaurants . . . I paid thirty percent of the cost. They didn't know the money came from me. Arundel made it look like Willesford was doing it to push its own product."

"When the Peregrine wine was poured at dinner tonight, I knew right away that you own Peregrine."

"Of course."

"Yet you subsidized the drinking of Willesford wine. . . ."

"The Peregrine vineyard is nothing. I bought it on a whim—many men have a dream of owning a vineyard. I thought of expanding it, then I lost interest. When the blue truffle came, the vineyard was a perfect cover. It's nothing compared to the market for the blue truffle. It will be worth millions, millions!"

For the first time, I saw a gleam in his eye that was not entirely normal. The man was a megalomaniac.

"You already have millions."

He shook his head vehemently. "You don't understand! It's not the money! I'll have absolute control over the supply of the most powerful flavor enhancer in the world. I'll make so many people happy—I'll be able to give them taste sensations like they've never known before!"

"You bought the title of the viscomte de Rougefoucault-Labourget," I said, wanting to bring him down from his gloating.

"I bought the château—the title came with it."

He was striving to find justification for his actions and I was getting irritated at his high-handed attitude.

"That doesn't make you nobility. You're no more a viscomte than I am."

His eyes flashed and he sat bolt upright.

"My family is French, on my mother's side. There was a title in the family at one time—it might have been one of the Rougefoucault family who deprived us of it. I was merely claiming my heritage."

I drank some coffee and tried to slow down. Most of what I had come to see of his elaborate scheme had been correct. As far as I knew, all the interfering elements had been eliminated. Except one . . .

I drank some more coffee. "You didn't send Johann Ditter to kill me, I'll give you that. I just learned today that the bees here are not deadly. The bee lady at the fair here told me that none of the bee varieties in the south of France are deadly unless one has a specific allergy to them."

It had been quite an instructive day at the fair. On another stand, I had learned from the pig expert that in the region around the vineyards, sanglier hunt singly. The 'terrifying' creatures that I had encountered in the cave were certainly in the plural so they must have been friendly pigs as Delorme said. It was while talking to the pig man that the use of pigs as truffle hunters had arisen.

"The bee episode was a warning—though it served the double purpose of getting me in a position where Monika could introduce me to you, quite "accidentally." When we went to the truffle market in Aupres, you wanted to find out how much I knew."

He made no reply.

"I knew nothing at that time—I guess you found that out."

It was a while before he spoke. "I was disappointed. I had hoped we might work together."

"In killing people?"

It was a reckless thing to say and it was out before I could stop it.

There was a glint in his eye that I wished weren't there.

"No, you didn't know anything then," he said in a

tone without emotion. "You were just a nuisance. I supposed you were another nosy parker, come to find out why Morel hadn't reported. I do so hope you'll be the last."

"Morel—yes, he found out, didn't he?"

He grimaced. "Instead of denouncing me, he wanted money."

"So you took him on your yacht to Corsica, tried to work a deal with him. It didn't work so you had one of your men kill him at Herculanum and try to frame Veronique and me for the murder."

He finished his coffee. I was dragging mine out—I didn't want to face what might happen next. "The viscomte is having a hunt tomorrow. I know you'll join us," he said silkily.

"Hunting what?" I asked, though I wasn't sure I wanted to know.

"Oh, there's lots of game around here. Even some—well, some fairly big game." He smiled without mirth and there was that maniacal flicker again.

A servant came in to say that Captain Gregali wanted to speak to him urgently. Masterson nodded. Gregali came in looking grim and I walked out of the study, leaving Masterson sitting there, unmoving.

One of the uniformed staff was outside the door. He stepped aside to let me pass. Another of them was at the bottom of the stairs and again I racked my brain to figure out why they all had such a similar look. Build, appearance, manner—what was it?

I walked on down the hall toward where I calculated the garages must be. Another of the ubiquitous men in uniform materialized—there had to be an army of them. "Can I help you, monsieur?" he asked politely.

"I'm looking for the garage," I said in an assertive tone.

"It is here but it is locked at night."

"I need something from my car."

"Monsieur le Viscomte has the keys."

"No one else?"

"No, monsieur, no one."

I gave him a dismissive nod and went back through the house, across the stone-flagged floor to the front door. It was locked. Another uniformed man appeared.

"I need some fresh air," I said. "Will you open the door?"

He nodded obediently and uncovered a small panel on the wall. He touched buttons and the door swung open.

"How do I get back in?"

"I'll be here, monsieur," he said imperturbably.

I strolled outside. The only gate was the one I had entered. Uniformed men patrolled in a tight pattern everywhere. I went back in the house and found Suvarov in the bar. I took him to a corner at the far end away from where most of the other guests were gathered.

"I want to get out of here," I said. "Tonight." He stared at me.

"Tonight? Why?"

I hesitated, then gave him the story I had unfolded before Masterson. He listened, becoming increasingly amazed.

"You told him you knew all this? What did he say?"

"He denied having anything to do with the deaths."

"What about all these people here?"

"They're all dependent on him, one way or another."

"Simone isn't. I brought her here. I know." He eyed me. "I'm not either—oh, he's been a good customer but I'd never condone murder." He paused, then asked, "What do you want me to do?"

"Fly me out of here—tonight."

His eyes widened. "I can't do that."

"Why not? You flew in here."

"It's illegal to fly an ultralight at night."

"What do I care about illegal?" I snapped at him. "My life's being threatened."

"It's not just that. It really is dangerous—ultralights have no navigation system. The pilot can only fly on visual and you can't see landmarks at night. They have no lights, so other aircraft can't see them. Worst of all, if there's no moon, the pilot can't see the line between earth and sky. This is hilly terrain—no, it's just too dangerous.

"Why don't you just take a car?" he suggested. I told him why not.

He shrugged. "I'd like to help you but I don't see how I can."

"This is ridiculous. Here I am, knowing I may be murdered tomorrow, and I can't do anything about it!"

"Did I hear someone mention murder?" a voice asked and Monika came over, detaching herself from a group in the corner. Suvarov glanced sideways at me. "We were talking about the hunt tomorrow," I replied. "I said hunting is murder."

She regarded me coolly. "You're not a sportsman, eh? Well, I think you'll get something out of it." She put down her glass. "I want to be sure of being fresh tomorrow so I'm retiring. Good night."

When she had gone, Suvarov said plaintively, "Listen, I'd like to help you but—well, what can I do?"

"We'll both try to think of something," I told him. "See you in the morning." As I left, I passed the study. I could hear the subdued voices of Monika and Viscount Masterson.

Up in my room, I dragged a chest before the door, put cushions from chairs under the bedspread, and created a fair facsimile of a body in it. I made myself as comfortable as possible in a chair in the corner. I knew I wouldn't sleep a wink.

It was a gentle but persistent rapping at the door that woke me. . . .

Chapter 45

"Who is it?" I called, but I could hear no reply. I quickly checked the mound in the bed. There was no knife handle protruding—so much for Gothic horror and 1930s Hollywood mysteries. It took a couple of minutes to push the chest away from the door and in the meantime there was another series of persistent taps. I opened the door to see Suvarov. "Let me in!" he whispered.

He pushed the door open forcibly and came in, closing it quickly.

"Do you still want to get out of here?" He was tense, not his usual debonair aviator image.

"Yes, but you said you couldn't fly at night!"

"It's five o'clock. The sun will be up in half an hour. We can take off at first light."

I looked at my watch in astonishment. I couldn't believe I had slept that long. "Well, yes, I—"

"Then dress fast." He went to the window and peered out cautiously. As I did as he said, I asked him why the abrupt change of mind.

"I had a chat with one of the staff last night after I talked to you. He's Nineteenth—says they all are."

"Nineteenth?"

"French Foreign Legion. When it was first

formed, it was attached to the French army, the Nineteenth Corps. Old Legion hands still refer to it as the Nineteenth. That's why they all have the same manner, the same bearing, the same close crop. They're disciplined and tough and many of them only joined to avoid paying for some crime. More than half the Legion today is German. They're ideal recruits for anyone who—"

I was struggling to pull on my socks but I caught the implication.

"Anyone ruthless and with a plan that needs men who'll do as they're told, men who like excitement and don't object to violence. So now you believe me?"

"That's not all," he said grimly. "I saw Ditter last night—the pilot who dropped the beehive on you. He was in the same uniform as the rest."

"I saw him too. Did he know you recognized him?"

"I don't think so, but Masterson caught me when I was talking to the other one. Masterson questioned me—he, well, he was different, sort of . . ."

"Different how?" I asked.

"He kept referring to the viscomte as if he were another person. It was scary, scary enough that I'm ready to take you out right now. Ready?" I pulled on shoes and we went out quietly. Night-lights shed low radiance in the corridors and on the staircase. No one was to be seen. Suvarov waved a hand and I followed him into the game room where a row of video machines gave off colored reflections. Suvarov closed the door carefully.

"I came in and played some games last night till I was alone, then I unlocked this window," he whispered.

We climbed out and crept across the lawn. The

château was a massive bulk in the darkness as we left it. We hurried to where Suvarov's ultralight was pegged down at the top end of a grassy slope. There was still no sign of any life and I reflected that we had been lucky to avoid the viscomte's private army.

Suvarov kicked the pegs loose and untied the ropes. He held a hand in the air and nodded. "Wind's just right. She'll take off like a swallow."

I looked at the aircraft, just visible in the predawn dimness. I had to be desperate to trust my life to this, I thought. A few flimsy strips of metal, some plastic sheeting, and an engine that looked as if it belonged in a kitchen blender.

"It's still dark," I pointed out.

"As soon as we're up in the air, we'll be able to see the dawn. We'll fly toward it."

Suvarov walked around the ultralight, examining it carefully but quickly. He took out a key and climbed into one of the seats.

There was a noise, a scuffling of the grass, and my heart froze. If it was one of the Legionnaires, we were caught. Suvarov heard it too and stared past me as a figure came out of the gloom.

It was Lewis Arundel.

He came close. The faint starlight was enough to show the black automatic pistol that he pushed toward Suvarov.

"All right," Arundel said in a taut voice. "Start her up. You're taking me out of here."

"Wait a minute!" I protested. "He's taking me!"

"Move aside!" he grated. "Are you ready to take off?" he snapped.

The hapless Suvarov looked from me to Arundel.

"Yes," he said in a low voice. "I don't want to start the engine till we're ready to go."

Arundel walked forward, past me, keeping the gun close to him. As dawn broke, the gloom was already crystallizing into shapes. Arundel heaved himself into the passenger seat with one hand, darting me a look.

"Too bad for you, but it's getting dangerous for me here," he said.

"You too? What's happened since yesterday when you were telling me about all the so-called accidents? Your memory started working? Or your conscience?"

"Ready?" Arundel asked sharply, and Suvarov nodded as he tapped one of the instruments in front of him. I was anxious to keep Arundel talking—anxious to do anything to delay the takeoff, to find a way to overcome Arundel. "You know plenty, don't you? From Morel, from Emil. . . ."

"I was on Masterson's yacht a few times," Arundel said to me but still keeping a watchful eye on Suvarov. "We often went to Ajaccio. Morel was on one of those trips too. Oh, I was on Masterson's payroll—he kept telling me how determined he was to buy the Willesford vineyard and that he'd have me run it for him. He made a lot of promises. I believed him—I didn't know then it was all a blind for this truffle scheme. I remembered too that Emil had told me that Chantier had been out on one of those trips."

He flicked an impatient glance at Suvarov, who was testing the controls.

"What did Morel find out?" I asked.

"I don't know for sure but he got Fox drunk one night. He also got something out of Emil and must have put together enough."

"Masterson had them both killed and then had to eliminate Morel, who was blackmailing him."

"I suppose, but I didn't have anything to do with the murders."

"One more thing . . . why did you—"

"Let's go!" Arundel shouted the order at Suvarov.

I stood there, poised for the opportunity to grab Arundel's arm and pull him out of the aircraft. Unwilling to relax his grip on the gun, he hadn't fastened his seat belt, and the gun was still aimed right at me. Suvarov turned the ignition key, darting me a helpless look. The engine gurgled into life, spluttered once, then settled promptly into a steady drone.

Arundel's sardonic manner hadn't deserted him completely.

"Give us a push—get us going!" he shouted over the engine noise.

"Not bloody likely!" I yelled and snatched wildly at his arm.

He might have shot me but instead he swung the gun, hitting me across the knuckles. I let go reflexively and the ultralight was already moving. It was out of my reach in seconds, picking up speed, moving down the slope at an amazingly rapid rate.

With a sinking heart, I watched it soar upward. It climbed, turning gently and becoming more sharply visible as it rose into the first splintered beams of the rising sun.

Then it changed. From pink-tinged it was instantly transformed into a boiling globe of red and yellow flame. The bellow of the explosion came before the horror of the sight impacted on my eyes. Black smoke foamed out as the fireball spread. Blazing pieces fell, dropping slowly through the air. One of them looked like a human arm . . .

I stared horrified. The flames were already burning out and I was appalled at how quickly two lives and an airplane could disappear. It was as if they had never existed. All that remained was a sooty cloud.

Voices were calling out and the sound jerked me back to reality—which was that I should have been on the ultralight and that the explosive planted on it explained why there had been no guards during the night. It would have been another "accident." Monica had evidently overheard Alex and I talking and the pilot, Ditter, had realized that Alex had spotted him. The ex-Legionnaire that Alex had pumped for information about Masterson's staff had obviously reported it, perhaps he had even planted further ideas in Alex's mind that had stressed his dangerous position.

The one advantage I had was that I was thought to be dead—and I needed every crumb of advantage I could gather. I had to get out of sight and fast. I made a run for the cover of the house.

Chapter 46

The viscomte's "army" was responding to the explosion with the same alacrity with which it had been mustered by a bugle call in the Sahara. Men in the familiar black uniform with red trim came out of the house; some took up positions by the wall, others went to the back of the château, and a relief team went out to the main gate.

I watched from a corner of the stable yard. I was safe temporarily but only as long as I was thought to be dead. I had to get out, but how? Some of the guests must be leaving today. I might be able to stow away in a car. I made my cautious way in the direction of the garages.

A servant came out of the kitchen with a barrel of trash and I ducked hastily out of sight. When he had gone back inside, I continued and reached the garage area. One glance was enough to show that the idea was not feasible. A pair of uniformed men were by the door, and inside, I could see two more examining vehicles.

All that was left was a getaway on foot. This presented two difficulties—first, to reach the wall unobserved, and second, to scale it. The former was the greater problem and as I reached that thought, a uniformed man came across the yard and went into the garage. Was that the answer? Put on a uniform and be like G. K. Chesterton's Invisible Man?

I headed back toward the kitchen area where the staff should be less militaristic and therefore easier to overcome. I thought of a chef's outfit but that would be out of place inside the house.

I went inside cautiously. A short corridor led past storage rooms, a couple of them with open doors and sacks, crates, and boxes neatly stacked inside. I went farther and came to another room, where steel filing cabinets covered two walls. A uniformed man wearing an apron was bending down, opening the lowest file drawer.

Planning had been my intention rather than precipitous action but this was too good a chance to miss. I planted a foot against his behind and pushed with all my body strength. His head crashed into the drawer and he went down on the floor like a sack of potatoes. This was easier than I had expected.

I kicked the door shut and was unfastening his buttons when he moaned and opened his eyes. His head must have been been baked hard by the African sun—to my horror, he started to struggle to his feet. I grabbed the lapels of his tunic and banged his head hard against the file cabinet door, then again. He slumped unconscious.

I stripped off my clothes, stuffed them into a cabinet, then pulled off his uniform. It wasn't easy to get off but at least it was a near fit. I couldn't find any rope but I came across a roll of heavy tape and used that to bind the man's wrists and ankles, gag him and secure him to the handles of a file cabinet. I grabbed an empty cardboard box and put it on my shoulder to use as a screen for my face.

I followed the corridor into a large room that looked to be a lounge. One of the staff came out of an adjacent room and walked toward me. For a long second, our eyes met. He went on. I fought the overpowering impulse to look back because I recognized him as the man who had wielded the crossbow that had killed Elwyn Fox.

His footsteps on the polished wood floor continued. Deciding where to go, I saw an alcove. In it was a telephone.

Communication was only secondary to getting out of the château and its grounds, but a message to Aristide of the Huitième Bureau would bring help—maybe I could survive until the French Marines arrived. I picked up the phone.

The voice that answered immediately was male, deep and stern. I asked for an outside line. "I'll connect you, sir," was the response. "What number do you wish?"

I didn't know Aristide's number offhand and the voice sounded as if it belonged to an in-house operator, so I couldn't ask for the police. I remembered Veronique's number, though, and I asked for that. There was a short pause, then the voice said, "I'm sorry, there seems to be a fault on that line. Please try again later."

I went on, turned near the foot of the grand staircase in the entry hall, and had gone only a few steps when a door opened ahead of me and Simone emerged. Her smart blue shirt with a white collar and darker blue skirt made her look more attractive than I would have believed. She stopped in midstride when she saw me and her eyes widened as she overcame the contradiction of the uniform.

"You! They said you were dead!" Emotions were

flashing across her face—first bewilderment, then fear, then horror. She raised a hand to her mouth in a little-girl gesture.

"But—but who . . . who was in the plane?"

"It was Arundel," I said softly.

"Oh, no," she moaned. Her hand dropped. Her body tightened. "Alex brought me here, I had hoped that we—" Her expression changed to anger. "You killed him!" she spat in a flash of fury. "You forced him to fly!"

"I wanted him to fly me out of here," I admitted, "but Lewis had a gun—"

She didn't let me explain. She beat her fists on me in a rain of blows and I was trying to protect my face when she shouted, "Murderer! Murderer!"

"Wait a minute! Let me—"

She raised her voice even more, screaming, "He's here! He's not dead! He's here."

I tried to clamp a hand over her mouth but she snapped at my fingers with sharp white teeth. A pair of strong hands seized me from behind and I was powerless. Another uniformed man arrived to help—the man I had passed in the corridor, the man who had shot Elwyn Fox with a crossbow. Simone took a step back, gave me a look of loathing, then ran down the corridor, sobbing.

"Well," said a voice in English. "You didn't take the last plane out after all."

Grant Masterson—or the viscomte de Rougefoucault-Labourget—came down the last few steps of the staircase. He looked suave, dressed for a day in the French countryside in a mint green polo shirt, cream slacks, and white shoes.

"A last-minute change in the passenger manifest," I said. "Lewis Arundel felt his need was greater than mine."

Masterson might be dressed in cavalier style but his voice and attitude were grim and uncompromising. "Yes, I noticed when I talked to him last night that he was beginning to entertain some wrong ideas about me. Pity, after he had been so useful."

"Same with Suvarov," I told him. "Your charm is fading fast—who's next, you must be wondering."

"You're an irritating fellow, you must learn to choose your words more carefully." His voice hardened. "But I'm afraid it's too late for that."

A peal of bells cut into his last words and all heads turned to the main door across the hall. The uniformed man on duty there opened it and spoke briefly to someone outside. He turned to Masterson.

"An ambulance is here. They say they had a report from the village that a body was seen to fall from the sky and land inside the grounds."

Masterson turned to glare at the crossbowman.

"Impossible," the man grated. "A kilo of plastic explosive was wrapped round that fuel tank. Neither of them could have remained in one piece."

"Send them away," snapped Masterson to the guard at the door. "Tell them we have found no bodies."

The guard pulled the door open a few inches and spoke quickly. A flow of voluble French came from outside. The guard argued. Voices were raised. Masterson glared in exasperation and was calling to the guard to get rid of the unwanted ambulance when Simone reappeared. She was pale and tense. One arm was behind her back and I thought she was coming for me but instead she confronted Masterson.

"I heard you," she said in a voice that trembled. "It was you—you killed Alex!"

Her eyes blazed fiercely and before either of the uniformed men could intervene, the arm came from behind her back and she swung a long, curved dagger, evidently pulled from one of the weapon racks on the walls. She slashed viciously at Masterson. Taken unawares though he was, he had enough presence of mind to throw up an arm in defense. The blade sliced deep through the fleshy part of his forearm and bright red blood spurted.

"Bring those ambulance men in!" I shouted loudly. "We have a man here bleeding to death!"

Behind me, the grip of my captor hadn't relaxed, but he didn't move, uncertain. Simone hefted the dagger for another swing. The noise had attracted another guard and he grabbed Simone's arm, saving Masterson from further damage.

The guard at the door stared mesmerized at the sight of the blood spattering the flagstones of the hall, then another peal of bells was accompanied by a thunderous banging. The door swung open.

A man in a black suit and a black homburg came in, carrying a black bag. He pushed his way past the flustered guard and behind him came three white-garbed attendants. The newcomer in black looked at Masterson, shocked and frozen, staring at his arm still spouting blood, then at Simone with the dagger still in her hand, and finally at me, immobile in the grip of the guard.

"Take care of that man!" he ordered in clipped tones. Unaccountably, his three attendants stood, unsure what to do, then one of them opened a large white metal case with a green cross and moved to the stunned Masterson.

I was looking at the doctor. Somehow, those black clothes didn't belong . . . and that black homburg seemed out of place . . . then I recognized the bristly black mustache and the round glasses. It was Aristide Pertois.

"I need medical attention too," I called out. "So does this woman." I nodded to Simone.

"Bring them all out to the ambulance," ordered Pertois in a voice of command. The grip on me hadn't relaxed, but I pulled against it, toward the door. We might have made it, but Simone called out in a high-pitched voice.

"This man is a murderer!"

She pointed to Masterson with the dagger, which still dripped blood, even though a guard hung onto her arm. "He killed Alex Suvarov and I will testify to it!"

"Bring them to the ambulance," repeated Pertois, but Simone turned to him. "You're a gendarme. Arrest him!"

The confused guards stared at Pertois. For a second, he looked nonplussed. He would have preferred to maintain his masquerade as a doctor and avoid a confrontation, but now it was too late.

It was Masterson, the viscomte, who recovered first. Still spurting blood, he sprang to the partly open door and dashed through. The engine of the ambulance roared and gravel screeched and clattered.

The guard released me and I ran to the door. The ungainly white vehicle bounced and swayed as it rocketed toward the main gates. The engine bellowed in a crescendo of noise as it gained speed.

The gates were closed. Masterson was leaning out of the driver's window, waving and shouting at the guards, but it was not until he was about a hundred meters away that they must have recognized him. The big gates began to swing open.

If Masterson had slowed, he would have made it through, but his foot must have been flat on the floor and he didn't relax it. Another meter wider was all he needed . . .

Instead, the ambulance hit the gates endwise and they sliced into the front of the vehicle like two giant knives. The frightful impact was transmitted to the stone pillars; one held firm but the other splintered with a crack like thunder and the ambulance disappeared in a cloud of dust and gravel.

Chapter 47

We sat in the Baie des Anges Café on the second floor of the Nice-Cote airport. A Swissair Boeing rumbled into the air and across our field of vision, but the double glazing was efficient enough to dim the sound of the aircraft's two engines and we did not even have to raise our voices.

Aristide Pertois sat opposite me. He looked like the proverbial cat that has swallowed the perfectly cooked canary and I told him he had every right to do so.

"My chief is very pleased at this successful resolution of the case," he said.

"I didn't mean that," I told him. "I meant figuring out where I was and then coming and saving my life."

He shrugged as if he saved lives every day.

"Naturally, we had been keeping close track of all those involved in this case. When Mam'selle Ballard drove out to the ultralight airfield and left with Suvarov in his aircraft, I was informed immediately. I had the flight log checked. Their château destination coincided with a fair known to be held there, a fair where both vineyards had exhibits. When Madame Ribereau told us—"

"Surely she's not a police informer!" I was horrified.

Pertois continued smoothly as if I had not interrupted. "She told us that a German girl had picked you up in a red Maserati. We alerted all road patrols, who reported her very distinctive car to be heading in the same direction as the ultralight. I arrived at the local gendarmerie that night and was aroused the next morning when phone calls came in concerning a huge explosion in the sky."

He paused to sip his pastis. "I hoped you were not in that explosion but I had no doubt that you were involved in some way."

"It should have been me in that ultralight," I said. "I feel responsible for both their deaths—Arundel and Suvarov."

"You cannot blame yourself," Pertois said firmly. "The man with the crossbow was also the explosives expert—he planted the plastique."

"Tell me something . . . if Masterson hadn't been killed, would you have had enough evidence to convict? With his money, he could have assembled a formidable defense."

"My colleagues in the Huitième Bureau had been very active," Pertois said. "They had compared dates and times of vessels in and out of the port of Ajaccio with the death by drowning of Andre Chantier. They interviewed all the officers and crew members of all those vessels. Among them was *Windsong,* M'sieu Masterson's boat. Then one of our people investigating the theft of the crossbow from the museum at Porticcio found that one of the museum staff had heard of an ex-Legionnaire known to have participated in many crossbow contests. It was found that he was in the employ of the viscomte, who had recently bought the château to which you had gone."

"Masterson received an urgent phone call last night from Gregali, the captain of *Windsong*. He must have been reporting your inquiries."

"He was," said Pertois. "We monitored the call."

"You tapped his phone? Isn't that unlawful?"

Pertois gave me a look of surprise. "Is it? I didn't know that. Anyway, we are now making further interrogations of *Windsong*'s crew. So far, we have confirmed that Chantier and Morel had been on the vessel. More revelations will follow, I am sure."

"Congratulations! You're an ingenious group in that Huitième Bureau."

"We are ingenious," he agreed. "And you—you are very lucky . . ." He nodded over my shoulder and I turned to see Veronique and Simone approaching, both looking stunning. "Lucky to have two such lovely ladies here to bid you farewell. It might have been three"—I looked askance and he went on—"however Fraulein Monika is still in our custody and likely to remain so for some time."

"What are you charging her with?" I asked curiously. "She was Masterson's mistress, obviously, but since when has that been a crime in France?"

"Poof!" he said contemptuously, "of course it is not. But in such a position, she must know a great deal about his operations and we intend to detain her until she tells us all she knows."

"Can you do that?"

His black eyebrows went up at least two millimeters. "Certainly! Why ever not?"

He finished his pastis and nodded to the waitress who was passing. He evidently had an "arrangement" here too. He rose to his feet and put on his cap. "Ladies," he said, bowing to Veronique and Simone, "I must go. I have other crimes to attend to. I leave this fellow in your gentle hands. Please make sure that he does not miss his flight. If he stays in France any longer, I fear for the future of our wine industry."

Here's an excerpt from *Death Al Dente* available from St. Martin's Press

"Cheese is like wine—it does not travel well," Gunther said as we walked through the packing shed. "You can see that there are several lines, each using a different packing material. You see, cheeses which continue to mature are wrapped in waxed paper and stored in wooden boxes. This way, the cheese can breathe after it has left the cellar. Other cheeses stop maturing as soon as they are taken out of the cellar and they have to be wrapped in plastic to preserve their humidity."

"What about this smaller line here?" I asked. "Aren't those soft cheeses?"

"Yes, and they require different packing too. Some are wrapped in leaves, some real some synthetic. Others travel on a bed of straw." He smiled at my expression. "Yes, even today this is still a popular method of packing certain of the more expensive soft cheeses. You'll find it amusing that health regulations of the European Union have been altered so that artificial straw can be used in some instances."

A further packing line was located near a massive spool taller than a man. It turned slowly, unrolling a wide sheet of aluminum foil. "That's for full sealing," said Gunther. "Some other soft cheeses are so sensitive, they must be dipped in liquid plastic."

The powerful smell was everywhere and Gunther told me of a nearby village with a cheese factory where an electrical failure occurred. Every operation was paralyzed, and the smell from the storage warehouses, no longer temperature controlled, was so powerful that the village had to be evacuated.

Electrical repair teams then went in wearing gas masks.

There was no sign of Pellegrini as we emerged into the sunlight so I took the opportunity to ask Gunther if mozzarella was the only cheese made from buffalo milk. "No, there are two others: provatura and provole. We make them both too but they have to be consumed within a day or two. They do not pack or travel well so they are consumed locally." He cast an anxious glance around. Almost half an hour had passed and I said, "Look, you must have to get back. I'll walk back to the farmhouse, Signor Pellegrini must still be there." Gunther protested, but I insisted and enjoyed the relatively clear air of the hundred yard walk.

I knocked at the door of the farmhouse but there was no answer. I went in and called Pellegrini's name but all was quiet. As I closed the door behind me, I noticed the robust aroma of coffee. It must come from that elaborate piece of Italian engineering on the table just inside the door and I instinctively looked there. The chrome-plated monster was quietly oozing steam but the big pot was gone.

I looked around the big room and the first thing that caught my eye was a trail of brown stains on the light-colored matting. They spread in a zigzag pattern and I followed them to find a dozen pieces of shattered china, apparently a coffee cup and saucer. Just beyond them was an overturned chair and the coffee pot, its contents a brown pool rapidly soaking into the floor covering.

Alarmed now, I called Pellegrini's name but all I could hear was the trickle of water from the giant waterwheel in the pond at the end of the room. The trail I had followed lined up that way and I walked tentatively forward.

Then I saw Pellegrini.

He was floating on his back in the shallow pond.

A loud scream came from behind me. An elderly, gray-haired woman with a large sack in one hand stood in the side doorway. She looked from me to Pellegrini and her face was contorted. She screamed again, pointed at me, then turned and ran.